one

LANA Rodriguez's eyelids narrowed suspiciously as she watched the buxom blonde in the minuscule bikini follow their surf instructor to a back room. She thought she recognized the expression of sly excitement on the young woman's face. Undoubtedly a man with their instructor's looks—the annoyingly potent, flashing grin and abundant, gleaming muscles—had female tourists throwing themselves at him with the consistency of a perfect Oahu day. Irritation bubbled up to the surface, an irritation that went far beyond her presence in Waikiki and taking a stupid surfing lesson.

Lana slammed the skin suit back into place, causing a brisk clang of the hanger against the metal rack. Her personal assistant and longtime friend's face fell at the evidence of her pique.

"Jeez, you weren't kidding when you said you hated Waikiki, were you?" Melanie pulled her skin suit's top down over her bathing suit. "You really *didn't* have to come, Lana. And you certainly didn't have to agree to take these surf lessons with me. I've taken vacations by myself before, you know."

Regret immediately lanced through Lana's flash of temper. Melanie was in the midst of a soul-scarring divorce that had already gone on for two years more than it should have. Sure, Melanie might have gone on a few vacations by herself before she married that sleazeball David Mason. Still, there was no way in hell Lana was going to allow her friend to be alone when she was still raw and hurting from her soon-to-be ex-husband's latest underhanded courtroom maneuver to get full custody of their four-year-old daughter, Shawna.

She gave Melanie an apologetic grin. "Sorry. Didn't mean to go diva on you."

Melanie laughed. "Girl, if you ever showed a *hint* of the diva gene, I'd have abandoned you years ago."

"Your shirt is too loose, hon." Lana chose a shirt that read *Jason Koa Surf Schools, Waikiki* over the left breast and handed it to Melanie before she picked one for herself. The tight long-sleeved shirt would partially protect them from the shearing Waikiki surf and the friction burn of surfboard against bare skin . . . as well as ensure that a woman's bikini top would stay in place.

Melanie shrugged out of the top and took the one that Lana handed her. "Why *do* you hate Waikiki so much?"

"Too touristy."

Melanie eyed her. "You seem really tense. And on the plane— jeez, Lana, I thought a few times you were going to have a panic attack like you used to have before you went onstage, back when you were still a kid."

Lana waved her hand impatiently. "Flying to Hawaii is worse

Paradise Rules
BETH KERY

ETERNAL
ROMANCE

Copyright © 2009 Beth Kery

The right of Beth Kery to be identified as the Author of
the Work has been asserted by her in accordance with the
Copyright, Designs and Patents Act 1988.

Published by arrangement with Berkley,
a division of Penguin Group (USA) Inc.

First published in Great Britain in 2013
by ETERNAL ROMANCE
An imprint of HEADLINE PUBLISHING GROUP

1

Apart from any use permitted under UK copyright law, this publication
may only be reproduced, stored, or transmitted, in any form, or by any
means, with prior permission in writing of the publishers or, in the case
of reprographic production, in accordance with the terms of licences
issued by the Copyright Licensing Agency.

All characters in this publication are fictitious and any resemblance to real
persons, living or dead, is purely coincidental.

Cataloguing in Publication Data is available from the British Library

ISBN 978 1 4722 0045 7

Offset in Sabon by Avon DataSet Ltd, Bidford-on-Avon, Warwickshire

Printed and bound by CPI Group (UK) Ltd, Croydon, CR0 4YY

Headline's policy is to use papers that are natural, renewable and
recyclable products and made from wood grown in sustainable forests.
The logging and manufacturing processes are expected to conform to the
environmental regulations of the country of origin.

HEADLINE PUBLISHING GROUP
An Hachette UK Company
338 Euston Road
London NW1 3BH

www.eternalromancebooks.co.uk
www.headline.co.uk
www.hachette.co.uk

I would like to thank my husband for his unwavering support and enthusiasm in regard to my writing. My deepest appreciation to Fiona Jayde and Robin Snodgrass for reading over all or portions of *Paradise Rules* and offering nuggets of wisdom and priceless feedback.

Thanks to Laura Bradford and my editor, Leis Pederson . . . for believing.

than flying to Europe. I should have asked my doctor for something to help me sleep."

For the whole damn trip, she added to herself.

"Are you afraid people will recognize you? You could be anybody under that hat and ginormous pair of sunglasses." Melanie's blue eyes dropped doubtfully over her friend's figure. "'Course . . . there's not much I can do about disguising your body when you're wearing a bikini. The boring, baggy clothes I usually buy for you just won't work in Waikiki. Even the homeless people wear swimsuits."

Lana was only half listening. Her gaze had wandered back to the corridor where their surfer-dude instructor had disappeared with the blonde on his tail.

"I'm not worried about being recognized. People don't care about the blues in Waikiki," she said grimly.

"There are blues and jazz lovers everywhere, Lana, and you know it."

Lana scowled. She hadn't actually been referring to a genre of music. "Waikiki is all surface and no substance—a flashy whore decked out in skimpy designer clothes, a perfect tan highlighting a perfect boob job . . . It's so fake."

So vicious. So primed to use the poor and underprivileged to serve the tourist industry's endless greed, she thought privately.

Melanie's eyebrows rose. Lana realized she'd allowed her bitterness to show and immediately made her face settle into impassivity.

"Well, it's certainly a happening spot," Melanie said. "I needed someplace with this kind of energy and excitement after what David has pulled over the past month. A secluded tropical island just wouldn't have done the trick." Melanie stretched the dark blue fabric over her generous breasts. "I need the distraction of a party atmosphere. And theses native guys are phenomenal. Don't tell me you didn't notice how gorgeous our surf instructor is. He's a walking god. He could be the inspiration for a tropical drink—Hawaiian Wet Dream."

"He's awfully tall to be a Hawaiian."

Melanie paused in the action of readjusting her bikini top.

"You don't think he's Hawaiian?"

Lana shrugged negligently. "Sure, he might have been born here and have some roots. I just meant there are few pure Hawaiians left. He's part Anglo. And he's got some Filipino influence, I'd guess, in addition to Hawaiian."

"Well, the combination is one hundred percent phenomenal." Melanie's blue eyes sparkled mischievously. "I'd *love* to have him help me forget about David on this vacation."

Lana smirked.

"Don't give me that look, Lana. Not *you*—of all people. No one knows better than me how single-minded you are when it comes to men. Surely you wouldn't deny me the pleasure of a few rounds of sex with a gorgeous stranger when you're such an expert on the activity."

Lana shrugged and leaned down to put on a pair of surf shoes. "You're right. I'm here to see that you have a good time, after all, and I'm going to make sure it happens. No better way to celebrate saying sayonara to that louse husband of yours than steaming up the sheets on your vacation. Hell, I'm only too happy to do the same." She nodded toward the back room. "Just don't count on doing it with our hunky surf instructor, though. It seems he's otherwise occupied."

Melanie checked her waterproof watch. "Jeez, he's already twenty minutes late. If he doesn't hurry, we're going to be rushing to make the luau I scheduled."

Lana clamped her back teeth together. "You have yet to learn about *Hawaiian time*, hon," she muttered with a scowl.

Melanie laughed. "Care to explain how you're such an expert on *Hawaiian time*? I've worked for you since you were a nineteen-year-old kid recording your first album. That was ten years ago, and I've never heard you mention Hawaii *once* in that time period. Did you spend time here before you came to the states from Mexico?"

"You know, this loser is really starting to bug the shit out of me," Lana said, choosing to ignore Melanie's questions. She dropped her beach bag on the floor and stalked toward the dim corridor at the back of the facility. "He's a little old to be playing irresponsible surfer dude, don't you think? I've got half a mind to report him to his boss."

"Lana, maybe you should just hang loose . . ."

But Lana ignored her friend. The familiar Hawaiian phrase made her clench her teeth even tighter.

She turned into a large room that contained several surfboards on tables in the process of being repaired or waxed. Her eyes immediately found the figures of the tall man and the curvy woman, despite the dim light. He leaned back casually, one foot propped against the wall, his hands tucked behind a pair of tight buns that Lana hadn't failed to notice as he strutted around, giving instructions about preparing for the lesson earlier. He looked down at the blonde, a half-amused, half-irritated expression on his shadowed face. His profile was as arresting as the rest of the package. That straight, bold nose had immediately pointed out his Caucasian heritage to her, along with his height.

"Excuse me. My friend and I have a schedule we'd like to keep. You would think you did, as well, considering the fact that between the two of us, we're shelling out four hundred dollars an hour for your services."

The woman started and gasped in surprise. Her hand jerked, and she hopped back with a guilty glance at Lana.

Lana was glad that she wore the dark glasses so neither of them saw how wide her eyes went. He had the nerve to not even hurry as he lowered the pant leg of his board shorts, covering a long, shapely, semi-erect cock. Even with his shorts lowered she could still perfectly make out the outline of it next to his thigh.

It was far from being the first cock she'd ever seen, and it wouldn't be the last. But that quick glance informed Lana it was the most beautiful. A flash of pure, primal heat surged through her along with a lightning bolt of irritation.

She was comforted by the fact that she knew her face gave nothing away.

"Four hundred dollars an hour should help you get over your discomfort. If you start doing your job now, I'll agree not to tell your boss about your negligence, Mr. . . . ?"

He didn't move from his lazy pose against the wall. She couldn't really make out his eyes in the dim room but sensed his stare boring into her. She'd noticed earlier that his eyes were a singular color—dark gray with flecks of green and amber.

"Koa. Jason Koa. And I'll be happy to reimburse you for the half hour of your lesson and still give you the full two hours."

"Good," she replied briskly, unmoved by the fact that he was apparently the owner of the two-bit surfing school. She started down the corridor, only to notice that he hadn't moved. "Well? Aren't you coming?"

"That gives me another eight minutes. I'll be with you in a moment, undoubtedly more comfortable and better prepared for teaching what I don't doubt will be a challenging lesson."

Lana stiffened when he reached for the giggling blonde. She thought of where she'd like to tell Jason Koa to stuff his insolent attitude and gorgeous smug face, but then she thought of Melanie. She imagined her friend's look of disappointment if Lana marched out there and self-righteously informed her that they were leaving.

She doubted her sunglasses disguised the glare of pure loathing she threw him before she turned away.

HE set down the board in the grassy area near the beach. "Okay. Which one of you ladies is up first?"

Jason was glad when the blonde with the round face and nice smile stepped forward. He'd have to work with her man-eater friend at some point, but he was still steamed by her insulting display of arrogance back at his shop. He wasn't sure why her bitchiness had gotten to him so much, but it had. He'd been so preoccupied by her frigid superiority that he hadn't been able to concentrate when pretty little Katie eagerly resumed her hand job.

Not that he'd really been interested to begin with. Katie had taken a lesson from him three days ago. He'd taken her up on her blatant offer of her body that night, but he'd quickly become annoyed by her pursuit of him. Her California-girl good looks, large breasts, and curvy hips and ass went a long way to making him forget his rule not to get involved with customers. He'd been irritated when she followed him into the back room today and thrown herself at him. His cock had responded to her eager hands but not with much enthusiasm.

Still, if she'd kept it up, he would have grudgingly let her finish him off. He was just a guy, after all.

But then the man-eater interrupted and ruined a little afternoon delight. He'd pushed Katie's industrious hand away after the woman left and made small talk with her about her job as a financial analyst. Apparently Katie had a hell of a head on her shoulders. That was the vacation mentality for you. Jason seriously doubted Katie was in the habit of throwing herself at males in the everyday business world, but give her the tropical breezes and the sensual rhythms of the island, and she was suddenly shameless.

He'd made his customers wait the full eight minutes, which caused him to feel a little guilty, he realized, as he positioned the blonde named Melanie belly-down on the board. Melanie was obviously nice and excited about her lesson. It had been rude of him to make her wait longer just because she had shit taste in friends.

Five minutes later, after he was satisfied that Melanie had the basics of paddling, kneeling, positioning herself in a standing position in the center of the board, and falling in the safest way, he suggested that she go and pick out a board from the beginner rack he kept on the beach.

He gave Melanie's silent friend a bland look. "You're up."

"I don't need instruction on the basics."

"Is that right?" he asked mockingly.

He glanced down over her. He had to admit she had the body of an athlete. It wouldn't surprise him if she knew exactly what she was doing. He'd immediately taken note of the casual manner in which she took off her sundress earlier in his shop. She was as used to baring her body as the female swimmers he knew—as most native Hawaiians, for that matter.

He hated to admit it, but she had excellent reason to be comfortable stripping down in public. She had a jaw-dropping body—strong and supple, but soft and feminine, too. And even though she wasn't tanned, her smooth skin held a golden hue that promised to soak up the sun thirstily. If she stayed on the island for two weeks, she'd probably be ready to contend in a Miss Hawaiian Tropic contest.

"I'll be the one to decide whether or not you need instruction. Get up on the board, and show me the basics."

Her muscles stiffened. For a second, he thought she'd refuse, which would be fine by him. He'd be more than happy to leave her on the beach.

She surprised him by stepping up on the board, however. He stopped her with a hand on her elbow when she started to go lie down on her belly.

"Take off the hat and glasses."

She started. Despite her frigid nature, her skin felt warm and satiny beneath his appreciative fingers.

"Why? What difference does it make?"

"I like to be able to look into the eyes of my students. Got a problem with that?"

He felt her stare on him from behind the dark glasses.

"Look, Waikiki isn't Waimea in March—or even Sandy for that matter," he said, referring to a few Oahu advanced surfer beaches. "But it ain't the wave pool at the water park, either, lady. Those waves can pound the hell out of you. If you don't do what I say, it can be dangerous. Call me an ass, but I tend to like to know what I'm dealing with before I take responsibility for you out there. If I can't look into your eyes, it makes it a little difficult for me to know what you're made of. Play by my rules, or don't play at all."

He realized he'd tightened his grip on her firm biceps. Without speaking she removed the straw hat and tossed it on the grass. Brown hair with golden highlights spilled around her shoulders. The glasses landed on top of the hat. Exotically tilted hazel eyes studied him coldly through thick, long lashes.

He knew those eyes. He knew that face. So did half the population.

He dropped his hand.

Okay, so half the population wouldn't recognize her. She wasn't pop-star famous by any means, but she did have a loyal following, not to mention the fact that her work commanded the respect of blues and jazz aficionados across the globe.

"Show me what you got," he said grimly. He watched her as she gracefully came up into a surfing stance.

"I told you," she said coldly over her left shoulder.

Jason spread his hand on the back of her thigh. "You know the actions, but you need to loosen up. You're too tight. Relax." He almost broke out in a huge smile when he slapped her thigh lightly. Her eyes widened in disbelief.

"Get your hand off me."

"Give me a break, lady," he muttered as he slid his hand down to her ankle, urging her to widen her stance an inch or two. "You saw me touching your friend as well. You need to relax more than just your body. Your attitude could use a Hawaiian adjustment as well."

"Think I should just *hang loose*, dude?"

He paused with his hand on her firm calf and glanced up at her. Her face was livid with fury.

"You know, I don't think I've ever seen you wear that particular expression on the front cover of a magazine. I guess that's for the best, considering the publisher wants people to *buy* their magazine, not be repulsed by it."

She clamped her jaw shut. He watched in fascination as her face smoothed into a beautiful mask of impassivity. He stroked her satiny skin ever so lightly, preferring her fury for some reason. Must be turning into a masochist in his old age. When she tensed even further, he knew she'd noticed his subtle groping. Out of the corner of his eye he saw Melanie approaching with a short board under her arm.

"Lana." Her name lingered on his tongue. "That wouldn't be short for *'Ailana* now, would it?"

This was interesting, Jason thought when he saw her cheek muscle twitch. He rose slowly until he looked down at her, holding her gaze all the while.

"It means 'loving' in Hawaiian. Of course without the *okina*, the word *ailana* refers to raw, fuck-me-till-I'm-blind sexual intercourse," he said softly, referring to the punctuation mark before the name. He saw the fury return to her expression and smiled insolently. "Ah—I see you already knew that, *'Ailana.*"

"There isn't a damn thing you can teach me that I don't already know and wish I didn't, Mr. Koa."

He leaned closer, catching her fresh, floral fragrance combined with healthy, sweet sweat. *Onaona*, he thought, instinctively using his admittedly primitive knowledge of the Hawaiian language to describe her scent. She even *smelled* like the islands.

"I beg to differ."

He saw her nostrils flare. His eyes fastened on her lush mouth.

"Is this board okay, Jason?" Melanie called out. He stepped back, glad for the interruption. He was only too happy to consider something else beside the fact that his cock had just stiffened to a lead pipe as he verbally sparred with a prima dona who clearly had some *serious* issues.

Not his problem.

So what if her personality was a far stretch from what he'd thought it would be given her low, sultry singing voice. Her voice, face, and body had thrilled many a male before him. He didn't need to be a fan of the entertainment industry to know that most famous people were whacked. Why should it surprise him that Lana Rodriguez was no different?

Still, Jason acknowledged he was disappointed. Her voice and bluesy arrangements brought out the pensive, moody side of him— the side he rarely showed others, certainly not in his role as an athlete or as an extroverted businessman in the Hawaiian tourist industry. In truth, he'd always been a little haunted by her songs.

He suppressed a frown when he fully registered his thoughts and gave an easy grin instead.

"Yeah, that's perfect, Melanie. Why don't you go and pick a board, Lana, and we'll catch a wave."

"*Bitchin*'," he heard Lana mutter scathingly under her breath before she walked away.

two

JASON nodded once when his bartender Manuel held up the coffeepot. He rubbed his eyes, took a sip of warmed-up coffee, and focused once again on the books. Even though it was two thirty in the afternoon on a Tuesday, there wasn't a seat available in Jace's. His beachside restaurant was arguably the most popular location for casual tropical ambience and high quality cuisine in Waikiki.

And the books informed him that it'd be yet another record-breaking month—at least for Jace's. So much for the price of a gallon of gas dampening the tourist industry. True, his surf school—at which he only occasionally taught these days—was doing only fair to middling in this economy. But Jason would never consider giving that up. He valued the opportunity to introduce people to his true love too much.

Of course, there were exceptions to that rule, he acknowledged grimly as he reflected on the lesson he'd given Lana Rodriguez yesterday. Not that he'd actually been able to *teach* her much. She was a natural on a surfboard. He'd heard her friend question her about it, and Lana had mumbled something about learning to surf as a kid in Cancun. He guessed it was possible for her to have learned there, but he somehow doubted it. He'd tried to surf in Cancun and Cozumel and thought the waves sucked.

She was lying, and he couldn't help but wonder about it. Why was Lana Rodriguez so intent on denying her Polynesian roots? He'd never caught a hint of her origins when he'd scanned her CD covers—usually too preoccupied to take much more in than her beautiful face and a body made for sin.

He rolled his eyes when he realized where his mind had wandered. Why did he keep thinking about her?

He redirected his attention to his books. The boat marina he owned in Honolulu also had taken a hit with the economy. Nothing major, but noticeable, nonetheless. Not too surprising, given the cost of fuel for powering a motorboat or Jet Ski.

People had their priorities on a vacation, it would seem. Fortunately, sipping an icy mai tai and munching on some seared-ahi tacos while they lazily watched the surf roll in was not something the typical vacationer was willing to sacrifice.

"What's the word?" someone asked from behind him. "If your business is doing as well as mine, we won't have to sell any of Grandma's farms—at least for another month."

Jason didn't bother to turn around when he heard the familiar voice. He tensed at the familiar theme of selling a portion of his grandmother's enormous estate—no matter that the topic had been brought up in a joking manner. Jason was Lily Koa's chosen executor; probably because Lily knew he wouldn't bow to family pressures and would carry out her wishes, no questions asked.

"Guess we picked the right industries. Food and sex are always in demand. Grandma's farm should be safe for a while," Jason replied in a light tone.

"Good news. There's no telling what Grandma would do if she discovered her golden grandson wasn't as perfect as everyone claims."

Jason calmly closed his account book when his cousin, Ipo— better known as just Po—tried to reach for it.

"Why so secret, cousin?" Po asked, scowling.

"My accounts are none of your damn business. What are you doing up and about so early? I thought the light of day would turn you to ash or something," Jason teased over his shoulder. He referred to his cousin's nocturnal profession as the owner of a nightclub and strip bar—Hawaiian Heat. Po also ran a high-class escort service, Hawaiian Nights, but that part of his business didn't go on the official books. It also was a major secret that members of the Koa clan kept from their matriarch, their energetic grandmother Lily.

Po's scowl didn't do much to ruin his good looks. His father may have been part Hawaiian, but Po favored his sophisticated French mother more than the Koa side of the family. With his slicked back black hair and expensive European clothing, Po called to mind a sleek, graceful panther. Jason noticed the way his cousin still stared at his closed account book. Was his cousin wondering if Jason kept any of Lily's accounts here in Jace's? Well, he could be as nosy as he wanted. Jason kept his grandmother's books locked up on the private sanctuary of his houseboat.

"You keeping secrets from me, Jace? Careful—I'll get you back," Po teased with a raised brow. The couple sitting next to

Jason at the bar stood and walked away. Po sat down next to Jason.

"Ipo, my man," Manuel said from behind the bar. The two men exchanged a handshake. "Can I get you something?"

"Nothing for me, Manuel. I'm just here to tempt my cousin." Something seemed to occur to Po as he stared at Jace's bartender. "Hey, did Pete Makala ever call you about working that big campaign event in Loa Ridge? I told him you were the best bartender on the island."

Manuel gave Jason a quick glance, but Jason's face remained impassive. "Yeah, Makala called. Thanks for the recommendation, but I have to work for Jace that night."

"You turned down Pete Makala?" Po asked dubiously.

"Maybe it's something you ought to consider doing as well." Jason's tone was mild enough, but the look he gave his cousin held a warning. Practically everyone in Hawaii knew that despite his influential political ties, Peter Makala was a major figure in organized crime in Hawaii. It just made things ten times as complicated that many of the people Makala dealt with were legit—at least on the surface.

Jason couldn't run Po's life for him, but he could certainly prevent his morally challenged cousin from involving the Koa family or Jason's employees with his sleazy acquaintances. When Manuel had explained to him about Makala's phone call several weeks back, Jason had frankly advised against working for the crime boss and then left the decision up to Manuel. He'd been relieved when Manuel had refused the offer.

The Koas were an old family with extensive land holdings and contacts all over the islands. Personally, Jason thought Makala was using Po for his connections—and possibly as an "in" for that windward strip of Koa land where Makala and his cronies wanted to develop a hotel-casino complex. Jason's warnings to Po had bounced off his cousin like rain on rubber, however.

"Makala's a good guy, Jace. He thinks the world of you. Always saying he could make you governor of Hawaii if you'd just let him get his hands on you. He says he could have gotten Grandma into the White House," Po said with a flashing grin and a pump of his dark eyebrows.

"You're not inspiring my confidence in our government officials if you're saying winning an office requires passing through Makala's hands first," Jason muttered in amusement. "Now . . . what did you really come down here for in the full light of day?"

"I knew you'd want in on this juicy bit of gossip I just got from Kathy. You're not going to believe who called for a date tonight." Jason chuckled when he saw the mischievous sparkle in his cousin's black eyes. He may not trust Po, but he liked him, nonetheless. His cousin had been gifted with no small amount of Lily Koa's famous charm. Besides, Po resided in Jason's earliest memories.

He knew Kathy Manx was the administrative assistant who did the scheduling and details for Po's escort service. Jason worried about Po's less than legal dealings in the sex industry . . . along with who knew what else, considering his connections to people like Peter Makala. It wasn't that Jason was being uptight; from all accounts, Po ran a pretty classy operation. The thing he resented—like many of his relatives—was the necessity for constantly having to hide the truth from their grandma Lily. Lily would erupt if she ever discovered her oldest grandson's shady dealings.

But worse, she would be hurt. Jason would do anything in his power to prevent that.

Po himself had a cavalier attitude in regard to Lily discovering what he did for a living, a fact that pissed off many Koas to no end, most especially Jason's cousin Kelly. But Jason knew from experience it was useless to lecture Po about his lifestyle. He'd just be dreaming about his next scheme for fun, sex, and profit the entire time you ranted.

"I've got a *celebrity* alert," Po chanted in a singsong voice, as though he were dangling a sweet in front of Jason's face.

Jason paused in the action of reaching for his coffee cup. Hearing the word *celebrity* immediately made Lana Rodriguez's beautiful, defiant face pop into his head. But surely Po couldn't be referring to *her*.

But how many celebrities visited the island on any given week? Strange to think of the brittle, cold woman he'd verbally sparred with yesterday paying for a night of guilt-free sex.

Even as Po leaned forward and whispered Lana Rodriguez's name, Jason altered his opinion. Lana Rodriguez was *exactly* the kind of woman who would want to make sure she called all the shots with her sex partner.

His lip curled in irritation.

"You don't look surprised. Has she already been to Jace's?" Po looked a little jealous.

"No, she hasn't been to Jace's."

"You don't seem very interested, cousin. The woman gives sexy a whole new meaning. I know how much you like her music. How many times have I heard her CD blaring when Harold has taken me out to your boat?"

"You got your lazy ass out of bed just to come here and tell me that Lana Rodriguez is hiring a male prostitute for the night?" Jason sidestepped. He didn't particularly like the fact that the overly curious Po had caught him during his isolative, thoughtful moods on two or three occasions. He preferred to keep that part of himself private.

"She hired an *escort*," Po corrected, clearly insulted. "And technically, she called to hire one for her friend. But I've trained Kathy well when it comes to sales. According to Kathy, when she smoothly asked Ms. Rodriguez if she'd need any of our services for herself, Rodriguez paused for a moment, and then said, 'Sure. Why not?'"

Jason could perfectly imagine her low, smoky voice uttering the question as blandly as someone might agree to another mai tai when Manuel offered. His focus fractured when someone tapped on his shoulder.

"Excuse me? Aren't you Jace? As in, *the* Jace Koa?"

Jason twisted around on his stool to see a sunburned, brown-haired woman in her early thirties. She pointed to a spot on the wall that displayed a photo of him, his eight gold medals from the 2000 Olympics fanned out over his abdomen. He gave a slow, practiced grin while his mind still churned over what Po had just told him.

"That's a younger, more in shape version of me, but yeah. I'm Jace Koa."

Her brown eyes flickered down warmly over his body. "You look like you're in *great* shape to me. Do you still swim?"

"As much as I walk."

The woman grinned flirtatiously. "I figured you had to do something to get a body like that. Can I buy you a drink?"

Jason chuckled. She was easy on the eyes, but that wasn't

saying much. In his opinion, even the drabbest of women bloomed in the sultry Hawaiian climate. He probably wouldn't have given this woman a second glance on the mainland, but the combination of the adventure of her getaway and the tropical nights had awakened the carnal woman in her.

It was just one of the many reasons he loved Hawaii so much.

"Oh, I forgot you own the place." She stepped closer. "How about if you buy me one, then?"

"Sure," Jason agreed without pause. He waved at Manuel, who immediately ceased his banter with one of the customers. "Have you tried one of our famous mai tais yet?"

The woman shook her head.

"You don't know what you're missing. I stole the recipe from my grandmother. It's become a Koa tradition. My grandma Lily traveled as far as Cornwall in England once, and as a result, she decided to add a splash of Pendrang whiskey to the Polynesian brew," Jason recited the familiar litany with a grin, even though his mind was otherwise occupied.

"Sounds like it'll have a serious kick."

"Well, my grandmother's a serious kick. Manuel, fix her up, will you? Free of charge." Manuel winked at the woman before he went to make her drink.

Po tapped him on the shoulder. "I'm going."

Jason leaned in closer to his cousin. "No. Hold on a minute," he said under his breath.

"I haven't got time to sit here and watch you seduce the tourists," Po whispered, scowling.

"I'm not *seducing* her. I'm doing business. Just let me make nice for a second. People don't tend to like a rude restaurateur."

Po rolled his eyes and started to get off the stool.

"Sit down. I want to talk to you about this Rodriguez thing," Jason hissed.

Po paused. His surprise at Jason's intensity segued to a sharp, speculative look. He sagged back on the stool. Jason turned and smoothly asked the woman what she thought of their beautiful island.

It was his job to charm the tourists, after all. Still, he had to admit it was hard to be charming when he was thinking about what he planned with Lana Rodriguez.

three

LANA finished tying the halter dress around her neck and walked over to the ringing phone. It would either be the front desk, announcing the arrival of her guest for the evening, or Melanie, calling in a panic as she waited for her guest. Her friend had already called her from her private suite down the hall four times, threatening to bail on plans for spending the evening—or night—with a paid escort.

"If you don't like him, tell him to leave," Lana had said matter-of-factly the last time Melanie had called. "That's the whole idea, honey—no hassles. You're paying for the service. You're in charge. He's paid—and paid *well*," she added with grim amusement, "to do whatever you want. That includes *leaving* the second you say the word."

It may sound mercenary, but it was true, Lana thought presently as she picked up the phone and gave permission for her guest to be allowed to come to her suite. She'd existed in the limelight for years now. She'd been soured by too many experiences with men who were more interested in attaching themselves to her in order to leech off the benefits of her talent, money, or both.

She'd learned to spot the type with amazing rapidity, given the experience of her childhood. There were plenty of individuals around who were programmed to take advantage . . . to use. It didn't matter if they vampirized man, woman, or child, as long as it brought 'em an ounce of self-respect and the unholy buck.

She fastened an earring as she checked the table room service had lain out while she was in the shower. Everything looked as it should—the champagne, the food she'd chosen either on heated salvers or, in the case of the shrimp and caviar, chilled in bowls surrounded by ice. She made a point of treating her guests well, and was only minimally disappointed if she wasn't attracted to them and politely ended the evening early. She appreciated the chance to meet a male in a controlled environment and fulfill her sexual needs if the opportunity was ripe.

Lana also was grateful for the fact that unlike many women—women who might have to do something they ended up regretting to satisfy their normal sexual desires—she had the money to pay for her needs. It wasn't a gift she took lightly.

When the knock came at the door, she glanced in the mirror quickly to check her appearance. Once again, she never shortchanged her guests. They had a right to find her as attractive as she was capable of being. It wasn't a one way street, after all. She slid her feet into a pair of high-heeled sandals.

"Just a moment! I'll be right with you," she called as she

fastened the strappy sandals around her ankles. She opened the door a moment later.

Her inviting smile melted.

"What are *you* doing here?"

"It's nice to see you again, too," Jason Koa returned with a flashing grin. She didn't have time to respond to his unexpected presence before he stepped into the foyer, forcing her back a few steps. He closed the door.

Lana gathered herself and straightened her spine. It would have been nice if he didn't still tower over her. She was five foot eight, and when she put on a pair of heels, it was common for her to look straight into a man's eyes.

Or look down at him.

Not so with Jason Koa.

"I asked you a question."

His smile widened. Despite her fury, something rippled in her lower belly—and it wasn't disgust. He had a smile that could almost literally bring a woman to her knees. The fact that he used that weapon with impunity infuriated her. Lana was all too familiar with men who could charm as easily as breathe.

"You're surprised that I'm your escort for the evening?"

She gave him a disbelieving look and snorted in contempt.

"I'll take that as a yes," he said softly. His electric smile faded for a few seconds as he examined her with a smoky stare. His gaze seemed to score her as it traveled down her body.

He moved past her abruptly and walked into the suite. Lana followed him, her mouth still hanging open in shock that *Jason Koa* was here. Just because he'd invaded her thoughts and her dreams didn't mean he had the right to barge into her real life.

He turned after inspecting the vivid pinks and oranges splashed across the sky. The view of the two-mile-long stretch of beach with Diamond Head to the left and the sun setting over the mountains to the right was breathtaking from her suite at the Moana Surfrider Hotel, but her focus was entirely on Jason. She took in his appearance for the first time, realizing the sight of him was more awe-inspiring than the Waikiki sunset.

He wore a pair of black pants and a white dress shirt, open at the collar. His beige jacket was perfectly tailored and highlighted his broad shoulders. He wore his dark brown hair longer in the front, but in the back it was neatly trimmed just above the collar of his shirt. The style perfectly set off his starkly masculine face. He held a paper sack. Her gaze lingered on his tanned, large hand gripping the package. He had great hands. Granted, *everything* about his body was amazing, but Lana had caught herself staring at his masculine, capable-looking hands frequently during her surf lesson.

Now she imagined what those hands would look like on her body—what they'd feel like.

"There's been a mistake," she said breathlessly. "I was expecting someone else."

"You weren't expecting someone from Hawaiian Nights escort service?"

She went still. Her heartbeat began to drum in her ears in the silence that followed. He slowly came toward her.

"What's the matter, Lana? I assure you that I'm capable of filling the requirements for the job."

She shivered at the impact of his low, raspy voice. "You work for Hawaiian Nights?"

He gave her a bland look and shrugged at what he must consider a statement of the obvious. "Why is that so hard to believe?"

Lana couldn't think of how to respond. He was certainly handsome enough for the job. He was *more* than sexy enough. In fact, he was *too* attractive. The effect he had on her made her uneasy.

"Did you know it was *me* you were meeting?"

"Sure."

She shook her head incredulously. "And knowing that, you actually agreed to come?" Her gaze lowered to his slow grin. His smile—that flash of white teeth against sun-bronzed skin—really ought to be outlawed for its mind-altering effects. Best not to think of what it did to her body. When he didn't speak, just continued to stare at her with a small, insolent grin on his firm lips, she prodded, "We took an instant dislike to each other. Maybe you didn't notice?"

"Bit hard not to notice a blizzard in Waikiki. The way I recall it, *you* took an instant dislike to *me*."

"Didn't like the experience much, did you? Well, there's a first time for everything."

He didn't appear overly dismayed by her sarcastic remark. As a matter of fact, he seemed so damn comfortable, Lana suddenly felt as if *she* were the interloper in *his* space. Like the whole damn island was his, and she'd just had the temerity to place a toe on his sandy beach.

Which there was a tad of truth to, she had to admit. This island paradise would never be her home, whereas Jason Koa embodied it.

Those singular dark gray eyes flecked with gold lowered over her deliberately, lingering on the swells of her breasts in the V of the neckline—checking out the bounty that had just washed up on his sovereign shore. She wasn't wearing a bra. She gritted her teeth when she felt her nipples tighten against the smooth, cool fabric of the dress. "We may not like talking to each other much, but you didn't call Hawaiian Nights for a chat buddy, did you?"

Lana stiffened. "I called for a fuck buddy. Is that what you're thinking, Mr. Koa?"

He surprised her by chuckling softly, the sound reminding her of something between a purr and a soft growl. His big male body looked entirely relaxed, making her hyperaware of her own anxious tension. "Christ, you're a piece of work. Do you ever let up?"

She considered him with an icy stare. The humor vanished from his face. Because of the flecks in his gray eyes, his gaze usually reminded her of hot smoke, but Lana learned at that moment they could also go hard and cold. Her tension mounted. Okay, so he was much more than just the big, sinuous panther lazing around in the sun that she'd just compared him to in her mind.

"All right. If that's the way you want to play it, fine. I might think you're a mean, cold bitch, but that doesn't mean I wouldn't love to have you under me, in front of me . . . on your knees." He closed the distance between them. Lana stared up at him warily when he leaned down over her, close enough for her to inhale his spicy cologne and natural rich male scent. Warm fluid flooded her panties. Just like that—in an instant—her body had readied itself for him. The strength of her response stunned her.

Frightened her.

"I've thought about all those positions, and a dozen other equally interesting ones, since yesterday," he rasped, his face just inches from her own. "So if you're asking me if I think you called Hawaiian Nights for a fuck buddy, I think the answer is yeah. But I don't want to be your 'buddy,' Lana. I don't want to be patronized by your champagne and your caviar and your small talk. I just want to fuck you. On *my* terms."

"Go to hell."

"Uh-uh. You're going to take me to paradise. And if you can manage to keep your mean mouth shut, I'll take you right along with me." His warm, fragrant breath fanned her lips. Despite the chaos of her thoughts, her body ruled her at that moment. She strained toward him.

He seized her mouth in a hard kiss. His male essence flooded her awareness, leaving room for nothing but a hot, erupting desire. She clutched onto his shoulders then desperately sank her hand into his hair, holding on for dear life as a tsunami of lust pounded through her. He penetrated her lips and made free with her mouth. She found herself striking out hungrily with her own tongue, ravenous for more of his flavor.

She was so overwhelmed with the power of his kiss she didn't realize he'd untied the halter of her dress until he lowered the material to her waist. He sealed their lips. She trembled. The man's kiss could more accurately be called an attack. That's how it seemed to her jangled nerves and screaming senses.

He stepped back to inspect her. His nostrils flared. Her nipples puckered in acute anticipation of pleasure. He surprised her by reaching into the paper bag he still clutched, his palpable gaze never leaving her breasts.

"I brought this for you," he said gruffly.

Her eyes widened when he withdrew a white lei. The velvety, cool petals tickled the hypersensitive skin of her breasts when he put it around her neck. He lifted her loose hair over the flowers and took his time releasing it, letting the strands run through his fingers. His other hand adjusted the flowers and paused near an aching nipple.

He seemed to be holding his breath. She *knew* she was.

She gave a small whimper when he touched the beading flesh with a calloused thumb and forefinger.

"It's made of orchids," he said in a low rumble as he watched himself pinch lightly at her nipple then sooth it with a caress. "My grandmother grows her own carnations, orchids, and plumeria, and makes them into 'flower jewelry.' She loves her flowers. She says they're the only accessory a woman should wear because they will remind her that she herself is a beautiful bloom." He glanced up and met her stare. The hand at the back of her neck shifted. A long finger slipped beneath the cool petals. "She always uses plumeria at the neck, even on her orchid leis." Lana inhaled the sweet, familiar fragrance of the flower traditionally used for leis. "The scent is released at the warmth of your neck. Perfumed jewelry, Grandma Lily says."

He reached around Lana's waist and unzipped her dress. At his urging, the fabric slipped off her hips and fell in a soft heap around her ankles. Her silk panties followed. She stood before him, wearing nothing but her sandals and flowers.

Her throat had gone dry. Her confusion—the paradox of anger, anxiety, curiosity, and desire—seemed to paralyze her muscles.

"It's beautiful. Thank you," she finally said.

His lips tilted. He seemed genuinely pleased by her compliment. He probably hadn't known she was capable of saying something nice. But it was only the truth. The gift of the white orchid lei struck her as perfect . . . simple, sensual, and astonishingly lovely.

In truth, his offering had disarmed her.

"You're the beautiful one, 'Ailana." He leaned in closer. "Now . . . I'd like to watch while you bloom for me."

She stiffened warily when he spread his big hand over her hip, fixing her in place while he burrowed the ridge of his forefinger between her shaved labia. He grunted in masculine appreciation when he felt how damp she was. Despite her surprise at his boldness, it felt delicious to have him slide along her clit, creating a sizzling friction that made her press tighter against his hand. She tried to kiss him, but he straightened and moved his face back. He watched her closely while he penetrated her slit with his middle finger, still rubbing and agitating her clit.

"So smooth and wet. I knew you'd have a sweet little pussy."

"Jason," she muttered thickly while he played her cunt to perfection. She put her hands on his shoulders and tried to pull him down to her . . . tried to gain some measure of control over the situation. But he refused to kiss her. It made her feel vulnerable and uncomfortable, but also incredibly aroused to know that he wanted to stare at her while she climaxed. A complete stranger. The fact that he was entirely dressed while she was naked also added to her strange combination of distress and arousal.

She moaned and ground against his hand. The friction was optimal . . . perfect. She tried once again to avoid his intense stare.

This time she unbuttoned his shirt and shoved a hand over warm, sleek muscle.

"No," he said softly. Firmly.

He spun her around. She cried out in protest at the absence of his gifted, strumming fingers on her pussy. Her eyes widened when she saw he'd turned her to face a mirror that hung over a credenza. He pushed her toward it, pressing his long, hard body to her backside. He nuzzled her neck with his nose, his eyes on her in the mirror.

"Look at you," he whispered hoarsely. "You're blooming right before my eyes."

She struggled feebly in protest. She didn't want to look at herself while Jason Koa pleasured her. The image she saw in the mirror was incredibly erotic—his dark, big hands stroking her hips and belly, her pink nipples trembling delicately next to the exquisite white flowers. But it also made panic rise in her for some reason. She felt too exposed . . . too vulnerable.

She needed to get back to her place of control.

He held her hips in place when she tried to turn around to face him. She gasped when he bent his knees and pressed his erection against her ass. Instinctively she ground back against him. He sawed his hips against her, stimulating himself and her at once. His low growl made her reach around, trying to get her hands on the cock she'd been thinking and dreaming about for days—despite her better judgment.

He moved quickly, grabbing her wrists and pinning them next to her abdomen. He held her with one hand, easily restraining her. She glanced at him in the mirror only to see his magnetic eyes were already on her.

"Let me go," she said, her mounting sense of helplessness making her sound angrier than she was. Mostly she was just spinning, knocked off balance by the knowledge of her desire.

"Maybe. After I watch you come a time or two."

She saw that her pulse leapt wildly at her throat. Her eyes dropped to his lowering hand. She bit her bottom lip, stifling a groan when he slid a finger next to her burning, erect clit. He had ample lubrication to work with, she realized with a trace of humiliation. The reaction he evoked in her wasn't a safe, *healthy* sexual hunger.

She was soaked. Ravenous to the point of foolishness. Which would eventually lead to regret, she knew.

He stroked her, and her anxieties turned to mist in the sultry air. She cried out when he once again penetrated her pussy with his middle finger. His hand and fingers moved in a concentrated, synchronous movement that caused heat to flood her cheeks and her juices to flow more abundantly around his fingers.

He watched her in the mirror as she went rigid with pleasure. Panic boiled in her belly at her stark vulnerability, but the desire pounding through her was stronger. She gritted her teeth together and closed her eyes a moment later, shutting him out in the only way she could as an orgasm crashed through her. Because she partially struggled against it, her climax had a sharp, almost painful quality to it. He tightened his hold on her wrists, pushing her back into his long, hard body. His hand became more demanding. A shout tore out of her throat.

He wasn't going to let her give anything less than her all.

"That was so pretty, I think I'd like to see it again," she heard him say a minute later as she sagged against him with her head forward, her hair falling into her eyes.

"No," she whispered. She felt strange—like she'd been turned inside out. It shamed her to reflect on how she'd submitted to his demands to control the pace of their lovemaking.

"Yes."

She inhaled sharply when she felt his calloused fingertips caress the underside of her left breast.

"You're softer than the flower's petals."

She moaned when he cradled her from below. Without looking up, she knew he studied the image of her breast in his hand.

"Look up, 'Ailana."

"Stop calling me that."

"I call you that because it's your name. Isn't it," he stated more than asked. He squeezed her breast softly, molding her flesh in his warm palm. "Now, look at me touching you. Would you rather I stop?"

She looked up slowly. She didn't want him to stop, and he knew that, the bastard. His gaze lanced right through her. Against her will, she pushed back with her hips, pressing her ass against his firm erection. His facial muscles tightened at her caress.

"You really want to be in the driver's seat, don't you?" he asked huskily.

She just stared at him while he fondled her breast, too aroused to find words.

"But we're playing by my rules, 'Ailana."

"Not if you want to get paid in full, we're not."

He grinned. "We'll see about that. I'm going to release your wrists now. But I want you to move your hands to the back of your head. Keep your elbows wide."

"Forget it."

"Oh, I'm not going to forget it. The vision of you granting me permission to play with your beautiful body will likely be etched in my memory until I'm an old man." He released her wrists. "Hands up."

He was entirely unmoved by her defiant stare.

"Put your hands on your head, 'Ailana."

The drum of her heartbeat escalated to a roar. She held his gaze and slowly raised her hands to her head. It was like someone else was doing it instead of her. She felt so strange, like she was both detached from herself and at the same time, more aware of her body than she'd ever been.

More *alive* than she'd ever been.

"That's a girl," he praised in a low voice. His other hand rose. For an excruciatingly arousing minute or two, they both watched in the mirror as he fondled her breasts and tweaked her nipples until they were stiff and aching. Lana felt trapped . . . deliciously held hostage by her own desire.

He held up her breasts from below, squeezing them lightly in his big hands, making the pink nipples poke out lewdly between his fingers. Lana held her breath and whimpered.

"Shhh," he soothed when he heard her sound of desperation. "Do you need to come again, baby?"

Air popped out of her lungs.

He released one breast and fingered the lei. He brushed the velvety petals over the nipple of the breast he still held in his palm in a deliberate yet lazy fashion.

"Go ahead. Say it."

Lana trembled as she watched him caress her nipple with the flower. Her need felt so raw she hurt.

"I . . . I want to come again."

She felt his cock leap against her bottom. Had admitting to her desire really aroused him that much?

"'Course you do," he murmured warmly. He pushed her hair back and pressed a hot kiss to the side of her neck, just above the fragrant plumeria. He raised his hand to her right wrist and forced it down to her pussy.

"Spread the lips wide."

Her arm jerked reflexively in his hold. She met his hot, steamy stare in the mirror. Not that she required further evidence of his arousal. His cock throbbed next to her ass, the sensation tempting her. The heat penetrating the fabric of his pants and resonating into her flesh was driving her crazy.

Slowly, she separated the lips of her shaved, slick labia. Her heartbeat slammed in her ears as she watched his rigid expression while he stared at her exposed outer sex for several tense seconds. She kept her eyes fixed on his handsome face, feeling too vulnerable to look at what was undoubtedly a flagrant display of her uncontrolled desire.

"Thank you for showing me how lovely you are. Let go now," he said gruffly. Lana didn't resist when he grabbed her wrist and placed her hand on the back of her head, once again. She was too eager for him to touch her . . . for him to make her forget herself once again. She tried to still her panting when he lightly pinched her labia together just beneath her burning clit. Then he slid his forefinger down into the fleshy pocket he'd made and stirred.

Lana cried out at the sharp pleasure. She clamped her jaw together, both ashamed and aroused by the moist clicking sounds caused by his agitating finger on her wet tissues. She shut her eyes tightly as orgasm loomed.

He paused in his wicked stirring of her clit.

"Open your eyes. Look at me touching you."

She groaned as her head fell back on his shoulder. Her eyelids remained sealed shut.

"Lana."

The hoarse, one word plea caused her to open her eyes warily. He snagged her gaze and glanced downward, magically forcing her stare to follow his.

He moved his long finger, agitating her clit. Lana's knees buckled as orgasm crashed into her. She was hardly conscious of him using one hand around her waist to steady her as pleasure shuddered through her flesh in powerful waves. She distantly was aware of the fact that he pushed her upper body down.

"Put your hands on the table."

She reached out blindly, her body still shuddering in climax. Her awareness zipped into full focus, however, when she felt his hand move behind her. She heard a paper ripping and realized he was putting on a condom.

Then he was pressing the thick head of his penis to her slit.

"Ahhh," she moaned tensely. He pushed. Her vagina stretched—and strained—to accept him. But she was so hungry, and slowly her need encouraged her body to accommodate his gentle but insistent thrusts.

Her entire body shook by the time he'd fully sheathed his cock in her. She felt so full . . . so hot. His hand caressed her hip, her waist, and the side of a suspended breast. His fingers rose to the nape of her neck, where he tugged on a handful of her hair.

She met his gaze in the mirror. He began to fuck her, deep and thorough. Her mouth hung open in shock at the cyclone of sensation that barraged her consciousness. He held her with one hand at the shoulder, the other at her hip. He made free with her, slamming their flesh together, creating a nearly unbearable friction. She realized through a thick haze of lust that despite his earlier actions, he was intent on his own pleasure at the moment. Selfish, even.

He wasn't going to wait for her.

For some reason, the realization satisfied her. Aroused her. She pushed back with her hands on the table and matched his hard, ruthless rhythm with her hips. His pleasure became her sole focus. She saw his snarl in the mirror, gloried in his savage grunts as their bodies crashed together stormily. He suddenly put both his hands on her shoulders, raising her until she stood before him. He bent his knees and fucked her in their upright position, fixedly watching her breasts in the mirror as he bounced the firm flesh again and again with his driving cock.

Lana cried out in mixed misery and bliss when he pushed her down hard on his full length and began to throb in release. He grunted gutturally. His spasming penis felt so good deep inside her. It pleased her to know she'd given him satisfaction, but her own need still festered like a raw, open wound.

He leaned over her, forcing her to bend at the waist. Her hands went out to catch them, supporting the majority of their upper-body weight on the table. He pressed his face against her back. Her pussy clenched around him. He groaned, and she wondered if he'd felt her unintentional caress. His breath struck her skin in erratic bursts of warm air.

It felt nice. Too nice.

When she tried to rise, he straightened. The feeling of his softened but still ample penis sliding out of her made her grit her teeth in a mixture of anguish and rising discomfort.

Thankfully, he said nothing as she walked away. She closed the bathroom door, took one look at the stranger in the mirror and then meticulously avoided the sight. She carefully removed the lei and set it on the marble vanity.

It was difficult to meet his eyes when she returned a minute later wearing a mauve satin robe, but it wasn't as hard as it might have been had she not taken the time to collect herself. She noticed he'd refastened his pants.

"Would you like something to eat?"

He looked irritated.

"Just a second," he muttered before he went to the bathroom. Lana realized he was disposing of the condom. When he returned a moment later, she was sipping a glass of champagne, staring at the star-encrusted midnight blue sky, trying to let the crashing waves on the beach calm her.

Instead, the pounding surf reminded her of Jason slamming into her body in a relentless, driving rhythm.

She handed him a filled flute when he approached her, but he refused to take it.

"I told you. I don't want your champagne."

"I'm not patronizing you, Jason," she said, referring to his earlier statement.

"You could have fooled me."

She inhaled slowly and set down both champagne flutes. Through the reflection in the sliding glass door of the lanai, she saw him scrape his hair back with his fingers in a gesture of frustration.

"Look, I'm sorry. I know I was greedy there at the end. I was . . . excited. Extremely so."

"You have nothing to apologize for," she said softly.

"Then what's with the ice-queen routine?" he demanded with a burst of irritation.

She turned around and faced him.

"If you don't want anything to eat or drink, I'm not sure there's anything left to say or do."

She was proud of how even her voice had sounded, how calm, despite the clamminess of her hands and the increasingly uncomfortable pressure on her chest. She'd had panic attacks before, and she didn't relish the prospect of having another one in front of Jason Koa. She hadn't had one of those frightening spells since she was in her early twenties, but the threat of them always lingered in the background. The panic attacks had been at their worst when she was a child. She could still feel her father shaking her, hear the fury in his voice.

Still smell the rancid scent of cheap whiskey on his breath.

Don't you dare play games with me. I know you're faking it. You'll sing if you want to eat tomorrow. You'll sing if you don't want to be locked out again. You didn't like sleeping on the beach last time, did you?

Jason's eyes widened incredulously at her cold words. His face settled into a rigid, furious mask. "So you got what you wanted, is that it?"

"Very much so," she assured him.

"I know I sure as hell did."

She stepped toward him, but her confused attempt to smooth the waves she'd caused was cut short when he said curtly, "Don't worry, I'll see myself out."

She turned and faced the ocean again. When she heard the door shut briskly behind him, she picked up the champagne glass with a shaky hand.

The icy fluid tasted flat and bitter on her tongue.

four

LANA swung open the door. Melanie looked flushed and pretty standing there in the hallway. Lana suspected her healthy glow had just as much to do with the escort named Eric, the man Melanie'd spent the last two nights with, as it did the tropical sun.

Lana's own tan had deepened considerably. But unlike Melanie, Lana couldn't attribute her glowing skin to great sex. She'd spent the last few nights alone in a cold bed, trying not to think about that night with Jason Koa. She couldn't imagine what had gotten into her—why she'd behaved so uncharacteristically.

Every time she recalled the graphic image of herself in that mirror—raw, unprotected, and shuddering violently in orgasm—something swelled uncomfortably in her chest.

"Another night in paradise," Melanie sighed.

Lana chuckled. She was glad Melanie seemed so relaxed. Still, a prickle of uncertainty went through her when she fully took in the contentment on her friend's face.

"Honey, you're not letting this guy—Eric—get under your skin, are you?" She felt like a hypocrite after she asked. Who was the one who had allowed a paid escort to get to her?

And Lana *knew* better.

"No, but I am going to miss him when we leave," Melanie admitted as she stepped into Lana's suite. Lana picked up her purse. "He's really made me forget about David—or at least, not obsess about him so much. Kind of hard to focus on all the nasty things David's been pulling in divorce court when you've got a beautiful man filling up your ... er ... thoughts."

Lana smiled. "Well, I'm thankful for that. Are you seeing him again tonight?"

Melanie blushed, making her cheeks turn even pinker beneath her sunburn. "He's stopping by at ten."

Lana checked her watch. "Guess we'd better get to dinner, then."

Since they were both wearing heels, they had to take the street instead of the beach. The mood on the usually bustling Kalakaua Avenue was uncharacteristically mellow in the soft twilight. Lana walked briskly, however, refusing to enjoy the beauty of the evening, the strolling tourists, or the caressing breeze. Her memories of the glitzy, touristy avenue fueled her hasty footsteps. Or maybe it was the sound of street entertainers in the distance—strumming ukuleles and a woman's voice.

A *woman*, not a child, she reminded herself anxiously.

"I think this is the entrance," Melanie said, referring to the restaurant where she'd booked a reservation.

"Jace's?" Lana asked when she saw the sign. Her footsteps faltered for an instant as she recalled the hotel front desk calling the other night to announce her guest.

A Jace says he's here to see you, Ms. Rodriguez. Shall I send him up?

"Yeah, apparently it's a Waikiki must. It's always so booked up, though. I couldn't get reservations until tonight. The food is supposed to be phenomenal, and I got us an ocean-side table. It came with the highest recommendation in my travel guide."

"Great," Lana murmured as they approached a native hostess wearing a pretty floral dress and a peach-colored lei.

"I love your lei," Melanie complimented amiably as the woman gathered their menus.

"Thank you," the hostess replied with a smile. She led Melanie and Lana down a walnut-panel-lined hallway. Out of the corner of her eye Lana noticed a blur of photos, all associated with sporting events around the islands—outrigger canoe races, swimming events, surfers riding shockingly tall waves. "They're actually for sale over there if you're interested. The owner's grandmother makes them. She always says flowers are the only jewelry women should wear."

One of the photos came into sharp, clear focus—the image of a lean, powerfully built male swimmer crouched to dive on the starting block.

"Jason Koa," Lana said.

The hostess's brow furrowed before she looked to where Lana stared. Her smile widened. "Yes, that's the owner of Jace's. He's an Olympic gold medalist, many times over. He still holds several world records. He's also a championship surfer."

"He's our surf instructor!" Melanie exclaimed. They'd all paused and were staring at the photo of Jason.

The hostess laughed melodiously.

"You were lucky to get him. His busy schedule usually only

allows him to squeeze in a couple lessons a week. He has enough staff to cover the lessons, but he usually tries to teach a few because he loves it so much. He also owns a boat marina in Honolulu, and he's always volunteering for charity and sporting events here on the island. The Koa family is very well known locally. Koa Farms exports a huge amount of island produce to the Orient and the mainland—pineapple, macadamia nuts, coconut oil, things like that. So . . . he didn't tell you he owned Jace's?"

"No, he never mentioned it," Lana replied coolly. She unglued her gaze from the photograph of Jason poised to dive. Even though he wore goggles, she still could see the intensity in his dark eyes, the expression of focused determination.

The look of a man who got what he wanted.

"Does he have any other . . . business ventures?" Lana asked, trying to hide the irritation in her voice. From the perplexed expression of the hostess, she hadn't succeeded very well.

"Not that I'm aware of. I can't imagine what else he'd have time for."

Lana smiled and nodded. The hostess resumed showing them to their table.

"Wow, we were taught how to surf by a local legend," Melanie whispered as they followed the hostess.

Lana hadn't revealed to her good friend that Jason Koa had enlightened her on a great deal more than just how to find her balance in the crashing surf. He's showed her the dizzying depths of her passion. As far as Melanie knew, Lana's guest on that first night had been enjoyed and subsequently forgotten.

She thanked the hostess distractedly when she placed a napkin in her lap and handed them the menus. She gazed out at the remaining swimmers frolicking in the waves.

Jason Koa may have fueled the flames of her desire into an inferno, but he'd done it dishonestly. Surely he'd lied about being a male escort. Why would a man like him bother being employed as a male escort—being employed as *anything*, for that matter, when he was clearly a successful entrepreneur and probably the most eligible bachelor on the whole damn island? Anger burned in her stomach when she considered his bald misrepresentation.

But so did curiosity.

Why had he done it? He didn't need to *trick* a woman to get her into bed. Was his motivation just to put Lana in her place after the way she'd treated him during the surf lesson? Had he just been soothing a bruised ego?

If that were the case, he should be triumphant. He'd brought her to her knees. She would have done anything he'd asked her—and gladly. She should be wild with fury. But although she was unsettled and, yes, angry, she couldn't help but recall the expression on his handsome face just before he'd stalked out of her hotel suite. It'd hardly been victorious.

She ordered a mai tai at the waiter's recommendation and made small talk with Melanie. But the question kept recurring to her again and again.

Why had he done it?

For some reason, her mind fastened on the question and refused to let go. Not until she found out the answer.

LANA was freshly amazed sitting in the traditional Polynesian vessel. She'd forgotten how narrow and sleek the hulls of an outrigger canoe were. It would immediately tip over if it weren't for the balancing outrigger support float—the *ama*—which was attached to the port side. The *ama* made the little boat much faster and more stable on the high waves than a single-hulled canoe. Not that the waves were high presently. Jason had chosen a secluded harbor for his boat marina, one with a natural stone breakwater that almost entirely protected the calm, brilliantly blue water from the Pacific's crashing surf.

The little man studied her with polite curiosity. Muscles and delineated tendons flexed beneath her rower's tanned, leathery skin. She'd learned not five minutes ago that his name was Harold. She'd been standing in the pleasant city park behind the boat marina, staring up at a ten-foot-tall bronzed statue of Jason Koa. In the custom of the islands, a half-dozen or more leis hung around the statue's neck. The flowers were wilted and brown near the bronze, but the top ones were still fresh—probably placed there by tourists after getting off a catamaran or chartered dinner cruise last night.

"Jace hates that," someone had suddenly said from behind her as she stared at the statue.

Lana had turned around to see a short, spry elderly man watching her with tiny, raisinlike brown eyes.

"Why?"

The man had shrugged. "Sometimes public officials try to kiss up to Jace, make him a poster boy to their causes. I guess they think he's the perfect image of Hawaii." Harold nodded at the statue. "A certain city councilwoman pushed for that thing. I think she thought it'd please Jace, but instead, it just annoys him. He never says he hates it, but I see the way he looks when people mention it. Probably makes him feel like a strutting rooster, having a statue of himself so near his marina. Are you looking for Jace?"

"Yes," Lana had admitted, caught with her guard down by his pleasant forthrightness. A brief conversation had ensued, after which Lana found herself being rowed out to Jason's home. It somehow seemed appropriate that he lived on the water.

"Rodriguez," Harold mused as he rowed. "Are you Mexican?"

"Yes. Partially. Are you?" she asked, recognizing his accent despite his obviously Polynesian features.

He nodded proudly. "I grew up in Puerto Vallarta. How about you?"

"In a tiny little village on the Yucatan peninsula—near Cozumel," Lana replied evasively. She smiled, feeling a tad guilty as she watched him labor for her. He wouldn't allow her to row, and had asked very politely if she would do him the honor of facing him while he piloted the craft. "Thank you again for taking me out to Jason's boat. Are you sure he won't be upset at the intrusion? If you'd just given me his number, I would have called first to warn him."

Harold shook his head. "I don't understand mainlander's obsession with the cell phone. Jace will be thrilled to have such a lovely lady drop in on him unexpectedly. Why would we deny him that experience?"

Lana couldn't stop herself from laughing when she saw Harold's grin, despite the fact that she was far from agreeing with his analysis of the situation. She had no reason to assume that Jason Koa would be thrilled to have her invade his privacy.

She examined the boat Harold rowed them toward with interest. It was enormous—*clearly* a houseboat in the literal sense. Its proportions must have been twenty by eighty feet, and that square footage didn't include the foredeck or the large canopied lounging deck on top of the main cabin.

Harold tied up the canoe, scurried onto the boat, and put out a hand to help her come aboard. He immediately got back into the little craft.

"Uh . . . you're leaving?" Lana asked, flustered.

Harold nodded matter-of-factly. "I've got to get back to work at the marina. Jace can take you back to shore."

Lana glanced around uncertainly as Harold paddled away, not at all liking the idea of not having a ready escape route.

Not comfortable at all.

She shouldn't have given in to the urge to see him, shouldn't have allowed her curiosity to get the best of her. If only she could have held out. She'd be safely back in New York in three days, after all.

But she *hadn't* been able to hold out. More fool her.

She padded across the deck in her white canvas tennis shoes, peering through the windows. The boat bobbed subtly in the gentle waves. Wind chimes trilled in the breeze, but otherwise everything was silent.

"Hello?" she called through one of the opened windows, but no reply was forthcoming. Nervousness fluttered in her belly.

What the hell was she doing here?

She knocked on the cabin door. When she got no reply, she made a quick circuit of the deck, but Jason was nowhere in sight.

She knocked several more times at the door and then tried the handle. It was open. She entered, wiping her shoes when she saw the gleaming wood floors. After traveling down a short hallway, she found herself in the midst of what might have been a luxurious condominium, complete with built-in cherrywood cabinetry, a gourmet kitchen with stainless steel appliances, and a living room with comfortable furnishings and a state-of-the-art entertainment system built into the wall. Her anxious gaze took in several fine examples of oil paintings of local landscapes. She also noticed two renderings of forbidding, gray ocean-side cliffs and frothing waves. Her brow wrinkled in confusion. The haunting landscapes depicted in the paintings stood in stark contrast to the colorful tropical coastlines of Oahu.

"Jason?" she called out hoarsely.

Again, there was only silence.

She distantly heard the sound of water splashing. She walked over to the window and watched, her breath burning in her lungs, as Jason arose out of the ocean with a flex and bulge of defined muscle. He'd obviously taken an afternoon swim. He used his fingers to wipe water out of his face, then casually swiped his hand over a ridged abdomen, making a stream of water splash off taut, sun-bronzed skin. Lana stood rigid, paralyzed by the sight of him glittering and flashing in the bright sunlight like an ancient Polynesian god.

She made a small, trapped sound of dismay—or was it longing?—when he suddenly went still and looked directly at her through the pane of glass.

five

JASON didn't say anything, just went to the refrigerator, opened it, and took out a bottle of water. He turned to face Lana Rodriguez and cracked off the plastic top with a brisk twist of his wrist. The silence that ensued was tense . . . charged.

He chugged down half the water.

She still stood where he'd first seen her by the window. She wore a pair of cutoff jean shorts, a fitted T-shirt, and white canvas tennis shoes. Her hair had been pulled back into a ponytail. He didn't see a trace of makeup on her face, but she didn't need it. He'd been right. Her skin soaked up the sun like it had thirsted for it forever. Her legs looked long, smooth, and satiny in the shadowed light.

He sensed her uncertainty, her anxiety, but he did nothing to soothe her unrest. The sight of her rattled him. That knowledge made him realize he needed every advantage he could get. Forget

Hawaiian hospitality. She was going to have to sweat for putting herself in his territory.

Just like he did.

She walked toward him silently, her exquisitely chiseled jaw held high. Damn, that woman had a chip on her shoulder.

"I'm sorry for intruding," she said. Her low, smoky voice made his damp skin prickle. "The door was open and I . . . couldn't find you."

"Why?"

She flinched slightly at his harsh question, but then her jaw went up again. He saw anger ignite in her tilted hazel eyes.

"I wanted to hire you again. As an escort."

He gave a bark of laughter before he chugged down the remainder of the water and tossed the plastic bottle in his recycling bin beneath the sink. "Give it a rest, will you? Angie—the hostess at Jace's—told me you were there last night. Did you think she didn't recognize you? She was telling everyone about her encounter with Lana Rodriguez, including me when I went in to close last night. You *know* I'm not really an escort for Hawaiian Nights. What are you *really* here for?"

Her backbone stiffened. "You don't seem to have any problems with the fact that you blatantly misled me."

He shrugged. "It's like I said the other night. I got what I wanted, and so did you. What if I did twist the truth a little?"

"*Twist* the truth?" she repeated incredulously. "I could have you arrested for what you did!"

"You could try." He watched her as he used the towel around his neck to dry his hair. "But you'd have to admit you solicited sexual services from Hawaiian Nights. That's not going to please the police any more than my little misrepresentation. I'll just say it was a mistake that you thought I was a male prostitute."

She stalked toward him, looking furious. He thought she was about to ream him out when she suddenly stopped dead in her tracks.

"*Why?*" The single word popped out of her mouth, seemingly against her will. "Why the hell did you do that?"

He paused before he let the towel drop to his chest. His cock stiffened to full, leaden readiness, as erect as it might have been after having a woman pamper it with her hands and mouth for long, delicious minutes.

All that from just the *sight* of Lana's vulnerability, just the *hint* of her softness.

"I told you. I wanted you. When the opportunity arose to take what I wanted, I took it."

She shook her head in amazement. "Just like that."

"Yeah," he growled as he came around the granite-topped island that set off his kitchen from the living space. He saw her eyes go wide as he stalked toward her. "Just like that. So why don't we talk about what's really important here." He opened his hand at the back of her neck and pulled her against him. He leaned down until their mouths were just inches apart. The light scent of flowers and sweet woman filtered into his nose. He breathed deeply through his nostrils.

"Tell me why you came, Lana."

She panted lightly in the taut silence.

"Come on," he coaxed, his gaze glued to her mouth. "Just say it."

For some reason, he wasn't shocked when a single tear spilled down her cheek. He'd sensed her inner conflict from the begin-ning. It was what fascinated him about her, what drew him like metal to lodestone, despite the fact that his brain blared a warning to stay away from her.

"I . . ." Her elegant throat convulsed as she swallowed thickly. "I . . . need you. Again."

He pressed his mouth against her forehead and then her warm, parted lips.

"Thank you for telling me. And you're willing to play by my rules?"

"Yes," she whispered.

She looked dazed as she stared up at him. And indescribably beautiful. He couldn't resist dipping his tongue fleetingly into the warm honey behind her lips. When he raised his head, he nodded toward the hallway.

"Go back to my bedroom and take off your clothes. Wait for me on the bed while I take a quick shower."

He saw her pulse beating madly at her throat as he waited tensely for her answer. He exhaled in relief when she merely extricated herself from his arms and walked toward the hallway.

Five minutes later he paused in the doorway to his bedroom. She'd pulled back the comforter on his bed, but she hadn't covered herself with the sheet. She'd released her hair. It spread over her shoulders and his pillow in a sexy spill.

He paused, his pulse drumming out a primitive beat in his aching cock. His raging erection hadn't abated in the least during the frigid shower he'd taken in the guest bathroom. The feeble attempt to regain some control over his lust hadn't helped in the slightest. He kept picturing the way Lana had looked in the mirror as he nursed her through her orgasm, kept remembering how tightly she'd sheathed his cock. The cold shower hadn't begun to penetrate his body heat when he imagined her stretched out on his bed, waiting for him.

And his vivid imagination hadn't even begun to approximate her naked beauty. The fact that she'd come there and exposed her need, despite her insecurity, amazed him.

It turned him on more than he cared to admit.

He saw her eyes lower and linger on his jutting erection. It bobbed in the air eagerly, as though she'd touched him instead of just looked.

"Spread your legs," he murmured as he approached the bed. It pleased him that she shaved. He liked to be granted full access to a woman's sensitive tissues during sex. He shaved his testicles because he wanted the same pleasure for himself.

But in Lana's case, it would be a true crime to cover any part of her lovely pink flower, he thought as she widened her legs and exposed her dewy petals to his hungry gaze.

"Now reach up and grab the posts," he instructed, referring to the cherrywood posts of his headboard.

She hesitated.

"My rules, Lana. You agreed."

She slowly reached up, stretching her torso. Her pale breasts thrust upward.

Jason reminded himself to breathe as he opened a drawer on his bedside table and drew out a blue silk scarf. She merely stared at him, her eyes looking enormous in her face as he tied her wrists to the headboard.

"Now you have no choice but to play by my rules." He knelt over her. She said nothing, but he heard her gasp as he lightly ran his fingertips along the sensitive skin at the side of her waist and over her ribs. Her large pink nipples pebbled at his touch. He couldn't resist the temptation of them.

He came down on his hands and knees and suckled the tip of one of her breasts. She cried out at the sudden onslaught. Her sleek body writhed beneath him, but he wouldn't be denied such delicious, firm flesh. He feasted on her plump, responsive breasts while she whimpered and moaned. He molded her in his palms, pushing her nipples together for his greedy consumption.

"Such pretty breasts. I think I'll fuck them later," he mused when he finally lifted his head, appreciating the results of the efforts of his hands and mouth on her flushed flesh.

He reluctantly left her breasts so that he could taste the skin next to her belly button and nip at the side of her waist. His hands wandered over her belly, hips, and thighs, relishing how soft she was, how smooth, how she flowed beneath his fingertips. She tasted good everywhere. Her shivers of pleasure were like nectar on his tongue.

He spread her lithesome thighs farther and swiped his tongue between her labia, letting her honey soak into his appreciative taste buds. She cried out sharply and twisted in her restraints. He held her hips.

"Shhh. Don't fight me."

Her hips settled on the bed. She stared at him as she panted. He saw the wariness that crept into her expression.

"If you close your eyes right now, 'Ailana . . . if you try to shut me out, I'll stop."

Her facial features went rigid in disbelief, but he hadn't read her mind. Not really. Her mounting anxiety had been broadcast loud and clear on her face.

He lowered his head, keeping his eyes trained on her face, and began to eat her succulent pussy while she watched.

After a moment, it was him who shut his eyes as the experience overwhelmed his senses. He turned his head, tonguing and suckling her most concentrated nectar off the smooth petals of her cunt. Ah, God, she was sweetness distilled. *Onaona*. He drowned in her taste, only distantly aware of her harsh moans and sharp cries of pleasure.

He vibrated her clit with his finger and drove his tongue high up into her weeping slit when she cried out in orgasm.

Her juices still slicked his lips, tongue, and throat when he came up on his hands and knees over her. His cock felt as if it would burst, he was so stiff. Her taste did something strange to him. He gritted his teeth when he took his erection into his hand and stroked the length. Lana watched him through narrowed eyelids as she panted, still recovering from her climax.

"Do you like to suck cock, Lana?"

She nodded, still watching him as he pumped his cock.

"Are you good at it?" he teased warmly as he came farther up on the bed, his knees straddling her chest. He put one hand on the headboard and leaned over her.

Again, she nodded, her eyes never leaving his cock.

"I'll just bet you are," he admitted grudgingly, wishing he hadn't asked. He caught a stream of pre-cum on his pistoning fist and spread it over the sensitive head with his thumb. She moaned softly and licked her lower lip. His cock lurched in his hand. He forced himself to release the heavy member. The weight of it made it drop. The crown brushed against her cheek and jerked up at the contact.

She turned her face, her lips parting hungrily.

With an extreme effort of will, he spread his hand on her jaw and straightened her head on the pillow, keeping her from fitting his cock between her seeking lips.

"I'm left in so little doubt about how good you are with that mouth, I think I'll feed my cock to you instead of letting you consume it, Lana."

Her brow furrowed in puzzlement.

"Open your lips," he rasped. He was so aroused that he was only going to last for about two strokes in her wet heat. Or maybe just the sight of her desire-darkened eyes and damp, lush lips would be sufficient to do him in, he thought grimly as she opened wide to receive him.

He pushed the head of his cock between her lips, stretching them even wider than she'd spread them. He grunted in pleasure at the sensation of penetrating her tight hold and sliding his cock against her warm, wet tongue. When she tried to raise her head off the pillow, he gripped gently at the hair at her nape, stilling her.

"Don't move."

Her eyes looked enormous as she stared up at him. He closed his eyelids briefly to stave off the potency of the erotic image she made with the first few inches of his cock in her mouth. He felt her flutter her tongue against him and groaned when he realized she rubbed against the slit, eager for his taste. She once again strained up, trying to slide more of his length into her mouth.

He tightened his hold on her hair.

"I'm going to *give* it to you, Lana. Stay still."

She froze, but he couldn't prevent her from increasing the suction of her mouth. Her cheeks hollowed out as she sucked. He muttered a curse and pushed into her farther. It felt so damn good he couldn't stop himself from stroking her shallowly . . . fucking her sweet, hot mouth.

"Is that what you wanted?"

She moaned, the sensation vibrating into his thrusting cock. He flexed his hips, filling her mouth to capacity. Her thirstiness, her unceasingly strong suction, stunned him. In a moment of mindless lust he thrust deeper. She made a muted choking sound and his eyes popped open.

"I'm sorry," he murmured. He felt her straining, trying to position herself to take him more completely. He resituated her head and gently probed deeper. This time, he watched her reaction carefully. All he saw was wild arousal in her eyes when he breached her throat and felt that tight ring squeezing him. He fell forward, catching his weight with one hand on the wall.

"Ah, God, Lana." He withdrew from her throat and fucked her mouth fast and shallow. She drew on him so hungrily it was too much to bear. His balls pinched in a mixture of pleasure and pain, and he knew he'd reached his limit.

He jerked his penis out of her mouth and arrowed it at her heaving breasts. Her nipple felt cool and erect against his steaming cock. He batted at it and roared as he erupted.

He blinked into partial awareness a moment later, still panting, still shuddering in the aftershocks of a mind-splintering climax. Her breast dripped and glistened with his cum. She stared fixedly at where his still spasming cock lay pressed to her nipple.

"Let me," she whispered. "Please."

It would have been an utter impossibility to deny such a sweet request. Not that he remotely *wanted* to deny it. He gritted his teeth and shivered when she sucked his hypersensitive member deep, cleaning him with her strong, quick tongue.

A short while later he used several tissues to dry her breast before he came down next to her on the bed. His body sagged in temporary repletion. Still, the delicious sensation of Lana's silky skin and firm flesh pressing against him told him his satiation would be short-lived. He nuzzled her breast lazily and kissed a stiff nipple.

"It felt so good. Thank you, Lana," he whispered against her moist flesh. Her nipple beaded tighter for him. He glanced up at her face when she remained silent. She looked like she was going to say something, but then she stopped.

"What?" he prodded.

"How . . . Why do you do that to me?" she asked huskily.

He sat up on one elbow. "What, precisely?"

She opened her mouth and then closed it again. He saw her pull on the restraint of the scarf.

"What, Lana?"

"Nothing," she whispered. "Will you untie me, please?"

He considered her for a long moment. He didn't like the way she avoided his gaze. Why did he get so irritated when she withheld herself from him?

"Not yet, I don't think."

She swallowed thickly. "Why not?"

He lowered his head until their foreheads touched. "Because I like having you at my mercy. You're a strong woman, Lana, but you're *aching* for this. Why are you ashamed of wanting to let go of all that tight control for a while?"

Her mouth twitched, but she remained mute. He began to stroke her languorously from hip to breast, all too eager to make her body speak if she refused him her words.

His boat rocked them ever so gently as he caressed her for

the next several minutes. The wind chimes trilled in the distance. Otherwise, the silence hung thickly around them as he explored her body with his hand and their gazes clung. She bit her lower lip as he brushed his fingers over her breasts and then trailed them down her belly. He knew she tried not to cry out. He was quickly becoming addicted to forcing her to face her desire head-on, and he resented her withholding it as he stroked her silky flesh.

His cock stiffened as he touched her. As much as he wanted to see her succumb, he realized his own need was quickly becoming untenable.

He reached in the bedside drawer for a condom.

six

SHE said nothing as he rolled the rubber over his cock and came down over her, supporting his upper body on one elbow and guiding his cock to her slit. But she gave a plaintive cry when he drove into her sleek pussy and pressed his naked balls to her dewy, swollen petals.

"Shhh," he soothed as he dropped kisses on her flushed cheeks. But he didn't know who he was trying to soothe, her or himself. He stroked her and clamped his eyes shut.

Christ, it was sublime.

He held her gaze and fucked her, slow and shallow, causing sweet little electrical sensations of distilled pleasure to pulse his cock and tickle up his spine.

Her pussy fit him like she'd been tailor-made.

Even though the room was cast in shadow, he saw how vividly pink her cheeks were. He suspected his tight thrusts were having the same effect on her that they were on him. His eyes fixed on her parted lips. She whimpered on his firm downstrokes.

He touched his mouth to her lips.

"Are you burning, Lana?"

"Yes," she whispered. She flexed her hips, trying to get him to ride her faster. Instead, he paused, fully sheathed in her pussy. He kissed her like he wanted to fuck her, pillaging her sweet mouth, desecrating it . . . loving it. The pleasant throb of his cock slowly mounted to a furious ache.

The sensation of her squeezing vagina eventually made him groan roughly and lift his head. He'd been slaking his thirst on her mouth for several minutes. It amazed him to realize it, but he wanted to kiss her even more. His cock wouldn't let him, though. He silently cursed the damn thing for putting limits on his ravishment of this woman.

She licked her upper lip anxiously. They were both covered in a fine layer of perspiration. Her eyes moved over his chest, the hunger he saw in her gaze making his need swell.

"Untie me so I can touch you."

He began to move, his actions firm and deliberate. Her beautiful face tightened.

"Not this time, Lana."

He *wanted* her hands on his body, all right. But the strength of the explosion that was building in him warned him it wouldn't be wise. She tested his control sorely. He watched her expression, fascinated, as he pounded their bodies together with longer strokes now, more than he'd allowed them before, but still denying them both the driving thrusts they craved . . . building their fire carefully.

"Jason," she pleaded. He felt her shaking but then wondered if it was his own flesh trembling. Her hips strained up for him, her pussy whispering promises to him of the deepest, sweetest orgasm imaginable.

"What, Lana?" he goaded between a clenched jaw. "What do you want? What did you come here for?"

She writhed beneath him, clawing at the silk scarf. "For *this*. Fuck me. Do it hard."

A drop of sweat rolled down his abdomen when he rose. He placed his hands on the top of the headboard. She keened when he lanced down into her tight pussy at the new angle. He set a hard, relentless pace. A fuse went off in his brain when she spread her thighs wider, granting him greater access to paradise. Tight control gave way to pure, unregulated lust and need. Their flesh slapped together in an intense, fluid fuck.

She lifted her head off his pillow and shouted out her release.

"That's right, give it to me," he grated out as he pounded into her spasming pussy and heat flooded around him. It was too much. He drove into her high and hard, and exploded. It felt so good it hurt. He fell down over her, seeking out her skin with his nose and mouth, some primitive part of his brain needing to breathe her in the midst of that agonizing, blissful storm.

He slowly came back to himself with the scent of Lana—desire-drenched flowers—flooding his nose. Something told him not to breathe too deeply of the addicting fragrance. She was cold and rigid and . . . mixed up. Not his type.

But it was too late.

He buried his nose in the damp, soft curve of a breast and inhaled deeply.

LANA felt as though her flesh had gone fluid. Her mind worked sluggishly, unable to work properly with the sensation of Jason's body pressing her down into the mattress and her nerves still firing madly after her explosive climax. She was quieting . . . but slowly, deliciously, her muscles going heavy and warm in the lazy descent. His nuzzling nose and mouth on her breast only added to the decadent sweetness of the still moments—the calm following the storm. His head pressed more heavily to her breasts, his warm breath caressing her perspiration damp skin. She wondered if he slept. Lana closed her eyes in profound contentment.

In the distance, a boat called a warning with its horn.

"Jason?" she whispered.

He lifted his head slowly. He hadn't been sleeping, after all. By the sight of his heavy eyelids, however, he hadn't been far from it.

"Sorry," he muttered.

He reached. With a flex of taut muscle, he untied the scarf. Her arms lowered and she experienced a moment of discomfort. She didn't know what to do with her hands. She'd wanted desperately to stroke his beautiful body in the heat of passion, but now that he'd released her, she still felt restrained.

Not by bonds—by her own uncertainty.

He paused after tossing aside the strip of silk, and Lana experienced a pang of regret for interrupting their profound lassitude. But it had caused that old, familiar pressure on her chest to consider what it would be like to have his head resting on her breast while he slept peacefully. Only this time, Lana couldn't decide if the sensation was caused by panic or some sort of . . . inner fullness.

Either way, she'd felt a need to put a stop to it.

He came up on his elbows, regarding her intently. One of her hands fell to the cool sheets, but she couldn't stop the other from caressing the dense muscles of his shoulder and upper arm. Her vagina tightened around his embedded cock at the sight of him . . . at the sensation of his thick, smooth, perspiration-slick skin beneath her hand. He looked magnificent with sweat gleaming on his bronzed skin, his long bangs mussed on his forehead . . . the gleam of a well-satisfied male in his dark eyes. His gaze swept down over her throat and breasts. His lips twitched in amusement, but she thought he looked pleased.

"We really worked up a sweat. How about a swim?" he rumbled, his stare still latched on her breasts.

"I doubt I could keep up with you."

She muffled a protest when he shifted off her. "Just a dip, honey. We've already done the workout."

She couldn't help but join him in a smile as he stood. He was in the process of removing the condom, his back to her, when he glanced over his shoulder. His smile faded.

"Jesus."

"What?" she asked, alarmed.

"I just realized I've never seen you smile."

Her mouth hung open for a second before she recovered. "Despite what you think, it's not such an unusual occurrence." When he didn't say anything, she cleared her throat uncomfortably. "I don't have anything to wear swimming, Jason."

"I disagree. You've got a beautiful bathing suit," he said, glancing over his shoulder at her naked body.

Lana couldn't help but notice that there was only the faintest of tans lines around his lean hips. He likely only wore swim trunks one out of every four times he was in the sun. His muscular ass was nearly as bronzed as the rest of him. She could only be thankful that he'd been wearing a pair of board shorts when he arose from the lagoon earlier, looking like a god arising from the sunlit waters. The vision of him had wreaked havoc on her senses, but if he'd been naked, he would have devastated her.

"Come on. I'll show you. It's private, so no one will see us," he said, forcing her to drag her eyes off the awesome sight of his bare ass.

Lana stood and followed him down the hallway, their bare feet padding softly on the cool wood floor. She waited while he paused in the bathroom, glancing around his home.

She'd noticed when she entered earlier that although he left his windows open to the sultry Hawaiian breezes, his air-conditioning had been set to a low setting. When it became too stuffy inside the breezy boathouse, the air conditioner kicked on, cooling the interior. A small roof surrounded the entire boat, casting the living quarters in a pleasant shadow that contrasted drastically with the brilliance of the sun reflecting off the Pacific Ocean.

Jason Koa had created a lovely, incredibly peaceful home for himself, Lana acknowledged as she waited behind him while he opened a pair of patio doors in the living room.

They stepped onto the deck. Lana blinked in the blinding sunlight. She looked out on a circular body of cerulean water. The waves were even gentler here than in the protected harbor. She hadn't noticed it before when she circled the deck, searching for Jason, but he'd moored his boat at the mouth of a lagoon. A hundred feet away she saw a white beach. To the left, a finger of land stretched out into the water. An enormous koa tree, its trunk possibly ten or eleven feet thick, persevered on the tiny spit of land. A few palms crowded next to it, along with a thick tangle of foliage. The inlet was protected on the opposite side by the curve of the land. In the distance she saw the vastness of the Pacific Ocean.

"Wow," Lana murmured as she gazed out at the calm blue waters. "A private swimming pool."

Jason laughed before he grabbed her hand and pulled her toward the edge. "I had my reasons for picking this harbor for the marina. There's a coral reef to the south of where I moor the houseboat. It protects the lagoon even more than the harbor. It's deep enough to dive here, though."

Lana just looked up at him and nodded. She dove. The rush of water over her heated, sensitized body felt delicious. A second after she surfaced, she heard a splash and knew Jason had followed her. His head and shoulders popped out of the water not ten feet away from her. His smile struck her like a flashbulb—not of light, but of concentrated sex. Something lurched in her breast at the sight. She couldn't help but wonder how may women he seduced with that smile on a daily basis. The image of the blonde with the curvy body and the eager hands popped into her mind's eye.

A shadow crossed his face as he came toward her.

"What's wrong?"

"Nothing," she said lightly. She laid her hot cheek in the cool water and began a lazy sidestroke toward the beach. Why should she care if Jason Koa seduced a dozen women a day? His effort-less sex appeal and skilled lovemaking were the reasons she'd sought him out, weren't they?

A moment later she sat in the soft sand and let the gentle surf caress her thighs, hips, and belly. Orange hibiscus flowers danced in the gentle breeze just to the right of her. Six foot and several inches of hard, delicious male glided up next to her on a wave, his muscular back and gleaming ass breaking the surface of the foaming water.

Paradise, indeed. Lana couldn't imagine why she'd gone so tense when she saw him smile.

He plopped down next to her, his forearms resting lightly on his bent knees. For several minutes they just gazed out at a sky so perfect it looked like a turquoise shellacked dome.

"Don't you get tired of it after a while?"

"What?" he asked, turning toward her.

"Perfection."

She glanced at him when he didn't reply. His head was tilted down, casting his eyes in shadow as he studied her. "No. I love this island. I grew up here. My family is here. I've been to a lot of different places, but no matter how much I enjoy them, I eventually want to come back. What have you got against my home, Lana?"

She swallowed uneasily when she heard the low, gruff quality of his voice. She hadn't meant to lead them into dangerous waters. "What makes you think I have anything against it? As you're always saying . . . it's a paradise."

She could tell by his sidelong glance that he knew he was being brushed off. "You don't think it's paradise though, do you?"

She shrugged and nodded at the calm azure lagoon. "Who would deny it?"

He bent his head and rubbed his cheek idly against his

forearm as he studied her averted profile. "Someone who's decided it's hell, I suppose."

She said nothing. Thankfully the tension of the moment eased with the help of the sunshine and the gentle surf. They sat for a long time, not talking, just enjoying the hot sun and cool water.

"I should go. I must be keeping you from work," she murmured eventually.

He made an irritated sound. "You're fine," he said. Then, after a moment, he asked, "Where do you live?"

"Manhattan."

He grunted. She glanced at him sharply.

"What's that supposed to mean?"

He shrugged. "It just makes sense."

"What?"

"You seem like a city girl," he stated vaguely.

"You mean I'm uptight."

Again, that vivid flash of white in his dark face.

"No. I meant that you seem like a city girl," he restated firmly. "You don't take any shit, that's for sure."

It hadn't sounded like an admonishment. In fact, his tone had been even and matter-of-fact. Regret seeped into her awareness, nevertheless, for always coming off so edgy with him. An apology would have required an explanation as to why she *was* so defensive, however, so she remained mute. It wasn't like she had a good answer, after all. She couldn't very well tell him he chafed her because he seemed to embody everything about this island paradise—the brilliant beauty, the effortless charm . . . even a career that kowtowed to the tourists.

"Is Manhattan your brand of paradise?" he asked, interrupting her thoughts.

She smiled as she stared into the distance. "No. Not really."

"Then why do you live there?"

"Because it's convenient for my work. My studio lets me record there, and I perform fairly regularly at a club in SoHo."

"I like your music. I never got a chance to tell you."

She glanced over at him, surprised at the sincerity in his voice. Surprised in general.

"Why are you shocked that I like your stuff?"

"I don't know," she mumbled.

He leaned closer. She caught the scent of his male musk and clean ocean water.

"Tell me. I'd really like to know."

She gave him an exasperated look. "You just don't seem like the type, that's all."

"And what type would I be? The type that listens to the Beach Boys and Jimmy Buffet? Surfboards, margaritas, and girls running around in bikinis . . . Do I have it right?" he teased.

"Well, you are sort of a . . ."

"Cliché?"

She blinked. This time he hadn't sounded so lighthearted.

"I . . . I'm sorry," she murmured. "I hadn't meant to judge."

He sighed, some of the tension that had built up in their exchange leaving him. He cupped his hand on top of the water and watched idly as a gentle wave submersed it. "My mother says I get my occasional bouts of moodiness from her side of the family."

"Do your parents live on Oahu?"

"My father does. My mother lives in Cornwall. Maybe it's my Cornish genes that make me appreciate the blues."

She realized her mouth hung open in amazement. It seemed so

strange to think of him anywhere but here on this vibrant, lush Polynesian island. She thought of that steely hard gaze that entered his eyes at times, his manner with her in bed minutes ago, and was forced to alter her opinion. The stark, harsh beauty of the Cornish coast suited him just as much.

He was a walking paradox.

She shook her head slowly. "A Celtic Polynesian. Well, it's no wonder you're a swimmer," she finally said with a small smile. She shivered when she saw his eyes glued to her mouth, and she glanced out at the sunlit lagoon.

"Are your parents divorced, then?" she asked delicately.

"Never married. Every year I spend a month with my mother. I love visiting Cornwall, but like I said: this is my home."

"But . . . your mother . . . Why didn't you live with her?"

He sat back, exposing his lean, muscled torso to the sun. She couldn't stop herself from turning and gaping at his male beauty despite her interest in the conversation.

"It's a long story, but the short version of it is: my mother didn't expect to get pregnant on her visit to Hawaii. She's a writer, and even back then, she'd made a career for herself. My father has never once set foot off this island. Never wants to. After they'd talked it over a great deal, they struck a bargain." He met her gaze, and Lana sensed powerfully that he was entirely comfortable with whatever his parents' decision had been. She surmised this because Jason Koa was entirely comfortable with himself. "My mother agreed to let me grow up on the island with my father and my grandmother as long as I came to visit her every year. Grandma Lily went to Cornwall to get me soon after I was born."

"You mention your grandmother a lot. She must be very special to you."

"She is."

His simple earnestness touched her. How many times did a woman hear a strong, confident, entirely masculine man speak of his grandmother with such gentleness?

Lana realized that several seconds had passed in silence as they stared at one another. The cool surf lapping around her belly caused her nipples to tighten. His gaze dragged slowly over her neck and chest, pausing on her breasts.

"You may not care for the island, Lana, but you look like you belong here."

The skin at the back of her neck prickled at the sound of his husky voice. Her nipples pinched tighter under his appreciative stare.

She pushed forward several feet and came down on her knees in the sand, covering her body in the water. If he seemed surprised by her abrupt movement, his face didn't show it.

"I should be going," she said.

He sighed. "Yeah, I guess I should, too."

He shoved off the beach, but instead of immediately swimming toward the boat, he paused, waist-deep in the water, and waited for her. She saw his heavy-lidded look of frank appraisal and knew he was considering going another round in bed before she left.

The cool water seemed to lick sensually at her suddenly tingling pussy.

But awkwardness crashed down on her at that moment, as well. She'd allowed him to tie her down. She'd lost all vestiges of control beneath his knowing hands and mouth, spinning in a cyclone of desire that had eventually splintered her into a billion little fragments.

And she'd be lying if she said she didn't want to do it all again. Right this second.

Her need for control made her plunge into the cool water instead.

Not surprisingly, Jason was already standing on the deck as she hauled herself out of the water, using a ladder. She was thankful that he handed her a towel almost immediately and was even more grateful when, after quickly drying off, he tucked his own towel low around his trim hips. It still left a startling amount of bronzed male flesh and rippling muscle exposed, but that rectangle of cloth at least helped Lana to keep her senses from overwhelming her brain.

She wanted him to touch her, to somehow acknowledge the intimacy that had passed between them. She longed to reach out to him, as well, even if they were engaging solely in a casual fling. But he seemed aloof at that moment, much more like the man born in the intimidating, harsh landscapes of his mother's country.

Ten minutes later they'd both showered—separately—and dressed. Jason came out of the bedroom wearing a pair of khaki pants that rode enticingly low on his trim swimmer's hips and an off-white short-sleeved cotton shirt that offset his healthy tan. His dark hair was still damp. She caught a whiff of his clean-smelling cologne.

Too handsome to be turned loose on an unsuspecting public, she thought wryly.

She knew what many of the businessmen in Honolulu wore to meetings—shorts or pants and brightly colored island shirts. He paused when he saw her small smile.

"What?"

"I was thinking about your clothes. It must be nice to dress so casually for work everyday."

"One of the many reasons I love Hawaii so much," he said with a grin. He went to the refrigerator and took out a bottle of water. When he held up one for her in offering, Lana shook her head. She hopped down from the bar stool next to the kitchen island, waiting for him so that he could take her back to shore. He cracked open the plastic seal on the bottle with a quick twist of his strong wrist.

"Can I take you out to dinner tomorrow night?" she asked briskly.

He stopped in the motion of raising the bottle to his mouth.

"No, I don't think so," he replied slowly.

She felt like something heavy landed in her hollow stomach, but she didn't flinch. "I see. Thank you for today, then. I appreciate your making the time for me."

He set the bottle of water down on the countertop so hard water popped out and splattered on his wrist.

"God damn it," he said softly.

She just stared at him, unsure what to say. His long, dark eyelashes narrowed as he studied her intently.

"Do you do that on purpose?"

"What?"

"Pull that Queen of the Bitches routine just to piss me off?"

She swallowed thickly. "I was trying to thank you, Jason."

"For fucking you? Well, it was my pleasure, Lana." He grabbed his keys off the counter with an angry slashing motion. He started toward the hallway that led to the door. "Let's go."

"What are you mad at me for? I'm the one who just asked you out and got rejected," she spat out.

He spun around. Lana barely stopped herself from taking a step backward. He looked furious.

"What did I tell you the other night? I don't want to be patronized by you. I'm not some kind of island pretty boy who's going to play stud for you while you pet me and feed me sweets."

"I don't think that Ja—"

"I don't know what the hell you're thinking in that cold, calculating brain of yours, but I do know that's what you *want*. I see it all the time, you know. Half the young men in my family have been led around by the nose at one time or another by a rich mainlander here for a good time, including a hot island fuck. Hell, my cousin Po, who runs Hawaiian Nights, has made a fortune off people like you."

White-hot fury bubbled up in her chest. How *dare* he judge her. How dare he so facilely make *her* out to be one of the thoughtless tourists who treated the natives like lovely, exotic little objects who existed for the sole purpose of a good time?

"Don't stick me in some easy category. You don't know *anything* about me," she seethed.

"That's the way you want it, isn't it?" He took another step, coming close enough for her to imagine she felt the waves of heat and anger coming off his big body, close enough that she was forced to lean her head back if she wanted to keep control and not avoid his lasering stare like a coward. His voice volume dropped to a low, intimate rasp, but Lana sensed his bubbling irritation, nonetheless. "You want me to make your vacation a little more memorable? Okay. I've got no problem with that. You may be stiffer than a frozen board most of the time, but you bend real nice in bed. You know where you can find me."

"Why are you trying to insult me?" she asked in a furious whisper.

He shook his head. She couldn't tell if he was disgusted with her, himself, or both of them. "I'm being honest. Believe it or not, I doubt there are many guys who would like being condescended to by you. Don't you get tired carrying that huge chip around all the time?"

Her throat ached when she swallowed. Still, she was glad her voice sounded reasonably calm when she spoke. "I see I'm not the only one around here with a chip on their shoulder."

He went still for a few seconds as he looked down at her. The rapid beat of her heart in her ears escalated to an uncomfortable throb. His nostrils flared before he stepped back. He made a motion for her to move in front of him toward the door.

"I've told you the rules. If you want to play . . . Well, like I said. You know where to find me, Lana."

seven

JASON headed toward the marina before he returned home the next afternoon. An icy silence had reigned between Lana and him when he took her to shore yesterday. His irritation had only frothed when he'd noticed Harold had been in the process of hauling one of the Superboats up the ramp. The hull had been damaged, though not pierced.

The Superboats seemed to send out a siren call to any idiot who didn't have a clue how to handle the sleek, powerful craft on the Pacific's rough waters. He knew he should question Harold about the damage and get an insurance claim filed, but he'd been cranky enough over Lana's frigid attitude. He hadn't wanted to deal with the annoyance of some drunk jerk wrecking his boats on top of that.

What the hell was *with* that woman? It steamed him yet again to recall that brisk, businesslike tone she'd used when she'd asked if she could take him to dinner. Which really meant that she wanted to contract his *services* again. Her cool, low voice still echoed in his pissed-off brain.

I see. Thank you for today, then. I appreciate your making the time for me.

Like he maintained a fuck schedule or something.

He'd never known it was possible for hot molten lava to exist inside ice until he met Lana Rodriguez. Too bad it was fucking phenomenal being buried inside her when she erupted. If things had been otherwise, he might have been able to stop thinking about her.

The strength of his anger surprised him a little. Sure, Jason liked to be in the driver's seat in bed, but he wasn't a die-hard dominant. If a woman wanted to crawl on top of him and ride him to the finish line, fine and dandy—as long as she realized he was going to have his way in the end.

But Lana's aloofness really bugged the shit out of him for some reason, and if he had to tell the truth, it *wasn't* because he felt like a victim of a vicious colonialist culture. Sure, the phenomenon existed. Vacationers frequently treated natives—both women and men—like they were exotic playthings. But he'd never been cowed by the thought of a woman who just wanted him for a good time in bed.

Maybe that was because it rarely occurred. Most women wanted him for a hell of a lot more than a night or two of sex. Usually he'd *rather* they saw him as a disposable sex toy. All parties satisfied; easier all around.

He didn't care to dwell on the fact that he wouldn't allow Lana Rodriguez to treat him like that. He could imagine her kissing the living daylights out of him at the airport, giving his cock one last flirtatious tug through his shorts, and pursing her lips in a sexy good-bye kiss.

The fact of the matter was, it was a familiar enough scenario for him.

But imagining Lana's face in the tableau really stoked his temper into a hot flame. What made his fantasies ten times stupider was that Lana *never* looked like some kind of sultry, contrived seductress. Her expression was a beautiful, frozen mask, defiant and furious, or so heartbreakingly somber it made him want to do anything to change it. When he'd finally seen her smile, he'd been stunned.

The weird thing about it?

It seemed as if he'd been waiting for that smile for a lot longer than the four days he'd known her.

A hell of a lot longer.

But he was just going to have to get over his obsession, wasn't he? He was carrying his longtime fascination with her music too far ... starting to act like a teenager with an infatuation on a rock star. For all he knew, Lana Rodriguez was in a plane over the Pacific right now. Best thing all around if she was.

A fleeting vision of packing up all her CDs and tossing them in the garbage hit his brain. He almost laughed aloud at the ludicrousness of it as he approached the marina entrance. Next thing he knew, he'd be drinking like a fish and blubbering pitifully to his friends and cousins. Disgusting. And just the kind of thing he secretly despised, whether it be a guy or a woman who was doing the blubbering.

All because of a few fantastic fucks with an uptight, frigid city chick.

Yeah, just keep telling yourself she's frigid, he thought

mirthlessly as he opened the screen door and entered the dim marina.

"Never mind," he heard a familiar voice say staunchly. "I'll drop them off myself. You're busy. What are you *doing*, Harold Akuna?"

"I'll take it to Jace's," Harold replied in his typical calm manner that never wavered. Much to Lily Koa's irritation, it *certainly* never wavered for her. Harold came off to many as being as mild as a spring breeze, but his even-keeled demeanor disguised a stubborn streak that went a mile deep. Jason's cousin—although Harold wasn't *technically* his cousin, just intimately enmeshed in the far-reaching Koa family web—would never allow Lily Koa to row herself out to Jace's houseboat. There was a knight in shining amor beneath Harold's wizened face and strong little body.

Besides, everyone knew Harold was sweet on Lily.

"Don't be ridiculous. There are customers out on the dock. You work too hard, Harold. Are you losing weight? Been eating those disgusting TV dinners again?" Lily snorted. "Those things ought to be outlawed. Come out to the farm tonight. I'm slow cooking a nice pork roast. Hopefully it won't overcook while I'm watching little Lily—"

"How come you're babysitting Li'l Lil?" Jason interrupted. "I thought there was an official ban on grandma babysitting the—what was it at last count?—seventy-two great-grandkids."

"Oh, Jason, good!" His grandmother flashed a smile that had warmed hearts for almost eight decades. She didn't look a day over sixty, Jason thought as he leaned down and kissed her. Her cheek felt smooth and soft beneath his brushing lips. Her brown eyes sparkled with life. Her curly white hair was cut fashionably short. Like many older people in Hawaii, including Harold, she was slender and well-muscled from regular exercise in the temperate climate.

"I was on my way to the restaurant to drop these off for tonight when Kelly called me," Lily explained. "She thinks Kane has the chicken pox. I told her I'd watch the baby while she takes Kane to the clinic, so I need to head back in the other direction."

"Li'l Lil is my goddaughter. I'll go watch her, Grandma," Jason said. Lily Cavanaugh, better known as Li'l Lil, was the infant daughter of Jason's favorite cousin, Kelly.

"Kelly's already expecting me. I'm going to finish the pies she was baking. Anyway, I was on the way to Jace's to drop these off." Lily shoved a large plastic bag into his arms. "Can you take these with you when you go later?"

Jason knew the bag was filled with leis. Lily liked to sell them at his restaurant, and Jason knew Jace's customers thought the flower necklaces added to the festivity of their evening out. He'd long since gotten over his amazement over the fact that Lily Koa spent most of her time making leis when she was a millionaire many times over. Her involvement with her flower gardens and arbors was more than just a hobby; flowers were an essential part of Lily's personality.

"I'll see you at church tomorrow?" Lily asked Harold as she dug in her purse for car keys. She referred to the Kawaiaha'o Church where she volunteered a good deal of her time. She often goaded Harold into attending. Harold grudgingly went most Sundays, despite the fact that he was raised in Mexico and didn't understand a word of the Hawaiian language service.

Harold sighed and nodded.

"I won't even bother to ask if *you'll* be there," Lily said with a disapproving glance at Jason. He just grinned.

"Just like your father," Lily muttered under her breath as she headed toward the door.

"I was in church for Li'l Lil's baptism," he called out.

"Li'l Lil's first birthday luau is next week! You haven't been to church in a year."

"I'm hearty, Grandma. I only require a dose of godliness every five years or so."

"Heathen," Lily said with an exasperated expression that segued to a fond smile. She pushed open the screen door.

Harold gave him an inscrutable look before he reached for the plastic bag Jason held. Jason chuckled when the older man carefully removed a brilliant white, yellow, and pink plumeria bloom from a lei and then ran out of the marina. He glanced out the screen door in time to see Harold tenderly tucking the flower behind his grandmother's ear. Lily beamed at him.

"I should take lessons from him," Jason muttered under his breath. Harold knew what he was doing when it came to the ladies.

"She's never going to slow down, that woman," Harold observed when he returned to the marina.

"Yeah, well, she says the same thing about you. When are you going to ask her to marry you, anyway?"

Harold scowled. "A woman like her—she owns a quarter of the island. What could I bring to a marriage to Lily Koa?"

Jason rolled his eyes at the old argument. "Yourself. It's all my grandma wants."

"Yeah, well, there are a few people in your family who think Lily marrying me wouldn't be in her best interest."

"Fuck 'em," Jason replied flippantly to a topic that he actually took quite seriously. His grandmother's happiness—not to mention his friend Harold's—was no light affair. Still, he knew he couldn't push a character as stubborn as Harold. He set down the bag of flowers on the desk and glanced at the customer sign-in log for the day.

"Do I even want to ask the story about the damage on the Superboat?" he asked.

"Not really. I have it spelled out in the report. You want it?"

Jason nodded.

"That was one pretty lady I took out to your boat yesterday."

Jason grunted as he accepted the paperwork Harold handed him. "No one can argue with that."

"More than just pretty though. She'll be back."

Jason realized he wasn't absorbing any of the report he was trying to read. He glanced up at Harold's wrinkled face. "She's a vacationer. What makes you say that?"

Harold just shrugged his thin shoulders and exited out the back door.

LANA zipped up Melanie's new sexy fuchsia dress. Both of them inspected her in the hallway mirror of Melanie's suite. They'd had fun shopping all day for the perfect outfit for Melanie's date this evening. She and Eric had decided to venture out of the bedroom for a night out on the town.

"You look gorgeous," Lana proclaimed eventually. "Are you sure you're not going to break a bone dancing in those heels?"

"More likely to break one in the bedroom later on. Eric likes me to keep on my heels when we fool around, and things can get pretty . . . *athletic*."

Lana chuckled. "That sounds dangerous. Nice, but dangerous."

Melanie's laughter faded. "Are you sure you're okay with me going out with him again tonight? I feel like a real heel, abandoning you so much."

"The purpose of this vacation was for you to have a terrific time. I couldn't be more happy that you are."

Melanie gave her an impulsive hug. "Thanks so much. If it weren't for you, I would have never met Eric and ended up spending all my nights alone, thinking about David and crying myself to sleep."

"Well, we couldn't have had that." Lana hesitated as she examined Melanie's glowing face. "But . . . you're sure you're not falling for this guy, right? Maybe it would have been better to try out one or two of the other guys from Hawaiian Nights."

"Don't worry, Lana," Melanie said distractedly as she turned to the side and examined her figure in profile. She inhaled and held her breath for a second before she exhaled, scowling at her curvy tummy. "Eric is a sweetie, and he's fantastic in bed. He's patient and kind. But he's not exactly Albert Einstein or anything. Not that I'm complaining. I just mean . . . Well, like I said, you don't have anything to worry about. I mean, come on . . . you can't actually imagine that I want to get permanently involved with a male escort. Jeez, can you see me trying to explain *that* to Shawna someday?"

"Some things are just better left unsaid between mother and daughter. I'm sure you'll feel the same about Shawna's secrets someday."

"Don't even go there." Melanie ruined her dire warning by joining Lana in laughter. "I just wish you could have had as much luck with your date the other night as I did with Eric."

"I was very happy with my guest," Lana murmured.

"Really? You sure didn't act like it was anything special, and you never saw him again," Melanie muttered as she reapplied her lipstick. She popped the tube back into her metallic evening bag. "I feel so guilty that you've been spending your nights alone."

"You shouldn't. I spend *most* of my nights alone. That's the norm, not the exception."

"Yeah, but we're on vacation in Hawaii. You're supposed to indulge the senses," Melanie waggled her blonde eyebrows.

"Maybe I will venture out tonight."

Melanie was clearly surprised. "You're going out alone?"

"Just for a drink, maybe." She glanced at her reflection in the mirror. "I'm a big girl. I should be able to handle it. And we're leaving the island the day after tomorrow. Might as well enjoy it while I can."

HUNGER pains urged him out of his office at Jace's at around eleven that night. He wandered into the kitchen, which was still operating at a frantic pace. Jace's did a booming late-night business. His chef, Andy Townsend, and his staff would be busy until the waiters and waitresses stopped taking food orders at midnight.

"Hey, Jace. Jessica was just looking for you," Andy said as he dumped a handful of scallions into a pan and gave the steaming skillet a few quick jerks, tossing around the colorful ingredients. "They sold all the leis, and she was wondering if you had any more."

"Damn. My grandmother gave me some, and I forgot to bring them when I came this evening. What's good tonight?" He asked as he peered into the many pans on the stove and myriad delicious smells wafted up to his appreciative nose. His stomach growled more vociferously.

"If you're really hungry, the butterfish I bought for the special is out of this world. If not, the pesto grilled opah is nice and light."

"I wouldn't be here if I wasn't hungry," Jason replied with a grin.

A minute later Jason walked out of the kitchen with a plate of butterfish prepared in a wasabi, ginger, and cilantro sauce. It smelled so good that when he paused at the bar to get a glass of ice water, he couldn't wait to get back to his office. He took the seat that was always reserved for him at the crowded bar and asked Manuel for utensils. He completely tuned out the lively crowd while he savored the decadently rich fish. As usual, Andy's culinary combinations orchestrated a sublime symphony on his tongue. The talented chef cost Jace a small fortune, but the man was a genius.

"Guess it was good," Manuel joked a few minutes later when he cleared Jason's plate.

"Don't tell Andy I inhaled it. He'll be insulted."

Out of the corner of his eye he noticed Po waving at him from the front terrace where he sat at a table with a bleached blonde and Pete Makala. Great. Jason wasn't in the mood for the sophisticated crime boss. Jason waved back, pretending to interpret his cousin's gesture as a greeting instead of the beckoning that it was.

Manuel laughed at Jason's comment, but he seemed preoccupied. His dark eyes fixed steadily on a moving target as he filled up Jason's ice water. His bartender saw a lot on any given day at Jace's. Manuel was in his forties and possessed the aura of a wounded Latin lover. Women seemed to adore his world-weary sexuality. If something caught Manuel's jaded eye, it must be worth looking at.

Jason glanced over his shoulder.

In a sea of brightly colored shirts and floral print dresses, she wore black. The blouse fastened around her neck, leaving her lithesome arms and silky-looking shoulders bare. The soft fabric didn't cling indecently to her breasts, but it ghosted them in a god-awful sexy manner as she moved, hinting at their fullness and shape. His cock twitched—his and more than likely, just about every other guy's in the room. It was obvious she wasn't wearing a bra. She met his eyes, but her expression remained inscrutable.

He held his breath as she slowly made her way toward him.

"Hello."

Had she sounded a little breathless? Jason wondered. Hard to say, given the noise level in the bar.

"You look like you're out to find some trouble."

Lana laughed. "I came looking for you."

"Like I said," he murmured quietly. He tapped at the ice in his glass with a straw, his eyes glued to her curving mouth. He couldn't believe she'd just walked into his place looking hot enough to ramp up the testosterone in the room to record-breaking levels, and cool enough to care less. Out of the corner of his eye, he noticed Manuel was hovering in the vicinity, probably hoping for an introduction. Manuel was one of the few friends he possessed who liked Lana's soulful music as much as he did, and he obviously recognized her.

"You're doing a good business," she said as she glanced around, her voice low and rich as premium scotch. "Not a seat in the house."

"It's a full moon. People are out on the prowl. I could find you a seat, but it'd be a heck of a lot quieter than this. If you're looking for a party, it might not suit."

She arched her brows. "I told you what I was looking for."

"Yeah. You did." He'd been pretty damn gratified by her admission, too. Surprised but pleasantly so.

He leaned over the bar. "Send Amy out to the patio when you get a chance, will you?"

Manuel nodded grudgingly. He still stared at Lana, but Jason wasn't in the mood to introduce her. He didn't feel like sharing her, even in that small way. He was still reeling from the shock of turning around and being unexpectedly treated to the sight of her cool elegance amidst a sea of rowdy, half-drunk tourists.

I came looking for you.

Jason grabbed her hand and led her through the milling, standing crowd out to the front veranda, where they could walk easier amongst the seated patrons. Too late, he remembered that Po and Makala were out there. His cousin stood up, his liquid black eyes glued on Lana.

"Po. You're out early tonight. Pete, nice to see you," he greeted as he shook both men's hands. He nodded at the blonde who had her red lips wrapped around a straw. She studied him with open curiosity as she sucked strong enough to hollow out her cheeks. His gaze lowered over enormous tits capped with nipples pointed enough to put a guy's eye out. He quickly surmised she was one of Hawaiian Heat's dancers. Po made a habit of sampling all the new strippers he hired.

"Yeah, well, Natalie here wants to get to bed early tonight," Po said suggestively, his dark eyes never leaving Lana's face. "And who do we have here?"

Jason hesitated, not liking his cousin's hungry stare. But Lana extricated her hand from his hold and held it out in greeting.

"Lana Rodriguez," she said smoothly.

"I'm Jason's cousin, Po. This is Natalie and Pete Makala."

Jason saw Lana's face stiffen slightly when Po gave his name, but she recovered almost immediately. She nodded a greeting to both Natalie and Makala. "So . . . *you're* the one responsible for my getting to know Jason so well?"

Po's wide grin was as guileless as a child's. He looked first at Lana then at Jace then back to Lana again. "That's right. I'm so pleased it turned out. We aim to please at Hawaiian Nights. Isn't that right, Natalie?"

The blonde giggled and gave Jason the same look she probably gave her customers as she gyrated on the stage. He noticed Lana's eyelids narrowing in anger as she considered Po. For a second Jason thought she was going to chastise him for breaching the confidentiality of his customers. It wasn't like Po didn't deserve a dressing down, but Jason was relieved when Lana just studied his cousin with arched eyebrows, a sarcastic smile tilting her lips.

"Please, join us, Jace . . . Ms. Rodriguez." Makala waved at the two empty chairs, his manner as suave and proprietary as if he owned Jace's itself. "We actually came here tonight hoping to see you, Jace. Maybe you've heard that the position of liquor commissioner is about to become available?"

"Yeah, I did hear that," Jason replied in a friendly manner. "Kind of hard for the former commissioner to do the job from prison, I guess."

Makala shrugged elegantly. The guy was Fred Astaire smooth, Jason had to give him that. The people he fucked over probably thanked him politely after the fact.

"I was hoping you might consider taking on the position," Makala continued. "We could use a good man there, and it'd be an ideal stepping-stone for other jobs in public office."

Jason tried to hide his annoyance. He knew perfectly well that the former liquor commissioner, who had been indicted for taking bribes from various Honolulu nightclubs and taverns, had been on Makala's payroll. Jason was about as likely to accept Makala's proposal as he was to shove his head in a hungry shark's mouth. Makala knew the exact same thing. The crime boss was just stalling. He obviously wanted to discuss something else with Jason, and that topic was more than likely the acquirement of a certain piece of Lily Koa's land.

"I thank you for the offer, but as I've told you before, I'm not interested in public office. You'll have to excuse us. We'd like some privacy." Jason grabbed Lana's hand and pulled her along the terrace, leaving Po with his mouth hanging open at the abrupt dismissal.

Just as they reached the end of the tables, a hand reached out and grabbed his forearm. Jason clenched his teeth in annoyance at being interrupted yet again.

"Jace Koa? Look, honey, it's him."

"Well I'll be damned, it is," drawled the man sitting beside her. His Texas accent was as thick as his silver hair. He had a sunburn and wore several flashy gold rings on his fingers. He stood and reached out a hand to Jason. "This is a mighty fine establishment you've got here, young man. I watched you win every one of those medals in Sydney. Hell of a fight you put up for some of 'em."

Jason shook the man's hand and then did the same with the next man who stood, never releasing Lana. He dutifully asked how the party of four was enjoying themselves, wanting to get this over with as quickly as possible. When he saw one of the women eyeing Lana with interest, he stepped in front of her, sending a subtle message that while he may be on display, Lana wasn't. He chatted up the two couples with practiced ease for the next half minute, finally breaking away after recommending the mai tais and the chocolate soufflé.

Amy was already at the table on the patio lighting a candle when Jason and Lana got there. She took their drink orders and hurried back inside. The noise of the busy restaurant was muted out here, as it was vying equally with the sound of the waves hitting the beach. He kept a few tables on the side patio for private use. The view of the beach wasn't as good as it was along the front veranda. He took one look at Lana's face cast in moon glow and candlelight, and doubted he would have glanced once at the ocean anyway.

For a moment neither of them spoke.

"So what did you and Melanie do today?" he finally asked.

"We went shopping," she said with a small smile. "I'm not much for shopping, but it was fun."

He glanced down appreciatively at her dewy shoulders. "It looks like you were out in the sun at some point."

"Believe it or not, this tan is just from yesterday."

Their eyes met briefly, and she looked away. He wondered if she, like him, thought of sitting in the lagoon while the sun gilded her naked body.

"So that was your cousin?" she asked.

Jason nodded.

"The one who sent you to my hotel room the other night?"

"Yeah," Jason admitted, looking away from her steady stare.

He'd been too horny and too irritated to feel any shame for his conspiracy with Po to get into Lana's bed, but he felt a little guilty now. Thankfully she didn't scold him.

Amy arrived and set the drinks on the table. Lana calmly took a sip after the waitress had left them alone again.

"That story you told those people over there about these mai tais . . ." Her voice faded off.

"Yeah?" Jason prodded.

"Why didn't you tell them you were part Cornish? You made it sound as if the drink only got the splash of Cornish whiskey because your grandmother randomly visited Cornwall once," she murmured, puzzlement and humor playing across her expression.

He shrugged. "People have a fixed idea about what I should be like. I don't like to rob them of their fantasies."

She bit down on the large slice of pineapple that came in her drink as she studied him soberly. He trailed the thin rivulet of juice that trickled from her full lips to her chin with his gaze. She took another bite of the fruit before she bothered to wipe off the juice.

"So you made up a lie about it? Just because it's good for business?"

He paused in the action of reaching for his glass of iced tea when he registered her tone. "It's not a *lie*. My grandmother really did add the Pendrang to her usual recipe for a mai tai after going to Cornwall. So what if I do tell the story to add some atmosphere to the restaurant?"

"And sell a few drinks?"

"You have a problem with good old-fashioned capitalism?"

"So that was the only reason your grandmother altered the recipe?" Lana queried back, completely unscathed by the edge of his irritation. "Because it strikes me as being a little more personal than that. She made it into a Cornish–Polynesian blend. Very unique. I'm sure she must have been thinking of you when she did it."

Jason gave a bark of laughter. He didn't know whether to be complimented or insulted. "My private life is my own. I don't feel there's a need to share the details with complete strangers."

She shook her head. "Never mind. I just don't know how you do it."

"Do what?"

"Work in the tourist trade. It seems so . . ."

"What?" Jason growled softly when she stopped. "Fake?"

She met his gaze. "You really have to be 'on' a lot."

"Publicity is a must when you do what I do. I could say the same for your profession. You perform constantly."

"*No*. It's not the same at all. I sing what I want to sing, when I want to sing it. Plenty of people have tried to convince me to do stuff for a mainstream audience, but I've refused. The second I start doing that, it'll be like entering slavery."

Jason's eyebrows went up at her adamancy. He'd never seen her so passionate . . . except when she was making love. "Don't you think you're being a bit black-and-white about it? Everybody makes small concessions for their career."

"I don't," she replied swiftly. "I'm a very private person."

Jason didn't want to insult her, but he couldn't help but grin widely. "Well, why don't you just tell me a few things you *do* bend a little for, Lana?" He placed his forearms on the small tabletop and leaned toward her. "Besides sex, that is."

Her mouth fell open. "Well, I enjoy . . . Do you *really* want to know?"

"I asked, didn't I? What? Are you worried I'm making chitchat so you'll buy another drink?" he asked irritably.

She watched her fingers as she carefully wiped the condensation off the side of her glass. "No. More like because you feel like you have to before we have sex again."

After an extended silence, in which Jason might have ground a layer of enamel off the back of his teeth, she looked up uneasily. "Don't feel like you have to. It's not necessary for you to charm me . . . seduce me. We both want the same thing. You can just be yourself."

"Who says I *wasn't* being myself? Who says I *wanted* to have sex with you again?" he demanded, not bothering to hide his fury. Damn it, he couldn't even try and find out a little about her without her throwing up the walls.

"You said I knew where to find you. You said—"

"That you'd have to play by my rules. And guess what? My rules are that we talk to each other like civilized human beings instead of being so mercenary about the whole damn thing. Having a normal conversation isn't the same as *kissing ass*, Lana." He stood abruptly and moved next to her chair. "Jesus, if I hadn't heard you sing, if I hadn't fucked you, I'd think there was a robot in there instead of a woman."

He stalked away from her down the narrow patio.

"Wait, Jason."

He paused against his better judgment.

"I'm sorry. I just don't want to make this harder on anyone than it has to be."

"So your bitchiness was really an attempt at being *kind*?" he clarified sarcastically. "I'll recover quickly enough when you leave, Lana."

"I have no doubt of it. I was actually referring to myself."

His mouth sagged open at her unexpected admission. Christ, this woman kept him on the starting block, hyperalert for the sound of the starting gun.

"When are you leaving the island?" The words were out of his mouth before he had the opportunity to censor them.

"The day after tomorrow."

He retraced his steps slowly. He touched the line of her perfect jaw with his fingertips. "There's still time, then."

She didn't blink as she stared up at him from her sitting position. "That's why I came. Because there *is* still time," she replied in a hushed whisper.

"If you come with me now, I want you to stay the night on my boat. You're mine until tomorrow evening." It surprised him a little that he'd said it. But damn his competitive spirit, he couldn't walk away from the challenge of her.

He saw her hesitate. "I came here with Melanie."

He brushed his thumb across her lower lip and pressed into dewy, firm flesh. Her humid breath flowed across his fingers. His cock responded like she'd exhaled along its naked length.

"I have the feeling your friend will be very understanding. What kind of friend *wouldn't* want to see you relax a little if they actually gave a damn about you?"

Her lip curved beneath his thumb. "I'm not as uptight as you seem to think I am, Jason."

"I'm just going by all available evidence." His hand stretched around the elegant column of her throat. She wore her hair up, and he experienced a primitive urge to delve his fingers into it and ruin her perfect, sleek knot. Instead, he nudged her head forward slightly until her chin came within inches of the fly of his shorts.

She stared up at him with that smooth, somber expression that he also wished he could shatter. The rapid flutter of her pulse next to his palm told him she wasn't as impassive as she appeared to be.

"I'm asking for twenty hours of your life. Nothing more. Nothing less. What do you say?" he asked gruffly. He felt her throat constrict as she swallowed.

"I'll leave earlier if you change your mind."

He grabbed her hand and pulled her up into a standing position. The sensation of her nipples pressing against his chest made him curse the twenty minutes it would take to get her to his boat. He kissed her softly at first. But when he caught a hint of her essence, he recalled why he almost couldn't stop ravaging her sweet mouth yesterday, even when his cock was buried inside her tight, hot channel, ready to burst.

A minute later he lifted his head. Silver moon glow revealed her dazed expression.

"I'm *not* going to change my mind," he growled.

He took her hand and led her off the patio.

eight

LANA wished she hadn't asked him not to make small talk with her, because she could have used something to alleviate her rising anxiety. Or maybe it wasn't anxiety exactly, she admitted as she watched Jason in the bright moonlight as he started up the motor on the small boat he used for daily transport to his house. It was sexual tension like she'd never known. It seemed to thicken the very air between them until Lana felt like it was an effort to draw breath.

Before she could settle shakily on the middle seat of the boat, he called out to her.

"Come here."

He'd said it so quietly, she almost couldn't be sure she'd heard him correctly. The motorized skiff chugged along in the water. She placed her purse on the seat and gripped the sides of the hull.

"Won't I tip us over?" she asked.

"Get down on your knees and come slowly."

Something in his terse tone made her pulse leap at her throat. So . . . he felt it, too, this unbearable sexual tension. He didn't even want to wait until they got to his houseboat. Somehow the realization empowered her.

Her pussy throbbed with excitement as she made her way across the little craft. He spread his knees and she entered the protective harbor of his long legs. His hand opened at the back of her head. She felt his long fingers finding the fasteners and then heard the plastic clips hitting the bottom of the boat. He tore through the knot. Her hair spilled down her back as he mussed it, his actions unapologetically, flagrantly possessive. He pushed on her head.

"Put your mouth on me."

When she heard the stark need in his low voice she began to unbutton his shorts with frantic fingers, but he surprised her by gently pushing her face to his lap before she could release him from his clothes. The ridge of his cock pressed against her cheek. She opened her mouth and caressed the stiff column with her lips. He pressed down tighter on her head, and she became more desperate, stiffening her lips and stroking him with a hard pressure.

He groaned. She whimpered as his heat penetrated the cloth. Once again, she tried to lift her head, wild to free him from his clothing, eager to feel him naked on her tongue. But he pressed down harder, even lifting his pelvis, grinding lightly against her seeking lips. A small growl of frustration left her throat. She widened her jaw and took his girth between her teeth. He hissed in pleasure, his grip tightening in her hair. Lana moved her head, gently stroking the thick shaft between her teeth. When she reached the ridge beneath the cockhead, her tongue snaked out. She held him between her teeth and pressed down hard on the rim, wetting the cloth. She waggled her tongue while applying a steady pressure, excited by the sensation . . . made even hungrier by the fact that she couldn't completely get at him.

Jason muttered a curse and pulled at her hair.

"Stay there." Lana remained kneeling in the boat, feeling dazed and hot with arousal. Jason expertly maneuvered the skiff next to his houseboat. He hopped out and had it tied up in record-breaking time. She took his hand when he reached for her and then hesitated as she glanced at the middle seat.

"I need to get my purse—"

"Leave it," he ordered starkly. She wondered if he regretted his harshness, because when he spoke next, he sounded gentler. "I'll get your purse later." When he drew her up next to him on the deck and pressed against her, she felt his straining cock and the damp cloth over it. Without a kiss or a word, he pushed down on her shoulders. She sensed his intensity—shared in it.

She went to her knees all too gladly.

She finally got his shorts and boxer briefs shoved down his thighs, and she fisted the root of his cock while she slipped the fat tip of his penis between her lips.

"Ahhh, yeah," he grated out when she lapped at the delicious cockhead with her tongue, dancing around the tip, making him groan, before she dipped her head forward. She stuffed herself with him, filled herself with his turgid flesh, but still she was greedy, wanting more. It was her, not him, who first bumped the tip of his cock on the back of her throat, so eager was she to accustom herself to taking him deep. She gagged and quickly slid down his length, only to swallow him and test herself again.

As if from far away, she heard him hissing her name in a tense, ragged whisper. But then all rational thought left her. Only sensation ruled. She gripped at his tight, smooth buttocks, using her hold to guide him in and out of her mouth at a pace that suited her rabid hunger. She filled her palms with taut flesh while she took him deep again and again. One finger slid down the crevice of his ass. She felt the muscles tighten around her as she sought the opening, but that only made her hungrier. She pushed into the tight, muscular channel of his rectum at the same time the tip of his cock pressed into her throat. Her gag reflex vibrated him, but she kept him deep.

Hungry. So hungry.

"God damn it."

His sharp exclamation penetrated her thick fog of arousal. She opened her eyelids into slits and slid his cock out of her throat, using her lips and a strong suction to stroke him shallowly. She looked up at him. His hair fell down over his brow. She could perfectly see the rigid lines of his face in the moonlight as he stared down at her.

She pistoned her finger in and out of his rectum and slid his cock deep again.

He groaned gutturally and took a firmer grip on her head.

"Stay still," he rasped.

Lana froze at his harsh command. He flexed his hips, sliding his rigid erection in and out of her mouth at his own pace now, shallow and increasingly rapid. When Lana tried to move and match his lusty rhythm, he held her fast. She stared up at him as he fucked her mouth. He looked pagan and ruthless and beautiful in the moonlight. Her lips and jaw grew sore from clamping so hard as he pistoned his cock between them, but still she sucked harder. It was the only control allowed to her as he held her head immobile.

Then she recalled her finger and she reached, massaging his prostate.

She saw the whites of his eyes at the same time that a shout erupted out of his throat. He swelled impossibly large in her mouth and thrust. Lana gagged and pressed against his restraining hand. He must have sensed her discomfort despite his mindless pleasure, because he eased out of her throat, his cum spurting thickly on her tongue.

She struggled to keep up with the amount he ejaculated. He filled her mouth so quickly, and his plunging cock made it difficult for her to swallow. Finally she found a position where she could milk him as he continued to climax powerfully.

Thick spurts of semen became thin, irregular spills on her tongue. Lana cleaned him thoroughly while he gasped for air, a content purr vibrating her throat. He said her name—her full name, the name she'd prefer not to remember.

On his tongue, it sounded like an endearment.

Jason grabbed her elbows and lifted her to a standing position. He wanted to taste her mouth, but she pressed her face to his chest, denying him. Temporarily weakened as he was by the crashing climax she'd given him, he didn't push the issue. Instead he raked his fingers through her hair and pressed his mouth to the top of her head, as though it were her body that still clamored to return to equilibrium and not his.

It struck his quivering brain eventually that he'd been soothing her. He tilted her chin back so that he could see her face in the bright, bluish silver light of the moon. She regarded him solemnly. Her cheeks were damp. He gathered the wetness with his thumb.

"I'm sorry. I didn't mean to be so rough—"

"I loved it."

Just like that. Simple. Sweet. He kissed her parted lips in thanks for her honesty. Her generosity. After a moment of sipping at her mouth, he grabbed her hand. "Let's get in the water."

"Okay," she muttered huskily.

Once they'd gotten to the other side of his boat, they both began to strip. He finished quicker than she and watched as she shimmied out of the formfitting black pants she'd been wearing.

"Let me do the rest," he said.

She straightened and watched his face as he removed her blouse. He brushed his fingertips over the petal-soft skin at the sides of her breast once he'd bared her. He spread his hands, caressing her back before he plunged into her panties and palmed both butt cheeks. It felt supremely good, and he reminded himself regretfully that he'd never before taken the time to really explore her body. His arousal had been too great on both occasions.

He growled and nipped at her mouth playfully, feeling like he'd just won a gold medal, when she laughed. She put her hands on his chest and stroked him while he continued to map out the contours of her silky thighs and squeeze the globes of her ass in his palms. They groaned in unison when he reached and touched a fingertip to her slit. It was like dipping into warm oil.

"Enough," he muttered as he whisked her panties down her thighs. He steadied her while she stepped out of them. "If I keep playing with you, we'll never get in the water."

"You don't have to hurry on my account."

He smiled when he heard the tight, choked quality of her

voice. He turned her toward the calm, moonlit lagoon and lowered his mouth to her ear, inhaling her sweet, singular scent.

"I know you're burning, *Onaona*. I'll bring you relief. You just have to trust me. Get into the water."

He felt the shudder that went through her flesh. She moved to the edge of the deck and leapt into the water like she believed she'd find salvation in its depths.

He hit the surface of the cool water with a smile on his face. He grabbed the snorkels and masks he'd placed at the edge of the boat. Lana looked puzzled from where she treaded water just a few feet away from him.

"What's this for?" she asked when he handed her one of the snorkels.

"You've never snorkeled by moonlight?"

She handed him back the snorkel. "I don't care for it. I'll swim with you while you do it."

"Come on, Lana," he cajoled as he put his mask on his head. "You'll love this. We only get nights like this, when the full moon is so intense, a few times a year. We'll be able to see tons of fish over the reef."

She shook her head. Jason didn't need the moonlight to know that her expression had gone solemn and tense again. She swam over to the side of the boat and grabbed onto the ladder before she placed the snorkel and mask next to the flashlights he'd put on the deck. "I don't like to snorkel."

"Why?" he persisted.

She hesitated. "I just . . . don't."

"Did you have a bad experience trying it?"

"Yes, I guess I did. It's not a big deal."

He treaded water, waiting.

Lana swallowed thickly when he continued to watch her with calm curiosity. He wasn't going to push her, but he wasn't going to let her off easily, either, she realized.

"I . . . uh, I get nervous . . . about breathing underwater," she muttered. Her cheeks flooded with heat. She'd been a child here on Oahu the last time she'd tried to snorkel. At first she'd been so excited, but she'd unexpectedly become terrified by the closed-in feeling of being underwater. A pressure had grown in her chest, the early warning of a panic attack. She'd been afraid to draw air. Unable to put her inchoate fear into words, she'd told her father the mouthpiece was letting in water. Her father had ordered her to give up the endeavor, as he didn't want the salt water affecting her voice.

Of course, her father would never have jeopardized his supper, let alone the source of his booze.

"How old were you when you last tried?" Jason asked.

"Nine."

He came toward her. "Sit on one of the ladder rungs."

She followed his instructions, mostly because he spread his hands on her hips, lifted her, and plopped her down where he wanted her.

"Jason . . . no," she protested when he picked up the snorkel from the edge of the boat.

"We're not going to go anywhere right now, and you can keep your hand on the ladder the whole time." She couldn't think of what to say in protest to such a reasonable proposal. She sat there uncertainly while he adjusted her mask, feeling foolish . . . feeling like she was a child all over again. Still, the lagoon called to her. It would be something special to see the moonlit beauty of its depths.

She reluctantly came into the water when Jason beckoned her. She bit down on the snorkel mouthpiece, already feeling her chest tightening as she drew breath through the long tube, and she was still *above* water.

"Lana, listen," he said when she pulled out the mouthpiece and gulped for air.

"Plenty of air is getting to your lungs through the snorkel. I guarantee it. You don't have to gasp for it."

She gaped at him for a few seconds before she nodded. Jason was practically a water god, after all, she reassured herself. If he couldn't make her feel safe breathing in the deep waters, no one could.

"I'm going to be right here next to you," he said quietly. He flipped on one of the flashlights and handed it to her.

She placed her face into the water and let her legs float out behind her, all the while gripping tightly to the ladder with her right hand. She felt Jason's fingertips skim her waist and shivered. Anxiety may be making her stomach froth, but her nerves were still humming from arousal. His hand on her belly, her awareness of his big, hard body just inches away, not only stabilized her but pleasantly distracted her from her nervousness.

She was a little surprised to find that the flashlight in her hand cast a concentrated beam into the watery depths. Jason's boat created a stark shadow in the moonlit water, but several feet to the left of her and maybe ten feet down, she saw a quick movement. She inhaled raggedly and felt Jason's hold on her become firmer. He relented, however, and she surfaced.

"I saw a fish," she sputtered after she'd ripped out the mouthpiece.

His laugh sounded low and mellow. "What'd it look like?"

Lana described the blue fish with the brilliant yellow stripes.

"Butterfly fish."

"I can't believe how well I could see it in the moonlight, even without the flashlight."

"If you get a little more comfortable, we'll venture out a bit. You'll be amazed how much you'll see in the shallows over the coral."

Lana nodded and put the mouthpiece back in. She paused when Jason tightened his hold on her—one hand spread wide on her belly, the other at the small of her back. His treading legs brushed against hers, their limbs tangling loosely in the swirling water. His firm penis brushed her hip. She was so caught up by the arousing sensations, she drew air through the snorkel without thinking.

"You held your breath that whole time until the end when you got excited. This time take a nice, easy breath right when you put your face in the water. I'm right here."

Again she nodded and stretched out on her belly in the calm water, thinking about the hoarse quality of his voice when he'd just spoken, wondering if it meant he'd become as aware of her in that moment as she had him.

Her inhalation through the snorkel was slow and even. She couldn't locate the butterfly fish again, but in the distance, just feet from the surface, she saw the outline of a school of fish dart through the luminescent waters. She jerked in Jason's hold, wanting to tell him what she'd seen—in truth, wanting to surface and draw air above water. But she felt him quiet her. He stroked the side of her body in a soothing, elusive caress.

Lana found herself going still . . . expectant. She breathed slowly and shallowly through the snorkel, her entire focus on

Jason's hand curving around her ribs just above her waist. Her skin pebbled when he slid his fingertips over the side of her breast. His other hand cupped a buttock before it caressed her hip and waist warmly.

Even though she tracked the fish with the flashlight, she hardly knew what she saw. All thoughts of being deprived of air melted out of her brain as she trailed Jason's featherlight touch with every ounce of her attention. His forefinger detailed her nipple, learning the topography of the beading flesh. Lana moaned and lurched up in the water. She pulled out her mouthpiece.

"What's wrong?" he asked, his deep, quiet voice causing her skin to prickle further with excitement.

"I can't see any fish," she lied. He shaped her ass cheek to fit his palm and stroked her flank.

"Why don't you go back down for a bit. If you calm down, the fish will come to you. You're breathing easier, but you're still nervous. Just lie in the water and let go, honey."

She had no doubt given the thick, gruff quality of his voice that he planned to keep touching her body while she was at his mercy. He came nearer, dropping a kiss on her forehead. The velvety soft tip of his stiff cockhead slid across her hip, quick and elusive as the darting fish she'd sighted.

Her chest felt tight when she bit down on the mouthpiece, but she couldn't tell if it was from nervousness or excitement.

"You can let go of the ladder now. I've got you."

She reluctantly released her death grip when she saw him reach for the ladder.

"Now stretch out. Let your arms relax in the water."

She followed his instructions, her heartbeat hammering in her ears. His free hand opened on her belly, supporting her lightly.

Then, just as she'd expected he would—just as she'd hoped—he began to stroke her everywhere. She floated in the water and watched several brilliant, exotic fish swim beneath her, feeling as if she were inside a tropical aquarium.

And the whole time, Jason made her nerves simmer by caressing her body as though it were his to do with as he pleased.

nine

HE stroked her belly, ribs, and breasts with warm, languorous caresses. She wriggled in the water when he teased her nipples with his lightly pinching fingertips. She moaned in anguished anticipation when he charted every inch of skin on her belly and hips, growing desperate for him to bank the fires licking at her pussy.

She froze when he trailed a long finger down the crevice of her ass and explored her intimately. A blunt fingertip pressed to her rectum, subtly threatening to pierce her body. Warmth spread in the cool water next to her slit. She panted for air through the snorkel, but she never thought about not getting sufficient air.

She had far more important things to focus on.

His hand lowered, cupping a buttock. Lana shut her eyes reflexively when he slid a long finger into her vagina. When she opened her eyelids again, gasping as he thrust into her sensually, she found herself staring at a bright yellow fish with white stripes.

Two clown fish swam into the beam of the flashlight, followed by a large fish that looked silvery blue in the moonlight. She moaned when he stroked her more forcefully and sent up a finger to massage her clit.

She felt her excitement cresting and experienced a strong need to surface . . . to draw air through her mouth. But then Jason shifted in the water. She realized with a burst of shock that he'd pulled his body partly out of the ocean with his hand on the ladder. His lap cradled her prostrate body. She bit down hard on the plastic mouthpiece when she felt the incredibly arousing sensation of his fully erect cock pressing against her belly.

She whimpered in anguish when his fingers left her pussy. But then she felt him move next to her stomach . . . felt as he grabbed his long penis and pistoned his fist over the length. She tried to reach back for him, wanting to be the one to stroke him, but he suddenly dropped again in the water. The denial of his beautiful cock brought home the helplessness of her situation, reminded her of her vulnerability. Her lungs began to strain and burn for a full breath of air.

She jerked out of the water and yanked the mouthpiece from her mouth.

"What's wrong? You were doing so well."

She panted as she glanced back at him. "Why won't you let me touch you?"

"Because I'm touching *you* right now, honey. *You're* learning how to get comfortable breathing using a snorkel." Lana just stared at him as her pulse throbbed at her throat. Why did she get the impression he was trying to teach her much more than how to breathe comfortably underwater?

"Are you going back down or not?" he asked, his tone mild enough but also holding a hint of challenge.

For a moment, she hesitated. She didn't like being backed into a corner and forced to face a fear . . . even a silly childhood one. But then she thought of the mysterious silvery-blue depths of the lagoon. She thought of Jason sensitizing and pleasuring her body with his hand.

She replaced the mouthpiece slowly.

"Let your arms float in front of you this time. Just relax and *let go*," he instructed.

She took one last steadying inhale and went facedown in the water.

His warm hand was back on her cool skin almost immediately, soothing and exciting her at once. She was immensely grateful that it didn't take him long to get back to business, especially considering how close that *business* had been to a glorious finale just moments ago. He opened his big hand over her genitals and slid his middle finger into her slit. He palmed her entire sex and applied a lovely pressure on her clit, rubbing her with a subtle circular motion. Lana moaned into the snorkel, her breath coming quick and shallow . . . but easy. Jason's hand became more stringent in its demands, agitating the water around her cunt.

She strained for her release, pressing against him desperately. Suddenly he surged up out of the water again, cradling her suspended body with his thighs. Her arousal magnified exponentially when she felt his heavy erection against her skin. He ground up against her belly at the same time that he pressed down with the hand at her pussy. She floundered in the water, wild to return the friction, wanting him to join her in this frantic, delicious struggle.

He vibrated her clit hard at the same time that he rubbed against her, getting the pressure he needed on his cock.

The moonlit waters seemed to fracture into millions of separate silvery blue crystals in front of her eyes. She writhed as pleasure tore through her, whimpering into the snorkel when she felt his pressing cock spasm next to her belly. His body jerked in orgasm. She *might* have been able to tear her pussy away from his ruthless fingers in order to rip the mask out of her mouth and swallow air in greedy mouthfuls.

But she *couldn't* forgo the exquisite feeling of Jason's warm cum spurting onto the water-cooled skin of her belly. So she continued to breathe through the snorkel as she did what Jason had told her to do.

Let go.

She opened her eyes dazedly a moment later, still breathing heavily through the tube. The yellow fish and the clown fish must have been frightened off by their tense, orgasmic thrashing in the water, but the large blue fish still remained. It stared up at her soberly. Lana lifted her head out of the water and removed the mouthpiece. She set the flashlight on the deck, pulled the mask off her face, and settled it on her forehead. Jason hung on to the ladder, his wet, gleaming shoulders rising and falling as he tried to catch his breath.

"I saw lots of fish," she said hoarsely.

His glance snagged on her smile. He laughed. "Well, that was the whole point, wasn't it?"

He looked surprised when she surged through the water and planted a kiss on his mouth. "I have a funny feeling it wasn't the point at all. But I still liked the fish. Can we swim out over the reef and look for more?"

He leaned down and plucked softly at her upturned lips. "Of course," he rumbled.

His grin was a little cocky, but she was in a forgiving mood. She'd conquered a considerable childhood fear with Jason's help, after all.

In point of fact, she felt wonderful.

JASON set Lana's flashlight up on the deck and then took her mask and snorkel. His own equipment followed. He urged her silently toward the ladder with a hand at her smooth hip. They'd seen a ton of marine life swimming out over the coral. Lana must have completely conquered her fear, because it'd been him, instead of her, that had finally signaled that they go back to the boat.

"Did you see that octopus?" she asked when he followed her up the ladder.

"Yeah. It was a cuttlefish, actually." He opened the plastic cabinet where he stored towels. He wrapped Lana in one, feeling her shiver through the absorbent material. She seemed entirely unaware of being chilly, though.

"Is it always so active in the lagoon? Can you always see that many fish? Or is it just because of the moonlight?"

He glanced at her face before he reached for a towel for himself. It pleased him inordinately to see her exultant expression.

"It's always a good place to snorkel, but certain fish only show themselves at night. They were having a real party in the moonlight, huh?"

She dried her face as she looked wistfully out at the lagoon. "It was amazing."

"We'll go again tomorrow, then," he said. He finished drying off and fastened the towel around his hips. Lana was still shivering slightly when he grabbed her hand. "Come on. I've got something to warm you up."

They climbed the stairs that led to his upper deck. He flipped on a light. She made a low, sexy sound in her throat when she saw the steaming whirlpool surrounded by deck chairs. Without a word, she dropped her towel and climbed the steps into the hot water. Jason turned on the jets from the control panel and came up behind her. She already reclined in the frothing water, her head resting on the edge and a sublime smile on her face. He stroked her damp cheek, and she opened her heavy eyelids.

"Do you want something to drink?"

"Yes, please," she whispered.

"Pineapple juice, iced tea, or something with a kick?"

"Better have pineapple juice. The hot water feels so good. If I drink any alcohol, I'll be asleep in under a minute."

"We can't have that," he murmured as he stroked the damp hair off her neck. She stared up at him solemnly. His gaze caressed the pale globes of her breasts just beneath the churning water. "I've still got plans for you, and they don't include sleeping."

The sight of her swallowing thickly made his cock twitch against his thigh. There was no doubt about it. The idea of her agreeing to come here on his boat, the knowledge that she'd agreed to play by his rules, aroused him hugely. She was his for tonight and tomorrow.

He was going to keep pushing at her rigid defenses. He was going to do it because he knew how tremendous the reward was when she submitted.

He'd be patient when necessary, but he *was* going to feast on Lana Rodriguez . . . whether she was ready or not.

When he came back upstairs a few minutes later, he carried two glasses of iced pineapple juice and a folded towel tucked under his arm. He'd made a pit stop in his bedroom and loaded up on some supplies. He handed Lana the glasses before he clambered into the steamy water with her.

"All warmed up?" he asked when he settled next to her on the bench and noticed her content expression and flushed cheeks.

"Hmm," she purred as she took a sip of frigid juice. "Almost too warm. My muscles are turning to mush. It feels fantastic."

"I'm glad you think so." She set down her juice and settled back into the water. "Will you go right back to the grind when you return the day after tomorrow?"

"Not really. I just finished recording a new album before Melanie and I came to Hawaii. I'll have to do a promotional tour for it soon enough, but right now, it's the quiet before the storm."

"I look forward to hearing it."

She opened one eyelid. "You really were serious about liking my music?"

Her tone was curious and a little wistful, not incredulous like it had been yesterday.

"I have all of your CDs. Should I put one on? I have speakers on the deck."

She rolled the one eye she had open. "Please don't. I'm supposed to be on vacation."

He grinned. "So how come you came here when you seem to hate Hawaii?"

Lana closed her eyes and snuggled down in the hot water.

"Melanie chose it. She's my personal assistant, but more important, she's a good friend. She's going through an awful divorce. Her husband is using every weapon in the arsenal to try and get full custody of their daughter. Melanie's gone through hell lately. I wanted to make sure she had a good time."

"And she picked the last place in the world you would want to come to?"

"Like I said, the most important thing was for Melanie to have a good time."

"And is she?"

"I think she's having a marvelous time."

"Lana?"

"Yes?"

She opened her eyelids and regarded him with a trace of wariness that hadn't been there just a few seconds ago.

"Almost all of us from the islands are mutts. You heard about my Cornish mother. My dad is half Hawaiian, a quarter Filipino, and a quarter Samoan. My goddaughter, Lily, has a half-Hawaiian, half-Japanese mother and an Irish-Swedish father. Why are you so uncomfortable with the fact that you're part Polynesian?"

LANA sat up slowly in the water. It took her a few seconds to realize she'd been holding her breath.

"How . . . Why would you ask me that?"

His expression was unfathomable. "Don't most people notice? It must be because I grew up here. I see it in your smile. I feel it in your skin. You carry around the warmth of the islands in your body whether you like it or not. It might be Samoa or Fiji or maybe even New Zealand, but given your distinct dislike of Waikiki"—he paused, his dark eyes lasering right through her—"I'd say Hawaii is the culprit. Was it your mother or father?"

She stared at the churning water.

"My father, actually," she replied briskly after a moment. "He was half-Hawaiian, half-white. My mother and he met at Hawaii Pacific University."

"Both your parents are from Honolulu?"

"No." She inhaled, striving to calm her rapid heartbeat when she heard the unintentional sharpness in her tone. "My mother was Mexican American. My grandfather was from Southern California—he was quite a talented jazz saxophonist, actually. My mother grew up in San Diego. When my grandfather died, she and my grandmother moved back to Mexico. My mother died when I was four of a rare form of leukemia. My grandma came to Hawaii to collect me. I lived with her in Mexico," Lana said, breezing over the fact that she hadn't gone to live with her grandmother until she was eleven years old.

"What about your father?" Jason asked quietly.

"He died as well, but his was a more protracted illness," she said with a mirthless smile. She picked up her glass and took a sip, not really tasting the sweet pineapple flavor. "He died of cirrhosis of the liver from chronic alcoholism."

She heard Jason exhale in the silence that followed.

"So Rodriguez is your mother's maiden name?"

Lana nodded, still not meeting his eyes. "My grandmother's name. It was easier for me to take it when I moved to Mexico."

"If your father grew up here and he was half-Hawaiian, there's a chance my grandmother will know him. Seems like she knows everyone of Hawaiian descent on Oahu. What was his surname?"

She surged up out of the bubbling water. "I'm getting too warm," she murmured as she climbed out of the tub. Instead of using the little steps that led to the elevated pool, she hopped down from the ledge to the deck, avoiding Jason's stare. She glanced at him uneasily after she'd dried off and fastened the towel around her breasts. He'd turned his head to watch her, but otherwise he hadn't moved.

"My mother is buried in Oahu Cemetery. We buried my father alongside her when I was thirteen years old. I haven't been back to Honolulu since then. I'm sorry I don't have the warm memories for this place that you do," she said defensively. "We can't all be as lucky as you."

He stood and stepped out of the tub. Steam rose off his bronzed, glistening muscles. Even though his penis was flaccid at the moment, it was still firm and beautiful. His testicles hung like round, full fruit between his powerful thighs. He was the very image of male potency. He reached for his towel.

"Have you visited their graves while you've been here?"

She shook her head, unable to speak temporarily because of invisible fingers gripping her throat. She couldn't say if her muteness had been caused by the distressing nature of their conversation, the sight of Jason's magnificent, steaming flesh, or some combination of both.

Why did it seem like Jason Koa was always creating the riotous paradox of anxiety and raw lust inside of her? It was an intoxicating yet disturbing brew.

"I'll take you there if you'd like," he offered.

She gave him a sharp glance before she sat down on the cushioned recliner. How could she tell him that she longed to visit her mother's grave . . . in truth, longed to see her father's, as well . . . but dreaded it in equal measure. It upset her to think of them lying there side by side. She carried a shadowy childhood knowledge of how much her mother had worshipped her father. Not that he deserved it. Michael Nahua had been as handsome as the devil. He could charm a viper into purring like a satisfied kitten.

In truth, her father could be as charming as Jason when he chose. Unfortunately, he didn't choose it often. At least not with Lana, he hadn't.

You're not a little girl, Lana admonished herself impatiently. She was a grown woman; a woman who knew very well that people everywhere had suffered much crueler fates in childhood than a mother's death and the tribulations caused by an alcoholic father.

But she hadn't been able to bring herself to go to the cemetery. Her weakness shamed her more than she could say.

There hadn't been an hour in the past six days when she hadn't thought at least briefly of those twin graves. She paid an annual fee to have an attendant clear the gravestones of debris. Her father hadn't had any living relatives in Oahu. It caused a heavy lump to form in the pit of her stomach when she considered how forlorn the two graves must be compared to others—no one to pay them tribute, no flowers or other mementoes on Memorial Day. She'd wanted to pay the attendant to adorn her mother's grave with flowers on holidays but had felt guilty because she hadn't wanted to do the same for her father. Her ambivalence had hamstringed her into inaction over the years.

So stupid, this lingering love for a woman she never really knew; this bitterness toward a man who cared more for a bottle of whiskey than he had her.

She wondered if the graveyard attendant ever placed old flowers from other headstones on her parents' graves, ones that hadn't yet withered when new fresh ones arrived from loving, attentive relatives. Anguish rose in her at the thought.

She didn't appreciate Jason agitating the old wound.

"I won't be going to Oahu Cemetery," she said coolly. "So you were thinking I'm a racist because I didn't shout out the fact that I'm part Hawaiian. Am I right, Jason?"

He paused in the action of drying off his chest. His eyelids narrowed as he studied her. Her heartbeat leapt at her throat when she saw the ice that entered his gaze.

He said nothing, just went over to retrieve their drinks. He sat on a long wooden bench near her recliner. Lana lay back on the chair and took several sips of juice, willing herself to calm. The night air felt good on her warm skin.

Unfortunately her attempts at soothing herself were futile. She felt as agitated and tense as the bubbling water in the whirlpool. Her heartbeat still drummed too loud in her ears. She let her head fall back against the chair, irritated she couldn't conquer her volatile emotions.

God it'd be good to get off this island once and for all.

"Lana."

She tilted her head and met his gaze.

"Come here."

"I don't want to," she replied before she could stop herself. The fact of the matter was, she *did* want to go to Jason at that moment. Very much. And *that* was what was stoking her anxiety as much as anything.

He set down his drink on the deck.

"*I* want you to come here, though."

He waited patiently while she stewed. How could it be possible to want him so much, and yet be so desperate to keep him at a distance?

It was just sex, after all. Just pleasure.

She stood. Her legs felt a little shaky as she stepped toward him. She would have liked to blame her slight weakness on the hot water but suspected Jason's stare had something to do with it. It reminded her of the way he'd looked in the photo at Jace's . . . the one where he was poised to dive on the starting block.

So hard and determined.

She stood in front of him.

"Lower the towel."

She did so reluctantly. She rarely felt self-conscious about her body, but she did at that moment. Jason's merciless stare made her feel more *naked* than usual. His expression gave nothing away as he inspected her nude body. His gaze eventually met hers.

"I wasn't trying to suggest you were a racist. I was trying to ask you about something that's been confusing me about you. But you already know that. You were just raising the defenses to get me to back off. Right, Lana?"

She just stared at him as she resisted a powerful urge to reach for her towel to cover herself. Her hands bunched into fists at her side to prevent her from doing just that.

When she didn't reply, his face stiffened with anger. He reached for her hips and drew her toward him.

"Lie down in my lap."

Lana planted her feet, resisting him. "What? Why?"

"Because I said so," he told her with a fierce glare. "And be-cause I'm going to spank you."

Her mouth hung open in disbelief. Her thighs instinctively

closed, tightening around the acute throb of lust at her core. "Get serious."

Jason's expression informed her he was about as serious as it got. "What are you afraid of? That you'll like it?"

She scoffed.

He nodded pointedly at his lap. "I know I'm going to like it, and that's all that matters at the moment. Come on, Lana. My rules."

He remained unmoving, but she experienced his hot stare like a push on the inside.

She wondered if he could hear her heartbeat; it thudded so unnaturally loud in her ears. Why had she ever agreed to his stupid *rules*. She knew she could tell him no; knew he would take her back to shore if she requested it. As worked up as she was, however, being deprived of the hot, mindless pleasure she knew Jason could give her was the *last* thing she wanted.

What the hell? It never hurt to expand the sexual repertoire a bit.

She held her breath as she came down on her knees on the bench and then stretched out over his towel-covered lap. When she felt the outline of his penis through the fabric, she lifted her belly up like she'd been burned.

"Oh!" she cried out when Jason smacked her bottom. Her skin prickled and tingled where his palm had landed. She swung her chin around to face him.

"Lay *down*," he said.

She let her weight sag into his lap, biting her lower lip at the beguiling sensation of the column of his cock pressing against her stomach through his towel. He put his hands on her hips, readjusting her until the lower curves of her breast brushed his outer thigh and her bottom draped over the other edge of his lap.

She braced her elbows on the cushioned bench and raised her upper body, but Jason immediately stopped her with a hand on her shoulder.

"Spread your arms out in front of you, like you did when you were getting used to the snorkel earlier." He pushed gently but firmly at the back of her neck until her forehead rested on the cushion.

She felt entirely vulnerable lying there naked in his lap. She squirmed in mounting excitement when he placed his hand on her ass and stroked her warmly. He leaned forward. His warm breath ghosting her damp neck made her shiver.

"You have a beautiful ass, Lana. While you're on this boat, it's all mine."

She clenched her eyelids shut when she heard the softly growled challenge. He was trying to provoke her . . . daring her to run. When she refused to reply to his taunt, he sat up and resumed caressing her bare ass.

"Okay, Lana. Let's see how well your pride and defensiveness last through a good spanking."

ten

JASON took his time playing with her, letting the anticipation build. She had a gorgeous ass, taut and muscular with plenty of round, curvy flesh. He gaped at the firsthand evidence of how correct he'd been when he'd thought she would tan easily. Her ass was markedly pale in comparison to the golden-brown skin of her thighs and back. He loved the way her cheeks fit his palm. His cock ached pleasantly as he squeezed and stroked her firm, sweet flesh.

He wanted to remind her she was his to do with as he pleased . . . for the moment, anyway. He needed to remind *himself* of that fact. Her haughty question still echoed in his head.

So you were thinking I'm a racist because I didn't shout out the fact that I'm part Hawaiian. Am I right, Jason?

Truth was, he wanted to watch the elusive, prickly, stubborn Lana Rodriguez squirm, and if that made him a jerk . . . well, so be it.

He swung his hand back and landed a firm spank on the lower curve of her right ass cheek. She hopped up at the brisk contact.

"Stay still," he said, his voice slightly hoarse from the lust that pounded through his veins. He spanked her other buttock, testing her. His cock lurched when she tensed, but remained still in his lap. He gave her two more brisk spanks in quick succession, enjoying the slight shiver of her taut flesh as it absorbed the blows. He heard her whimper and paused to soothe her, rubbing her bottom softly, easing the sting in his palm as much as her ass. He grabbed a handful of firm flesh possessively.

"This ass was made for spanking. Among other things."

"Jason . . ." She moaned. He smacked her again with his palm, the resulting *whap* of skin against skin making his cock throb uncomfortably. He cursed and pulled at the towel still in his lap, lifting Lana slightly to release it from between their bodies.

A satisfied grunt popped out of his throat when he pressed her naked body against his straining cock. He felt her ribs expanding and contracting against his thighs as she panted.

He popped her bottom several more times, fascinated by the pink blush that rose on the smooth, pale cheeks. Every time he heard her whimper he paused and rubbed the firm globes, quieting her firing nerves. When she'd sag into his lap, panting, he'd spank her again, increasing the tension in her lithe muscles, building the excitement.

Then he'd soothe her all over again.

"Jason . . . no more," he heard her mumble as he rubbed her ass. She was nice and pink now. The curving flesh felt velvety soft and hot beneath his appreciative fingers.

"You want me to stop?" he murmured.

"Yes," she mumbled against his thigh. She gasped when he

abruptly plunged his finger into her warm cream. He grunted in animal satisfaction at the stark evidence of her arousal. He immobilized her squirming hips with one hand, keeping her still while he fingered her drenched pussy. "Your body is saying differently, Lana. Your body's telling me you like being spanked."

He couldn't help but grin when she started bouncing her pink ass, riding his finger for all she was worth, grinding her damp, tender outer sex against the ridge of his palm. He hated to withdraw, but her bobbing butt was too sweet of a moving target to resist. He swatted her several more times, more for effect than anything. Her bottom had been spanked enough, truth be told. His spanks were just light, brisk swats for sound effect . . . and to remind her that he was in charge.

He parted her fiery bottom cheeks, exposing her asshole. She seemed to sense his gaze on her, because she whimpered and squirmed in discomfort.

"Stay still, Lana," he murmured as he tightened his grip to still her. He leaned forward and snagged the towel he'd brought up earlier. He'd wrapped several items from his bedside drawer inside it. She came up on her elbows, peering around her shoulder when she sensed his movement. He saw her eyes widen when he sat back on the bench with a bottle of lubricant in his hand.

"Put your head back down on the bench. Arms out. I'm not going to tell you again," he admonished, a hint of humor curving his lips. She looked singularly lovely at that moment, her eyes wide and wary, her blushing bottom a carnal confection too sweet to resist. His cock lurched against her ribs. He grimaced in discomfort and shifted his hand beneath their bodies.

He settled his erection next to his abdomen and pressed Lana's body back against his aching balls and the root of his cock.

"You see what you're doing to me?" he grunted when he noticed she'd turned her head and watched as he rearranged his cock. The sight of her parted lips and hungry stare made him desperate. He spanked her gently to get her attention.

"Head back down, beautiful," he whispered when she met his gaze.

She slowly lowered her upper body.

LANA'S breath burned in her lungs as she heard him pop open the top of the bottle of lubricant. Like the night in the hotel room, when Jason had overwhelmed her with his bold lovemaking, she felt a sense of dissociation. Part of her seemed to watch this highly erotic encounter from a distance, while another part seemed hyperaware of her body: the warmth and tingling of her bare ass; the dull, nearly untenable ache of her pussy; the surging blood in her veins. Her heart pounded like she was running from an enemy despite the fact that she remained still and anticipatory.

She jumped when he parted her bottom cheeks again.

"Shhh," he soothed softly. She felt him caress her hip, his touch light and elusive, just like it had been in the water when he'd accustomed her to using the snorkel. She felt his finger on her rectum, lightly rubbing the sensitive ring . . . pressing. Lana forced herself to inhale slowly when he penetrated her.

"That's right," he murmured. "Keep breathing. Try to relax.

It was easy for him to say, she thought distractedly as he slid his lubricated finger all the way into her ass. *He* wasn't so horny that he felt like he might explode from the stimulation of a stiff breeze. *He* wasn't entirely naked and exposed lying in someone's lap.

She whimpered when he plunged his finger in and out of her ass. She heard her throbbing heartbeat, the gentle waves hitting the shore in the distance . . . and the squishy sound of his finger moving in the lubricant. The intimacy of what was occurring overwhelmed her. She clamped her eyes shut and moaned when he pistoned his finger more forcefully in her ass.

"You like that?" he whispered gruffly.

Lana gritted her teeth in frustration. Wasn't it enough that he had the power to bring her to her knees again and again? Why did he always have to make her *say* it was true? It infuriated her. He finger fucked her more forcefully. She turned her mouth into her upper arm, trying to restrain a groan of pleasure or a sob of uncertainty; Lana couldn't say which. He stimulated her ass, but it was as if he made every nerve in her pelvis simmer. She felt an overwhelming urge to push back on his hand harder, demand he take more of her. Her raw need humiliated her.

"Tell me you like it, Lana."

"Why are you always pushing me? What do you want from me?" she asked irritably.

His arm paused in its plunging motion.

"I told you before," he rasped. "I want you to let go."

"You want to break me or something! You want to—" She paused, biting down on her lower lip. She'd almost said *weaken me*, but she'd stopped herself just in time. "Expose me."

"What if I do? Would that be so bad?" He resumed stroking her ass, but this time he worked his hand between their bodies. A cry burst out of her throat when he began massaging her clit in tight little circles. Lana writhed in mounting pleasure, grinding her pelvis first against the pressure at her clit and then against his finger pounding into her ass. He applied optimal friction both from above and below. She felt so hot . . . so lost . . . so needy.

"That's right," she heard him say as if from a great distance. "Let go, 'Ailana."

She blinked open her eyes when his words penetrated her awareness. Her bobbing hips stilled. He noticed and slowed the taut, frantic pace he'd set. She whimpered at the loss of the delicious pressure.

"What's wrong?"

"I . . . don't. . . ." But she couldn't finish. Desire and confusion sealed her throat shut.

"You *don't* or you *won't*?" Jason queried from behind her, his tone hard.

Lana lowered her perspiration-damp forehead to the bench cushion. A warning blared in her brain, but her body screamed for release.

"All right," she whispered.

"All right, *what*?"

"You can continue."

When he withdrew his hand from her cunt and slid his finger out of her ass, Lana realized she'd pissed him off yet again.

"What are you doing?" she asked when he leaned over her body and groped for something on the floor of the deck. She came up on her elbows and twisted around as she watched him.

He didn't respond. She saw the grim, hard line of his mouth before she saw the dildo he'd just recovered from the towel on the floor. He must have brought it up earlier along with the lubricant, Lana realized. She shivered in anxious excitement as she watched him smear a coat of lubricant onto the sex toy. Unlike the vibrator she owned, this was purely a dildo meant for penetration. It was blue in color and shaped like a small penis with a thick head. Given the size of it, it was specifically designed for anal penetration, she realized.

He spread her pink bottom cheeks with one large hand, pressed the cool dildo to her rectum, and met her gaze. When she just stared at him, her excitement, uncertainty, and arousal likely writ large on her face, he pushed the dildo into her ass.

Her body tensed at the invasion.

Jason's facial muscles looked rigid as he slowly slid the dildo farther into her. Air popped out of her lungs when he pressed the base of the little blue cock tightly against her ass cheeks. It looked lewd, wedged as it was inside her most intimate flesh.

Jason swatted her ass from below and then palmed the flesh possessively, grinding it around and against the dildo.

She trembled. He pushed down on the base, jiggling it ever so slightly, holding her stare all the while.

He began to thrust the dildo in and out of her.

Sweat slicked her face and neck. A droplet ran frantically down her chest. She burned with sexual excitement.

"Jason—"

"Look at it. Watch your ass getting fucked."

She twisted more in his lap, unable to resist the compelling lure of his demand. She bit her lip and whimpered at the sight of him holding her in place with his long fingers while he plunged the dildo into her.

"Damn," he muttered under his breath. He released her bottom cheeks, still fucking her with the sex toy. Lana strained over her shoulder when she realized he was stroking his dense, ruddy erection where it pressed against his belly. That first time at his surf school she'd thought his penis was the most beautiful she'd ever seen. But even then, he hadn't looked like he did now, so swollen he seemed near to bursting. Raw lust slammed into her.

"Oh God . . . Jason, please . . ."

"Please what? What do you need?"

"I need you to fuck me," she admitted hoarsely, even while another voice in her head shouted that she was out of her mind. Her heart slammed in her ears as Jason removed the dildo from her ass and slid her lower body to the deck. He was lifting her back onto the bench again almost immediately after he'd slid out from under her. He stood.

"Come up on your hands and knees," he said.

It gratified her to hear his lust-thickened voice. At least she had the small satisfaction of knowing that even if he did bring her to her knees, she had nearly as great an impact on him. That realization helped to quell her mounting anxiety as she came up on her knees. Jason placed one knee on the bench and remained standing on his other foot.

Lana twisted her head around anxiously when she heard the pop of the lubricant bottle. Jason glanced up and caught her stare on him as he rolled on a condom and added lubrication. She swallowed thickly. He looked stunning . . . magnificent, every muscle in his body rigid with restraint, his smooth, bronzed skin gleaming with perspiration, his cock glistening and furiously erect.

He'd been so irritated with her earlier, she was a little surprised when he made his characteristic soothing sound as he came closer to her, his cock in his hand. Lana gasped when he pressed the impossibly thick, hard crown to her rectum.

"Press back. It'll be okay, Lana," he whispered roughly.

She did. She cried out shakily, her head falling forward, when the fat cockhead slipped into her body. Jason paused behind her, allowing her to become accustomed to his presence. She trembled when he ran a hand along the sensitive skin at the side of her body. He caressed her breast softly while his cock throbbed in her ass.

Lana's harsh groan scored her throat. She pushed back on him, seating him farther in her ass. She felt ready to explode into a million pieces. The anticipation combined with the pleasure hurt like an open wound.

"Please . . . just finish it. You're killing me," she cried out.

His harsh grunt informed her that he was in complete agreement . . . for once. He flexed his hips and fucked her shallowly. Lana bit her lip to still an overwhelming instinct to howl. The sensation he built in her was duller than what she experienced with vaginal intercourse but fuller, too. More incendiary. And his cock was so thick, it caused a burning indirect pressure on her clit.

He pumped once forcefully, causing a shout to erupt from her chest at the same moment his pelvis and thighs smacked against her butt cheeks. He hissed loudly before he strengthened his hold on her hips and begun to fuck her long and deep, smacking their flesh together again and again.

At first Lana merely stared blindly, her mouth hanging open. It was really too much. His cock was too large, his strokes were too powerful. He was going to split her . . . break her, just like she'd accused him earlier of wanting to do. But then his hand was on her cunt, rubbing and agitating her hungry clit, demanding without words for her to join him in his mindless orgy of pleasure.

And she did.

She pushed with her hips, pistoning his cock in and out of her ass with mindless abandon. Orgasm slammed into her at the same moment that Jason smacked against her body. She shuddered in a torrent of bliss. He continued to fuck her ass powerfully as she came. Even after she heard the shout of incredulous pleasure that signaled his own release, he continued to fuck her. When she fell forward on her chest and whimpered, he jerked his cock out of her.

Lana panted desperately for air, her cheek pressed to the bench cushion. He must have been concerned when he'd heard her cry out, but she wished he hadn't withdrawn. Even though his forceful orgasmic strokes had hurt a little, it'd also felt sublime to feel him throb in release while he was inside such a private place in her body. It'd struck her as beautiful to experience his vulnerability while he was in the midst of such a display of raw, powerful domination.

She remained unmoving when he encircled her waist with his arm and pressed his forehead to her back, his breath hitting her skin in erratic puffs. She replayed what had just occurred between them. Now that the demanding hunger of her lust had been satiated, it seemed a little surreal that she'd allowed it . . . that she'd participated there at the end with almost violent desire.

The depth of her need made her inwardly cringe.

He grunted softly in surprise when she reached for the towel beneath them on the bench and slid out from under him. She wrapped the towel around her and murmured an "excuse me" before she hurried down the stairs.

She locked the bathroom door behind her.

Ten minutes later she opened the door, pausing when she saw Jason standing in the dim hallway, leaning against the wall. He wore a pair of cargo shorts, but he was shirtless and barefoot. The humidity from the whirlpool had caused his hair to wave. He looked mussed and sex rumpled and so damn good it took her a few seconds to really take in the concern in his dark eyes.

"Are you okay?"

His gruff voice in the still hallway caused her damp skin to roughen.

"I'm fine. I just wanted to clean up."

He didn't say anything, but she had the impression he wanted to. She suspected he was irritated at her again and felt helpless because there was nothing she could do about it.

"I'll let you have the bathroom, then."

When she started to move past him, his hand snaked out and encircled her upper arm. He pulled and Lana landed face-first against his bare chest with a soft thud.

"I already cleaned up in the master bath."

"Oh, I'd forgotten you have another bathroom."

He grunted with impatience at the inane conversation. She pressed her cheek against his chest and inhaled shakily, absorbing his clean, soapy scent. He whisked his hands over her bare arms and pressed a single kiss on the top of her head.

"You must be tired. Let's go to bed."

Lana didn't really sleep with men. She might have drifted off a half a dozen times or so after a round of especially exhausting sex, but she didn't *do* spending the night together. Why had she agreed to spend the night with Jason, anyway? She suspected it had to do with the raw lust he always inspired in her. He'd made clear the rules of the game, and she'd been all too eager to agree as it meant she could have him. She wondered if Jason sensed the tension rising in her when he paused in his arm rubbing.

"All right," Lana said quickly before he could accuse her of being cold. How hard could it be to sleep in the same bed with a man? "Do you mind if I call the hotel first and leave a message for Melanie? I should let her know where I am."

He studied her face in the dim light. "Sure. You can use the phone in the kitchen. Just turn out the light when you're done."

Lana was left with the uncomfortable impression he'd seen more than she cared for him to with that laserlike stare of his. What was new? She had no right to complain, though, when she'd been the one to throw herself into the line of fire.

eleven

SHE woke to the sound of a boat gunning its motor in the near distance. As she blinked sleepily, the jarring noise faded only to be replaced by the soothing sound of the wind chimes Jason had hanging from the canopy on the upper deck.

The realization of where she was struck her suddenly, and she rolled onto her back. She rose from the empty, mussed bed a moment later. She saw through the partially closed blinds that it was another brilliant Oahu day.

She noticed that at some point Jason had brought her discarded clothing from the deck and placed it on the dresser. Her purse sat on top of the folded clothes. She retrieved her cell phone and then fingered the dressy blouse doubtfully. The outfit seemed far too constraining for the comfortable environment of Jason's ocean home.

A minute later she padded down the hallway, appreciatively

catching the aroma of freshly brewed coffee. Jason appeared to be nowhere in sight as she poured a cup of the rich brew and found some creamer in the refrigerator. She carried her coffee to the partially opened double doors that led to the deck and stepped outside.

The lagoon winked at her cheerily in the bright morning sunlight. Lana sat down on the deck next to the ladder and let her feet dangle in the water. She sipped the hot coffee, enjoying the sultry breeze and the feeling of the warm sun on her legs. She dialed the number for the Moana Surfrider and requested Melanie's room. Her friend answered groggily after three rings.

"Sorry to wake you."

"Lana?" Melanie asked, sounding considerably perkier all of a sudden. "I picked up your message last night. What's going on? Did you meet someone when you went out last night?"

"Yeah, I did," Lana murmured. "What about you? Did you and Eric have a fun time?"

"Oh my God, we had so much fun. You were right, though, I nearly did break an ankle dancing in those heels. We went to this place called the Green Turtle and danced until two in the morning—but what about you?" she interrupted herself abruptly. "You must have met someone amazing for you to spend the night with him. You never stay all night with a guy. Don't you try and get out of giving me all the juicy details."

"I did meet up with someone pretty amazing. You actually already know him. It was Jason Koa."

Lana heard the waves lapping gently against the side of the houseboat in the stunned silence that followed.

"*Jason Koa?* I thought you couldn't stand the sight of him."

Lana chuckled softly. "Come on, Melanie. I doubt there's a woman alive on the planet who couldn't stand the sight of him. I'm only human, you know."

Melanie gave an incredulous bark of laughter. "Jeez, Lana, leave it to you to get that gorgeous man into bed. How did this come about?"

Lana spied Jason in the narrow channel between the lagoon and the expanse of the ocean. He knifed through the water with breathtaking power. Lana knew it took a special kind of strength and experience to be an ocean swimmer, but Jason made it look as natural as breathing.

"It's a long story. I'm going to stay here with him on his houseboat for the rest of the day. If that's okay with you, I mean."

"Of course it is. I'll be fine . . . I'm just still in shock."

"It's not that shocking, Melanie. Pretty cut and dry, actually. It's like you said last night: I might as well live a little while I'm here."

Lana managed to quiet her friend's questions with a promise to give an explanation later. "I'll call you this afternoon, okay?" she asked before she hung up. She leaned back and sipped her coffee while she watched Jason come toward her, his back muscles flexing and gleaming magnificently in the brilliant sun.

"Good morning," she greeted when he finally surfaced near her dangling feet.

"Hi." He wasn't even out of breath, Lana realized with a touch of admiration. He yanked off his goggles and wiped off his streaming face. He looked down at her body and grinned.

"Sorry. I hope you don't mind," she said, referring to the huge T-shirt she'd pulled out of his bureau drawer. "I didn't feel like putting on my pants and blouse yet." The shirt featured an illustration of a female with a Pamela Anderson–type body with a surfboard under her arm. It read *Maui High Wave Patrol*. Jason chuckled before he dipped his head back in the water, efficiently getting tendrils of hair out of his eyes.

"I don't mind at all. Might have been nice if you'd found something that didn't validate your stereotype of me being a surfer dude."

"Aren't you?" she teased before she took a sip of coffee.

"Well, yeah, but that's not the point." She caught the glint in his eye and grinned right along with him. He draped an arm over the bottom rung of the ladder. "You know . . . I think I like you in the morning."

"But you're still undecided?" she asked in mock disbelief.

"No, I've decided," he said, his tone mellow even if his stare on her wasn't.

Lana looked pointedly out at the ocean, trying to minimize the effect of his gaze. "Do you still compete in swimming?"

He shook his head. "Not since the World Championships in 2004."

"And do you miss it?"

"Yes and no. I miss the competition but not all the stress and training."

She met his eyes. "Now you get to enjoy it for what it is. I can tell you love swimming. You'd probably live in the water if you could, wouldn't you?"

He nodded toward his houseboat. "I do live there, re-member?"

She laughed. "Some people are just naturals at something. But if they're pushed too hard at their talent, forced to perform and compete . . . they run the risk of losing their love affair with the thing they're good at. It becomes a task . . . a duty."

"You sound like you have firsthand knowledge of that. Is that why you're so adamant about not selling out with your music?"

She paused in the motion of lifting her coffee cup to her lips. "Yes, I guess it is. Do you want a cup of coffee?"

She saw his brow furrow as he studied her. For a second, she thought he was going to pursue the topic. But then he inhaled slowly and grinned.

"Are you flying?"

She was already standing up by way of an answer. "How do you take it?"

"Just a splash of cream."

He was sitting at the edge of the boat and drying off his chest and arms with a towel when she came out with his coffee.

"Thanks," he murmured when she handed him the cup and sat down next to him on the deck.

"Not a bad way to wake up every morning," she said, nodding to the cerulean lagoon.

"Yeah," he mumbled. She touched her hair self-consciously, wondering if that's why he looked at her with that odd expression. She'd gone to bed with it damp and hadn't combed it yet. It probably looked like a rat's nest. She finger combed it idly as they sipped their coffee in the silence that followed.

"Is Jace's closed on Sunday?" she asked.

He blinked like his mind had been far off. "No, we do a good brunch crowd on the weekend."

"Oh. I thought because of what you'd said yesterday you must close on Sundays. Feel free to go any time you—"

"*Lana.*"

She stopped abruptly when she heard the exasperation in his tone. "I told you I wanted you to spend the day here with me. If you want to go back to shore, just say the word, but don't make it seem like I'm the one who changed my mind."

"Oh, no . . . I don't want to," she insisted, feeling flustered. "Go back. Until later, I mean."

"It's not really that much to ask, is it? For you to just let go and relax—take it easy—for a few more hours?" he chided softly.

"No, of course not."

His hand came up to cradle her jaw. He turned her face until she met his stare. "It actually is, though. Isn't it? A lot for me to ask."

"It's fine, Jason."

His eyebrows went up skeptically. She was glad when he didn't comment further. He just stood and took her coffee before he grabbed her hand and helped her up. "Come on, let's sit in the sun on the front deck. After I dry off, I'll bring you some breakfast."

Lana trailed after him, wondering if she'd imagined that brief charged moment. She'd half convinced herself she had after Jason led her to several padded loungers and he fell back into one of them, his hands over his head. He proceeded to soak up the heat like the sun-worshipping male animal he was. Lana scooted back in her chair and submitted to the drugging effect of the warm rays. She might have even drifted off for a few minutes as she lay there next to Jason in the sunshine.

When she blinked open her heavy eyelids a while later Jason was gone. She was still rubbing the sleep out of her eyes when he came around the corner carrying a tray.

"What's this?" she asked drowsily when he pulled a metal table between their loungers and set down the heavily laden tray.

"Your breakfast. Nothing fancy. Some fruit from my grand-mother's farms." He snagged a chunk of mango with his fingers before he sprawled in the chair. She smiled. She'd never before known someone who was so supremely confident in his own skin. It was admittedly a wondrous sight: him lounging around wearing nothing but a pair of very low-riding trunks. He had a torso that made her wish she was a painter or a sculptor so that she could make some feeble attempt to replicate its glory. Her gaze reluctantly transferred to the tempting sight of fresh pineapple, mangoes, strawberries, bananas, and papaya heaped onto a platter. He'd included a bowl of what looked like strawberry yogurt for dipping.

"Oh, this looks wonderful," she murmured, reaching for a pineapple wedge.

"I can make some toast, too."

She shook her head emphatically as she chewed the succulent fruit. "No, this is perfect for me. Thank you for cutting up all of the fruit." She paused and blinked. "How long was I sleeping for?"

"Forty-five minutes or so," he replied before he snagged a piece of papaya and popped it into his mouth.

Her eyes widened in surprise. She'd thought she'd drifted off for a minute or two, tops. Rarely did she lose herself so utterly. When she was singing a particularly good song, she lost track of time, but that was one of the few occasions she could think of when she let go so completely.

Of course she'd let go last night when Jason had coaxed her into breathing through the snorkel. And later, when he'd had his way with her on the upper deck, she'd become a primitive creature existing solely for pleasure: a raw, exposed bundle of nerves whose sole agenda was sexual release.

"What's wrong?" Jason asked. Lana realized he sat up slowly from his lazy, reclining pose.

JASON tensed when a queer expression came over Lana's face and she placed the piece of mango she'd been holding back on the platter. He'd been pleased—and relieved—to see how relaxed she'd seemed this morning when he returned from his swim.

It'd taken him a while to fall asleep last night. One warning alarm after another had blared in his brain, starting with the one that went off when Lana had separated herself from him after he was still struggling to recover from the most intense orgasm he ever recalled having.

The truth of the matter was, he felt guilty for pushing her so hard. But, Christ, something about the stiff, bitchy attitude she donned occasionally like a bulletproof cloak royally pissed him off. As soon as she jerked that facade into place, Jason was filled with an irrational desire to rip it off her . . . to strip her bare once again.

The second alarm blared in his brain when he saw her face after she'd walked out of the bathroom last night. She hadn't realized he was standing in the hallway at first, and ever so briefly he'd caught a glimpse of the vulnerability on her face. When they'd gone to bed, he'd seen her hesitation after he stepped out of the shorts he'd been wearing. She'd dropped her towel and gotten into bed with him naked, but at that moment he'd known for a fact he'd misplayed his hand.

He'd most definitely pushed her too far. And it wasn't because she couldn't handle some kink or a hard fuck. It was because he'd used a little kink and a hard fuck to get her to drop her defenses. He'd have been better off being gentle with her, coaxing her like he had in the water into letting her rigid defenses slip.

But he'd been so desperate he'd gotten stupid.

Even though he'd felt her stiffen when he pulled her into his arms in bed last night, he'd refused to let go. He'd waited until he felt the tension melt out of her body and heard her even breathing. It'd taken a good hour for that to happen. He'd finally fallen asleep, determined to make it up to her the next day.

When he'd awakened just after dawn, his arms were empty. He'd rubbed his eyes, pausing when he saw her huddled at the far side of the bed. Her figure had looked as slight as a child's as she curled up into a small ball beneath the blanket.

Something had tightened inside his chest at the sight.

He'd taken out his misgivings on the Pacific Ocean. By the time he'd returned from his strenuous swim, he was convinced he had his head on straight again. Lana was a fascinating woman who was so sexy she could spin a guy right off his axis. But she had issues. Most people did. He'd be a hypocrite to blame a woman for having intimacy issues when there were probably dozens of females out there who would accuse him of the same thing.

He'd been lucky enough to be granted her company for a small period of time. He should make the most of it. She'd leave later today, and that'd be that. He just needed to spend the next few hours making up for forcing her to bend to the breaking point—all so that he could exhibit that *he* was more powerful than her rigid defenses. If he spent the day fully enjoying the experience of being with her and trying to make her forget his insensitivity last night, he could let her go with an easy mind.

Or so he'd thought until he'd taken off his goggles and seen her sitting on the deck of his boat earlier. She'd looked as sexy as an unmade bed with her hair tousled around her shoulders and a sublime smile on her beautiful face. Having Lana Rodriguez tease you with that whiskey-smooth voice first thing in the morning wasn't something a man could easily prepare himself for.

It was just her stardom plaguing him, he realized; his fascination with her bluesy, sexy voice. Her gloss would wear off, if not with the rapidness of a normal lust infatuation . . . quick enough, nonetheless.

She'd been relaxed enough to fall asleep up on the front deck, and she'd seemed comfortable enough when he brought out the fruit just now. But then he'd seen that shadow fall over her features, and she'd dropped the fruit back on the tray with stiff fingers.

"What's wrong?" he asked as he sat up slowly.

She glanced at him furtively and smiled. "Nothing. I was just thinking . . . how strange it was that I'd fallen asleep for so long. I don't usually drift off so easily." She picked up the piece of mango again, not seeming to be aware that she'd ever dropped it.

"It's the sunshine and being out on the water. Lots of people don't realize how lulling even the slight movement of the boat can be."

She sighed as she chewed her fruit and stared out at the opening of the harbor and the Pacific Ocean. "Actually, I've been known to get seasick on boats. But the waves are so gentle here, and your boat is so large that it absorbs most of the waves. It's nice," she admitted, but Jason heard her tentativeness.

"You sound like you're not sure about that," he teased.

She grabbed another pineapple wedge, dipped it in the yogurt, and bit off the tip. "Well, there's got to be storms . . . typhoons, even, right? What do you do then?"

"I just batten down the hatches. We get warnings for typhoons, you know. It's happened twice since I've owned this boat that I've had to go weather a storm at my grandmother's farm. Other than that—I have good insurance. Nature will have her way, no matter how much planning I do. Maybe you were too young to remember much about living here, but this *is* a typical day. It hardly ever varies."

"I remember one," she said softly after a minute of silence.

"One what?"

"One storm," she replied huskily. "A really bad one. I'd been . . . accidentally locked out of the cottage where I lived with my father."

Hadn't she implied she'd left the island soon after her mother died? She must have only been a tiny thing. How could her father have "accidentally" locked out a little kid in a storm? But then he remembered what she'd said about her father being an alcoholic and wondered how much that grim fact of life had played into the story.

"You must have been scared to death. When a bad storm hits the island, it can be ugly. Was it a true typhoon?"

"I don't think so. Just a bad storm. I survived." She finished off her pineapple and wiped her hands on one of the napkins he'd brought out. "I'm getting warm."

He almost called her on changing the subject so abruptly, but then remembered he was supposed to be patient with her. It galled him just to let things slide like that, but he'd promised himself.

"Want to take a dip?"

She hesitated for a moment, and he wondered why. Then he

realized that every time they'd swam before they'd done so after fooling around, when her inhibitions had been held in abeyance by lust. At the moment, they were highly aware of each other—or at least he was highly aware of her—but they'd hardly touched since last night. He watched her, curious as to how she would respond to the idea of stripping down to the only bathing suit she had available—her beautiful skin—with no sexual prelude.

"Sure," she replied. His eyebrows went up at her unruffled agreement, but he wasn't really surprised. Lana personified smooth coolness when she chose to. He stuffed a few more chunks of juicy mango into his mouth before he stood along with her.

"I'll put the fruit into the refrigerator until we get back from our swim," Lana offered, picking up the tray. Jason just grabbed several more chunks of mango and grunted agreeably, since his mouth was full of fruit.

When she came back outside, he'd already stripped out of his trunks and gotten in the water. She glanced at his discarded swimsuit and met his gaze before she reached for the hem of the shirt and matter-of-factly whipped it over her head. His tread in the water faltered slightly at the sight of her wearing nothing but some tiny black bikini briefs. He loved how small her waist was. It made the curve of her hips and the fullness of her breasts so much more pronounced—so much more exciting. Her breasts looked pale next to her tanned skin; the flesh soft, vulnerable . . . tender. His cock lengthened in the cool water.

"Leave on your panties," he called out when she started to remove them.

She looked up sharply. "Why?"

"Because I like your ass white."

So much for being patient and going easy on her. So much for the sexual fires being banked. Just like that, the flames surged into a full-fledged inferno. He saw her mouth drop open, noticed her sudden stillness.

He hadn't been the only one who'd noticed the heat flash.

She slowly removed her fingers from her panties. She dove into the water, surfaced, and swam toward the shore without pause. The urgent tug on his penis made him knife into the water after her. A few seconds later he reached and grabbed her windmilling wrist. She whipped her head up, her long hair splashing water in his face. Her lips fell open in amazement at being halted so abruptly.

Jason plunged his tongue between them.

He sealed their mouths together, swallowed her gasp of shock, and sent his tongue deep. He felt her slip slightly in the water beneath his ravaging kiss and pulled her closer to his body, letting his treading legs support most of their weight. The sensation of her silky skin sliding next to his, her soft breasts and pointed nipples pressing against his chest, caused his cock to surge like a snake at the strike.

"God, you feel good . . . taste good," he muttered a moment later as he kissed the salt water off her lips and cheeks and filled a hand with a breast. When he heard her soft moan, he covered her mouth again with his, kissing her feverishly. His excitement was like a flash flood, coming upon him unexpectedly and with torrential force.

He was so temporarily insane with lust that he would have driven into her pussy right there in the middle of the lagoon; fucked her like a madman if he could have managed it without drowning them both.

He ripped his mouth from hers. She blinked up at him dazedly when he grabbed her hand and tugged her alongside him.

"Jason," she sputtered through a mouthful of seawater.

"Bed," he replied monosyllabically. He'd gone caveman under the influence of his furiously throbbing cock.

"Just let me swim," she said.

He realized that it *would* be more efficient for them to swim to the boat instead of him dragging her through the water. He swam slowly next to her, not wanting her out of his sight for some reason. Maybe it was just his cock influencing him—making sure its source of relief didn't get too far out of striking distance. He'd have laughed at himself if he wasn't horny enough to tear barefisted through a wall to get to Lana at that moment.

When she reached for the ladder, he placed a hand above hers, stilling her. He held her hip and pressed his aching cock against her ass. His hand found her panties and shoved them down to her thighs. He flexed his hips aggressively, searching for her heated core. She whimpered when he encircled her waist firmly and skewered her with his cock. He pushed her down on him at the same time that he thrust. A harsh shout tore out of his throat when he fully embedded himself in her sleek, tight pussy.

"Ah, God, I'm sorry," he muttered between clenched teeth as he began to fuck her, making the water churn wildly around them. "But you feel so damned good. I won't come in you, but . . ."

He clenched his eyes shut as he lost himself in her. She was so hot, and she gloved him so tightly. He slammed into her with short, hard thrusts, feeling like a wild, feral animal had taken up residence between his legs . . . invaded his brain, even. Every time he withdrew slightly he experienced a blinding mandate to be back in her. Her pussy sucked at him like a hungry, hot little mouth, taunting him to test her depths higher and harder and faster.

He used his hold on her waist to slam her down more forcefully on his driving cock, creating a frantic tempo. The water surged and boiled around them. He plunged into her to his balls, his cock lurching viciously inside her hot, muscular sheath.

He shouted in anguish when he jerked out of her. He clung to the ladder for dear life and turned his body slightly away from her. His cock felt unbearably sensitive when he pumped himself. Climax tore through him. He shot off what felt like a geyser of semen into the water.

He shuddered when he felt her cool, small hand fist his cock. He kept his eyes closed, overwhelmed by pleasure as they both milked his spasming member together.

When he came back to himself and opened his heavy eyelids, he saw her watching him with huge eyes. She was still holding on to the ladder, but she'd twisted around to stare at him. Her hand still fisted his softened cock. Her lips and cheeks were flushed bright pink, signaling her arousal.

It'd likely been five minutes tops since the moment she'd removed his T-shirt and dived in the water.

"Sorry," he mumbled, embarrassment overcoming him when it slowly began to dawn on him what he'd just done. Talk about being hit by a bolt of sex lightning. What would he have done if he'd been struck by it in the midst of a public place? Probably would be being pulled off Lana and arrested right about now, he thought with a stab of amusement. He didn't realize he was smiling until he saw Lana's lips curve.

"Little anxious for it, weren't you?" she asked in that low, husky voice that he craved.

"I don't know what'd make you say that."

The sound of her laughter was as good as fucking her had been. Almost.

"Come on, let's go inside and I'll make it up to you," he assured her with a kiss.

twelve

LANA felt a little awkward when they stepped into the dim interior of Jason's houseboat. She tried to determine why she felt self-conscious—it'd been Jason who had fucked her like a horny teenager just now, after all. But then she realized his exuberant honesty in regard to his need was what had her feeling uncomfortable.

In truth, his inability to control himself until they'd gone to the bedroom surprised and gratified her. It also aroused her. She hadn't come while he'd skewered her with his cock and fucked her with frantic abandonment, but her pussy felt tender and swollen. Just thinking about the rough, wild ride made her vaginal muscles clench with excitement.

He grabbed her hand from behind, halting her as she headed toward the master bedroom.

"Wait here for a minute," he muttered gruffly. "I want to get a couple things ready for you."

The sight of him watching her with a sexy, heavy-lidded stare made her impatient. He was still gloriously nude. She longed to put her hands all over his gleaming, delineated muscles and hard male flesh. She didn't want to *wait*. Her pussy felt enflamed and empty. She thought of how indescribably arousing it'd been to stroke his swollen, spasming member while he climaxed in the water. She wanted Jason's cock back inside her and *soon*.

She eyed the arousing slant of his torso that angled up from his narrow waist. His back, shoulder, chest, and thigh muscles were stark in their strength; the honed tools of a world-class athlete. She reached but he caught her hand before she could stroke his abdomen.

"Can't you hold on just a minute?"

"*You* couldn't. Why do I have to?" she asked irritably.

He flashed that sexy laser grin.

"*Hurry*, then," she whispered, surprising herself by not censoring the need in her voice. His former exhibition of unbridled horniness had given her permission to show her own. Jason's widening grin told her he liked her impatience.

"Stay right there," he ordered as he let go of her hand and moved past her.

Lana felt her pulse thrumming with excitement in the tense minute that followed. She'd just started to edge toward the hallway that led to his bedroom when he stalked out of the hallway, looking magnificent and utterly comfortable in his nudity. She couldn't help but notice that his penis had lengthened while he'd been back in the bedroom.

She also couldn't help but wonder what he'd been doing back there that made him re-aroused.

He held up the silk scarf he'd used to tie her up to his bed several days ago, a gleam in his dark eyes.

"Come here. I'm going to blindfold you."

Lana went to him. She couldn't have stayed away from him in that moment if he'd proposed something ten times as anxiety-provoking. What did he have in mind, precisely? She thought of how ruthlessly he'd spanked her and then fucked her in the ass last night. Arousal pinched at her clit as he covered her eyes and tied the scarf behind her head. She wasn't sure she could handle something that intense again . . . but part of her wanted it, nevertheless.

"Come on," he coaxed, his voice low and gravely and sexy as hell.

"I can't see anything," she fretted a moment later after he'd tied the scarf over her eyes, but he took her hand before she was done speaking.

Lana padded barefoot after him. When they got to where she assumed was his bedroom, he turned her in his arms. She felt his big hands on her hips, his fingers sliding beneath her wet panties and pushing them off her legs. He held her arm and guided her back until the back of her legs touched the bed.

"Lie down."

Lana sat on the bed. The cool, soft sheets felt delicious against her heated pussy. She started to lie on her back but he stopped her with a hand on her thigh.

"Facedown."

Her breath burned uncomfortably in her lungs when she followed his instructions.

"Now spread your legs and raise your hands over your head." His deep voice reminded her of a low purr. She hesitated. "Come on, Lana. My rules, remember? That's a girl," he said when Lana spread her thighs and reached over her head. She wasn't entirely surprised when she felt him loop a cloth-covered restraint over her left wrist. Bondage had never been her thing in bed. She preferred to be the one who set the parameters for her sexual pleasure, making sure she got what she needed in a safe, efficient manner.

Nothing about Jason's lovemaking was safe. He'd never made a secret of his dominant tendencies, so realizing that he planned not only to restrain her hands but also her legs while he made love to her wasn't much of a shocker.

What *was* shocking was how aroused it made her.

But anxiety mixed with her lust in increasing strength as she felt him restrain her ankles. She was making herself wholly vulnerable. What if he hurt her? she thought with rising nervousness.

She felt him come down on the bed. He brushed her hair from her face and neck gently. As if he knew what she was thinking, he leaned down and spoke quietly next to her ear. "I'm going to make you feel good, *Onaona*. If you trust me, it will intensify your pleasure."

"Why do you call me that?" she whispered, finding it hard to find her voice because she was so preoccupied by the feeling of his mouth pressing kisses against the side of her neck.

"It means lovely"—he paused as he inhaled at her nape—"sweet, inviting . . . fragrant."

"Sweet and inviting? Surely you're not referring to me, Jason. You're always telling me I'm stiff and cold."

She felt his smile against her neck. It caused warm liquid to seep out of her pussy. "I think you're named correctly. On all counts, 'Ailana."

Her chin came off the pillow when he moved away from her.

She heard a drawer opening. Her anxiety ramped up again when she heard a plastic cap popping open. "What are you going to do?"

She felt his weight shifting again on the mattress. A whimper popped out of her throat when he straddled her and his muscular, hair-sprinkled thighs bracketed her hips. Large, warm hands spread on her back. Lana groaned in pleasure as he kneaded her flesh, his skin sliding against her own in a friction-free glide thanks to some sort of lightweight, fragrant oil.

"I thought I'd give you a nice massage. I figure you deserve it after the way I used your body solely for my pleasure just now," he replied, amusement tingeing his tone.

"Ohhh, that's nice," she moaned as he rubbed the tension out of her upper back muscles. "You actually know what you're doing, don't you?"

He chuckled. "When you're an athlete, you get pretty familiar with massage techniques."

Lana opened her mouth to respond, but her tongue seemed to be going heavy and relaxed in sympathy with the muscles melting beneath Jason's strong hands. He surprised her a little by spending twenty minutes or so methodically working the kinks out of her shoulders and back. Clearly, he hadn't offered the massage merely as a means of sexual titillation.

Not that it wasn't arousing to lay there, naked and tied up to the bed, while Jason used his knowing hands to turn her flesh to mush. She was hyperaware of the velvety tip of his thick cockhead brushing against her lower back. He wasn't iron hard, but Lana could tell as the languorous minutes passed that he became increasingly erect. Her pussy throbbed with a slow, delicious ache.

He transferred his attentions to her lower back, spanning her hips with his hands. It required him to scoot down on the bed. His erection dragged down her ass, smearing a light coat of pre-cum on one of her butt cheeks. She pressed her hips down on the mattress, suddenly in desperate need of pressure on her clit. His cock remained resting on her right buttock, warm and throbbing. As he continued to work her back muscles, it stiffened notice-ably. She wiggled her ass slightly, made horny as hell by the sen-sation. His cock lurched at her squirming, batting her bottom.

"Jason," she pleaded hoarsely.

He laughed softly and lifted one of his massaging hands. For an anxious few seconds, she couldn't feel his cock anymore, and she realized he must have lifted it off her ass. She groaned in intense excitement when he matter-of-factly parted her bottom cheeks and slid his now-enormous erection in the crevice. He held her buttocks in both hands, sandwiching his oiled cock tightly in her flesh. He flexed his hips.

"There," he said gruffly as he massaged the cheeks with his hands and slid his cock in the tight crack. "How's that for a nice butt massage?"

She moaned in excitement, grinding her bottom against his cock. "I hope this isn't a technique you learned from your sports masseuse."

He chuckled as he continued to stroke and rub her. "No. This is a creative technique inspired solely by your gorgeous ass."

Lana bit her lower lip hard when he pressed deeper. The thick cockhead burrowed in the crack until it slid against her lower spine and his balls pushed tightly against the lower curve of her ass. His big hands held her possessively, massaging and squeez-ing her flesh against his cock. She found herself pressing down desperately against the mattress, trying to alleviate the ache at her clit.

He abruptly lifted her hips an inch off the bed, depriving her of the delicious pressure on her pussy.

"Burning, *Onaona*?"

She turned her head, wishing she wasn't blindfolded. She could only imagine how glorious he must look poised with his arm muscles flexed, her ass in his hands and his cock buried between her buttocks.

"You know I am," she whispered.

"I think we're going to have to turn you over, then."

She moaned in misery when he withdrew his cock from the crack of her ass. It had felt so good, and now he was going to deprive her of the pressure she could get against the mattress.

"I'm not trying to torture you," he said humorously when he heard her groan. He unbound her and encouraged her to roll over with a hand at her hip, then proceeded to restrain her arms and legs all over again. When he spread her legs, she couldn't stop from gyrating her hips, hungry even for the elusive kiss of the cool air against her enflamed pussy. "I have a surprise for you."

"If it's another surprise out of that drawer over there, I'm not so sure I want to know about it."

"What? You mean the drawer where I keep my instruments of torture? Damn, I didn't mean for you to discover that secret so quickly," he said, his tone thick with laughter.

"Jason?" she asked when she felt him move off the bed. He'd worked her muscles expertly, but at the same time, he'd built a powerful arousal in her body. The mixture of relaxation, intense sexual excitement, and nervousness in regard to being restrained and blindfolded created a strange brew of emotions she'd never experienced before.

He spread his hand over her abdomen, as if to still her anxiety. "I'll be right back. I need to get something out of the spare bedroom."

Did he have so many sex toys he needed to keep some in the extra bedroom? she thought as she listened to him pad out of the room with hyperalert ears. She lifted her head when she heard him return, straining for any clue as to his intentions. When she heard the rattle of what sounded like a plastic bag, she called out, "Jason? What are you doing?"

"I have a little tribute for you," he said.

"Wha . . . !" She cried out in amazement when what felt like thousands of cool, velvety-soft *somethings* fell over her body from neck to toe. Sweet fragrance filled her nose.

"*Jason,*" she whispered in disbelief. He'd just buried her naked body in flowers.

His laughter caused a shiver to ripple down her spine. "I couldn't resist. Grandma left a bag full of leis here for me yesterday afternoon, and I forgot to take them to Jace's." She felt his weight press down on the mattress. His hand swept away some of the cool petals from her belly, and she trembled even more.

"You always smell so good," he muttered, sounding distracted. "Seems like you and flowers go together. One or two leis around your neck didn't seem like enough, though." He trailed a string of flowers across her ribs and her nipples drew tight against the covering petals. "I wanted to bury you in them, and I was right to want it." He gently whisked the flowers away from her breasts and let them fall to the sides of her body. "A prettier sight I couldn't have imagined if I tried."

She made a choking sound when he put his fingertips on a nipple and plucked up on it with a featherlight caress again and again, stiffening the turgid flesh even more. Then he picked up a string of flowers and used it to caress both straining peaks at once. Arousal flashed from her breasts to her pussy like a heat wave.

"Stop it, please," she whispered as he plucked at her nipples with soft petals sandwiched between his fingertips. When he paused, however, she groaned in agony.

"You don't really want me to stop, do you?"

Her hips shifted restlessly, and flowers scattered softly over her hips and thighs. When they fell to the side, she was still surrounded by inches and inches of cool petals. The scent of the fragrant oil Jason had rubbed into her skin, the plumeria blooms, and their combined arousal overwhelmed her, making her feel dizzy with desire. She hated to beg, but . . .

"I need to come," she said. "I hurt."

He gave a satisfied grunt, like he'd been waiting for her admission the entire time. "Then that's what you're going to get, *Onaona*."

He plunged a thick finger into her slit and then pushed another in alongside it. She gasped at the abrupt jolt of pressure, moaning as he finger fucked her.

"You're so wet," he muttered, his voice rough with excitement. "You're dripping in my palm." As if he wanted to prove it to her, he swept his fingers up between her labia, bringing her juices with him. He slid his fingertip up and down on the hypersensitive bud of flesh, then pressed the heel of his palm over her swollen labia and massaged her bull's-eye fashion.

When he went back to rubbing her naked clit, the soles of her feet burned in sympathy with her pussy.

She went taut, her back arching off the bed, her wrists pulling forcefully on her restraints. She knew a moment of animal fear that she wouldn't survive the enormity of the climax that loomed over her. But there was nowhere to go, nowhere to escape. She was tied to the bed, and Jason was unrelenting in his precise stimulation.

He'd overwhelmed her by burying her with flowers. Now he demanded that she drown in pleasure.

Orgasm slammed into her with typhoon force.

She lost herself. After a moment, she became aware that he was untying her blindfold. She still shuddered in orgasm, her feet flexing hard in the ankle restraints. Jason wouldn't let up; he just kept right on stimulating her. She blinked open her eyes to see him pinning her with his stare. Lana wouldn't have called his kneading of her pussy rough, necessarily, but it wasn't gentle, either.

She glanced down at her naked body buried in colorful blooms and moaned shakily. He was on his knees, supporting his upper body with one hand. Every muscle in his beautiful body was tensed. He looked like a wild animal prepared to spring. His erection hung heavy between his legs, pre-cum causing the smooth head to glisten. Her vagina flexed inward painfully. Her pussy still felt supersensitive and achy.

Jason slipped two fingers back in her slit and finger fucked her slowly while she panted for air. All the while he watched her, like he was waiting for her to say or do something. Her powerful orgasm had made her temporarily mute, however.

"I think that's long enough," he said quietly.

Lana didn't have time to ask him what he meant before he withdrew one finger and started massaging her clit again. And sure enough, just as he must have guessed, the soles of her feet began to burn and her clit sizzled beneath his ministrations. She began to strain for another orgasm.

When he leaned down and slipped a stiff nipple between his lips, Lana knew nothing but the white-hot flames at the center of her desire.

She blinked her eyes open again some untold amount of time later. Jason had straightened, his knees still on either side of her flower-strewn body. His erection looked almost intimidating . . . furious. She licked her lower lip before she glanced up at his face. His dark brown hair had fallen in a side part and fell over his forehead. His chiseled features were rigid. For a few seconds he didn't move a muscle, but then his gaze dropped to her breasts. He placed one hand on the headboard, leaning over her. Lana whimpered at the sensation of his cock thumping on her belly.

They shared an electric glance before he leaned back up, the bottle of massage oil in his hand.

The air itself seemed to crackle with tension as he opened the bottle and poured a small pool of oil between her heaving breasts and then a small amount in his right hand. He replaced the bottle on the bedside table and came back to his kneeling position over her restrained body. Lana watched, mesmerized, as he began to stroke his erection with the oiled hand.

"What am I going to do, 'Ailana?" he whispered gruffly.

She bit her lower lip to restrain a moan of longing. It was

mind-blowingly hot to watch him spread the oil over his swollen cock and pump it with his fist.

"Fuck my breasts?" she asked breathlessly.

"That's right. There'll be little pleasure in it for you, but I'm going to love it."

She met his stare. "There'll be pleasure in it for me."

A muscle leapt in his cheek. He let his heavy erection drop and leaned over to unfasten her wrist restraints. He situated his knees farther up her body and placed his hands on the headboard. When he lowered over her, his cock fell heavily between her breasts, smack dab in the puddle of oil. Excitement seemed to have robbed him of his voice, because he merely nodded ignorantly to her chest.

Lana obediently took her breasts in her hands and plumped the flesh against his cock. The weight of his erection on her chest made the juices flow again between her legs. Part of her wished he would fuck her pussy. She felt so empty inside. But a larger part sensed how aroused he was, how much the idea of fucking her breasts excited him. And she wanted to please Jason at that moment, more than anything.

He thrust, grunting in a satisfied manner as his cock burrowed between her breasts. Lana was so thankful he'd removed her blindfold, because the image was erotic enough to cause an orgasm from visual stimulation alone. His cock was ruddy and dark in comparison to her pale breasts. Her nipples poked up lewdly; the peaks dark pink in color and standing at rigid attention. The sight of the plump head of Jason's cock and the thick, glistening shaft sliding up between her breasts and then disappearing again between them left her spellbound.

"Christ, that's beautiful," she heard Jason mumble, and she

realized he'd been watching himself fuck her breasts with just as much attention as she had. "You have the prettiest tits I've ever seen. I'm glad you wear a swimsuit all the time. I like your breasts and ass pale. Makes them so much more fuckable."

"Jason," she whimpered.

"Rub those pretty nipples," he demanded roughly.

Lana complied, rubbing and pinching lightly at the sensitive peaks. Jason thrust more exuberantly, causing her breasts to bob up when he smacked his pelvis against them, his balls popping against the firm flesh before he withdrew. He groaned in excitement and grabbed the headboard tighter, putting more of his body weight on his hands.

He drove between her breasts with frantic excitement.

Desire swamped her all over again. She pressed tighter on her breasts, changing the angle on the trajectory of his penis. She twisted her head and caught the thick head of his penis between her lips as he surged forward. The oil had a sweet, fruity taste, but she could have cared less about that. She was hungry for the taste of his cum. Her tongue danced across the crown, capturing his essence frantically before he withdrew again.

"Ahhh, *yeah*," he hissed as he paused for a moment with his cock in her mouth. He pulsed up slightly, pushing it even farther along her tongue, before he slid out of her mouth and back between the furrow of her oiled breasts. He seemed eager to be back, however, now that he knew what waited for him on the upstroke.

"You're gonna make me come doing that," he informed her tensely after she'd sucked his penis into her mouth for three more strokes. Lana merely sucked him further and looked up at him. He snarled and flexed his hips, bouncing her breasts up and overfilling her mouth with swollen, throbbing flesh. He growled, deep and feral, before he withdrew rapidly.

Lana watched, wide-eyed, as he fucked her breasts fast and furiously while he came. By the time he slowed, a thick pool of warm cum had been deposited in the deep furrow between her breasts. His musky scent intermingled with that of the flowers that covered the bed.

She shut her eyelids tightly, overcome by sensation.

Overcome, period.

thirteen

JASON blinked the sweat out of his eyes. He saw when Lana clenched her eyelids shut, noticed the expression on her beautiful face that was something close to pain. Compassion overcame him. She was hurting again, and he'd been so involved in his own pleasure he hadn't noticed.

Then again, he probably wouldn't have noticed an explosion in his living room while he'd been fucking her beautiful breasts. He slid his still quivering cock out of the sweet furrow of her flesh, leaned down, and kissed her parted lips.

"You make me crazy, you know that?"

Her eyelids opened heavily. The fact that she looked disoriented pleased him—maybe more than it should have given the circumstances of their short, convenient affair. Maybe he *was* going to have to throw away her CDs . . . and not because he was irritated with her.

Not this time, he thought grimly.

Knowing she'd gotten almost as much gratification from giving him pleasure as he had taking it made him temporarily forget about her leaving in a few hours. She was here with him now.

And now was all he wanted to think about.

He plucked at her lips languorously. "I'll bet you're mad at me."

She blinked in surprise. "What do you mean?"

He nipped at her succulent lower lip. "I'll bet you want to be filled. You want to be fucked, and I don't mean your breasts."

Her soft laughter fell across his lips.

"You must be a mind reader, but you're wrong about me being angry. I loved every second of it. And Jason?"

"Yeah?"

"Thank you for the flowers. No one's ever given me flowers in such a . . . unique way."

He raised his head and examined her. "You're welcome. Lana?"

"Yes?"

He became fully cognizant of what he was about to say and edited himself at the last second. "It's a shame you're leaving tomorrow."

He saw her throat convulse as she swallowed. "Yeah. It is."

He kissed her, this time not so playfully. He closed his eyes and gave himself to the experience. She had an addicting mouth, no doubt about it.

He lifted his head a while later and nuzzled her nose.

"You know, I think I have just what you need," he mused while he used some tissues to mop up the cum between her breasts.

She glanced between his legs. "You most definitely do."

He chuckled and reached toward his bedside table again. "Yeah, but you might have to wait a little bit before I can be of any use to you in that department." He rifled around in the drawer.

"I'm sure it'll be worth the wait."

"I don't like to make a lady wait," he said as he found what he wanted and pulled it out of the drawer. He hadn't even opened the box yet. Her eyebrows went up when she saw what he withdrew.

"Oh."

He couldn't help but smile at the mixture of dubiousness and doubt mingling in her tone.

"Do you want a smaller one?" he asked as he held up the new vibrator. She licked her lower lip, her eyes glued to the purple plastic.

"No," she whispered.

He liked her answer. Liked it a lot, he thought as he hastily put batteries in the vibrator. The thick plastic shaft was narrower than his cock, but it'd fill her nicely and give her just what she needed until he was ready to take its place. Which might be sooner than he expected, Jason realized with mixed amusement and amazement as he set the vibrator on the table. His cock throbbed when he grabbed one of Lana's wrists and attached the cuff and then repeated the action with the other wrist.

"Why do you have to restrain me again?" she asked.

"Purely selfish. Turns me on to have you at my mercy."

He picked up the vibrator and set the top portion of the shaft to spinning. He pressed the rotating, pulsating nubs against Lana's belly. She inhaled sharply and moaned. He scooped plumeria and orchid blossoms onto the floor and reclined next to her on his side, wanting to press next to her skin to skin.

He lowered the vibrator and pressed it to her glossy labia, letting the spinning nubbins do their work. She gasped.

"You're going to come for me several times, aren't you," he stated rather than asked. The truth of what he said was in her shiny eyes and brilliantly flushed cheeks.

"I . . . I don't think I have much of a choice in the matter."

He grinned. "I don't see how we guys stand half a chance of getting laid when they make these things," he murmured, referring to the vibrator.

Her hot gaze caressed his chest and flickered back up to his eyes. "You obviously don't know a damn thing about women, Jason Koa."

His smile widened. Her lips curved beguilingly.

"Okay, stupid accusation. You clearly know plenty. But you don't get *something* if you think most women would *choose* that piece of divinely inspired, motorized plastic instead of you, Jason."

"Thanks for the nod," he murmured, all the while wondering if her comment warranted the intense rush he got from it. He pressed the vibrator into closer contact with her clit. "But the only woman I'm interested in at the moment is you. And like I said—you're going to come for me several times."

He peppered her cheeks, eyelids, and nose with kisses while she gasped for air. Either it'd been worth it to spend the extra money on this new vibrator or she was just primed to explode.

Or maybe both.

He continued to rain light kisses on her neck and then on her flushed breasts while she whimpered and moaned under the influence of the spinning shaft on her clit. Just when he sensed she was about to pop, he pushed a button that increased the rate of the spinning nodules. He pulled one of her turgid nipples into his mouth and suckled her hard. She writhed beneath him as she came. The sensation of pressing against her while she abandoned herself to pleasure was brain frying in its intensity.

Jason couldn't understand how she could be so uptight and anxious, and yet lose herself so utterly under the influence of desire. But he was eternally grateful she could.

He pushed the fat, penis-shaped crown of the vibrator into her drenched slit, watching her face as he did so. She still shuddered in orgasm, so he massaged her clit with his fingers as he slowly, firmly slid the toy into her vagina. Her entire body shook. Watching Lana spinning in a vortex of pleasure, completely at the mercy of her desire, was heady stuff. His cock was semierect again, despite his former powerful orgasms.

"Oh, God! *No*, it's too much," she grated out between clenched teeth.

"You can take it," he soothed. He replaced his fingers with the clitoral stimulator—a purple pair of butterfly wings—but he didn't switch the gizmo on.

He waited until she stopped shaking, soothing her with his hand on her waist and the side of her ribs. She inhaled raggedly, catching her breath after her orgasm. He kissed her belly and the upper part of her mons, inhaling the delicious scent of her arousal combined with the fragrance of the flowers. He salivated and had to resist a primitive urge to yank the vibrator out of her honeyed pussy and replace it with his tongue.

"Okay?" he asked.

She still panted, but she glanced down at him and nodded her head. He smiled his approval and turned the clitoral stimulator on at a low setting. She moaned.

"Can't you give me the tiniest break?" she accused as her hips shifted restlessly against the pressure of the beating butterfly's wings.

He pressed a grin to her belly button, his eyes on her face the entire time. "How's it feel?"

She shut her eyes and whimpered, her head falling back on the pillow, and Jason had his answer.

He turned the stimulator up to medium and let it go about its work while he occupied himself with familiarizing his tongue with the satiny skin at her belly, ribs, and lower breasts. The scent of her sex juices hung thick in the air now, mixing with the fragrance of the flowers. Jason felt himself getting drunk on the sweet intoxicant. Not only her honey perfumed the air; some indefinable scent that she seemed to release every time she climaxed filled his nose. He found it everywhere on her skin, but he kept seeking it out in undiscovered locations.

Jason wasn't sure how long he kissed and tasted her while the vibrator stimulated her clit, but at some point her increasingly desperate moans and cries penetrated his entranced state. He activated the waving motion on the vibrator's thick shaft and then the spinning nodules just beneath the crown.

Once again, he watched in fascination while Lana strained against her bindings and exploded in climax.

He wasn't ever aware of removing the vibrator from her pussy or releasing her ankles from their restraints. The next thing he knew, he had her knees pushed back into her chest, and he was mounting her. She cried out sharply when he thrust into her slit and pushed the shaft of his cock halfway into her.

It felt like being submersed in a tight tube of liquid heat. He clamped his eyes together and growled in animalistic frustration.

"*Fuck*, you're warm and tight," he hissed as he jerked his cock out of heaven. "Sorry," he muttered a few seconds later after he'd slid on a condom.

"It's okay," she replied shakily.

He was mad at himself for forgetting such a routine thing. And not just because wearing a condom was so crucial for safe sex, either.

He was pissed off because twice now he'd allowed himself to experience what it was like to be inside Lana Rodriguez naked. He'd never forget it. He'd never forget *her*, now.

Not that there'd ever been a good chance of that, he thought grimly as he pushed her knees back and mounted her once again.

LANA gave him a glance of amusement when she realized he'd eaten the two grilled cheese sandwiches she'd made for him before she ever finished her one.

"What? I worked up a hell of an appetite earlier," Jason defended. He grabbed a piece of pineapple and reclined on his elbow. They'd gone for a swim in the lagoon after they'd finally risen from bed, both of them sweaty, exhausted, and completely sated. After they'd come aboard and dried off, she'd heard Jason's stomach growling loudly. She'd laughed and gone inside to investigate what he had available to make for lunch. She'd loaded a tray with sliced grilled cheese sandwiches, the fruit from their breakfast, and two glasses of iced tea. Instead of eating on one of the decks, they'd opted to spread out towels and dine picnic style directly next to the edge of the boat and the sun-dappled lagoon.

She studied Jason from beneath lowered eyelids as he lounged there on the floor of the deck and munched on his pineapple. He'd refused to dress after they'd had sex and swam, and reclined there in all his naked-male splendor. He'd protested when she'd shrugged into his big T-shirt before she prepared their lunch.

"I'm not making our lunch naked," she'd laughed as she struggled to pull on the shirt while Jason yanked at the hem, trying to pull it off her. She'd attempted to reason with him when he finally let go and leaned against the kitchen counter, arms crossed under his chest and scowling. "Jason, you'll get sick of seeing me naked if you see me that way all the time."

He'd rolled his eyes in disgust and stalked back out on the deck, his attitude stating clearly that her statement was too ridiculous to even warrant a response. Lana had just stood there, staring at the magnificence of his long legs, muscular back, and tight ass. Okay, so Jason was most definitely the exception to the rule about getting sick of seeing someone naked if you saw the sight too often.

She thought the same thing presently as she chewed her grilled cheese and watched Jason lolling on the deck. The temperature was a delightful eighty degrees, comfortable in the shade and plenty hot in the sun. While they'd swum in the lagoon earlier, their attention had been caught by a thick bank of storm clouds over the mountains to the east. Lana knew the storm would never reach them—clouds frequently gathered in the high regions and never made their way down to the coast. Just before they'd returned to the boat, Jason had pointed out a rainbow arcing from the storm clouds down to the ocean. She was surprised to see when she came out with their lunch that it remained, although it had faded.

"I remember seeing rainbows all the time when I was a kid," Lana said as she stared at the ephemeral arch of light. She hummed the melody to "Somewhere Over the Rainbow" wistfully, her thoughts far away. When she finally came back to herself, she saw Jason watching her with an expression she couldn't quite identify.

"'Somewhere Over the Rainbow,'" he muttered.

Lana laughed, trying to shake off the uneasy feeling of having exposed herself in front of Jason's piercing stare. "I used to sing it when I was a kid. Did your grandmother ever tell you the story about the Rainbow Maiden?"

"Kahala?" Jason asked. "Sure, her jealous lover killed her and buried her under a tree just like that one," he said, tilting his chin toward the enormous koa tree on the finger of land that helped separate the lagoon from the harbor. "But her true lover resurrected her, and so she plays on the island to this day, casting her rainbows between the sun and the mist."

Lana smiled. "Funny. I'd almost forgotten about the Rainbow Maiden."

He sat up, his eyes still fixed on her face. "Don't see too many rainbows in Manhattan, I can imagine."

"No. And even when a rainbow myth is referred to, it's not to the Rainbow Maiden."

"Right. On the mainland, you get the stories from my mom's side of the world—leprechauns and pots of gold at the end of the rainbow."

She nodded her head in agreement and took a sip of tea.

"Maybe it's time for you to reclaim some of your heritage."

Lana glanced at him. His hair brushed his sculpted cheekbones. His face looked shadowed and intent.

"Like the Rainbow Maiden?" she teased, trying to lighten the moment.

He shrugged. "You haven't been back here since you were a kid. I'm sure there are a lot of things you must remember about the island. Surely not all of it was bad, Lana."

"I suppose," she said evenly, avoiding his gaze.

"It's too bad you can't stay for a few more days. There'll be a luau at my grandmother's farm Wednesday night to celebrate Li'l Lil's first birthday."

"Li'l Lil?"

He nodded. "She's my goddaughter. It'd be nice if you could come. The minister will do a small ceremony in the Hawaiian language. You'd like one of my grandmother's luaus. She's an amazing cook. Maybe that'd remind you of some nice things about Hawaii—close families, good food, a tendency to celebrate life in the moment."

Lana didn't miss his upraised eyebrows or significant look at the latter comment.

"Jason, I *do* have the ability to celebrate life in the moment. Why do you insist on portraying me as being so uptight?" she asked, exasperated.

"Tell me one thing that you do on a normal basis that would lend credence to your allegation that you aren't . . . living-in-the-moment challenged."

She made a scoffing noise. "I do pretty much whatever I want, whenever I want. I travel all over the world. I perform in front of thousands of strangers."

She noticed his doubtful expression and realized he didn't think any of those things counted as celebrating-the-moment activities.

"I take Tae Kwon Do classes. What?" she asked peevishly when he rolled his eyes.

"Imagine—*you* doing something that involves bolstering your defenses."

She felt her ire rising and took a long swallow of iced tea. "I do live in Manhattan, you know."

"And I'm glad you know how to defend yourself. That's not the point, though. We were talking about being spontaneous, living in the moment. I have an idea that'd show you can celebrate what's happening in the now."

She appraised him coolly. "I'll *bet* you do. What do you want? For me to go shark hunting after we clean up the lunch dishes?"

"I was thinking you could change your plane reservations and not go back to New York for a few days . . . a week . . . maybe two."

A boat sounded its horn in the harbor in the silence that followed. She scoured his face, looking for signs that he was joking. He looked like he had in the photo on the starting block: set, focused, and determined.

"Jason . . . I can't." She laughed uneasily when he just continued to pin her with his stare. "You weren't serious, were you?"

"What do you think?" he asked wryly before he popped a chunk of mango in his mouth.

"But I thought we agreed that this"—she waved her hand in the space between them—"was just a . . ."

"Fling? A guilt-free fuck fest?"

She inhaled slowly. "Why do you do that?"

"What, Lana? Does it hurt when you hear your personal version of the truth spoken out loud?" he asked quietly.

The line of his jaw was hard when he glanced out at the lagoon. He was angry again and trying to calm himself. She blinked in surprise when he stood up abruptly. Her thoughts fragmented and collapsed like a falling house of cards. It was a bit difficult to keep focus on a tiff while you were staring point-blank at Jason's long legs, muscular thighs, and jaw-dropping package.

She forced herself to look up at his face. "You wanted me to come out to your houseboat for last night and today, and I agreed. I'm not trying to make you mad, Jason. I'm just going by the map we set out for this before we came out here yesterday."

"Yeah, but here's the thing Lana: you don't really use maps when you're being spontaneous and living in the moment, do you? So what if I said one thing last night and changed my mind? Don't you ever do that?"

"Of course I do, but—"

"Then why can't you do it right now? You already told me you don't have anything big going on when you get back. 'The quiet after the storm,' that's what you said."

She gaped up at him, stunned by his challenge.

"You're not just a little curious about this?" he asked softly, waving his hand in the air between them just like she had earlier. He sighed after a moment, clearly disgusted with her when he saw her uncertainty. "I'm not asking you to marry me, Lana."

She felt her cheeks warming. "I realize that. But it just seems so . . . extreme for me to change my plans because of . . ." She trailed off, realizing too late that she'd probably insulted him yet again.

"I've never asked a woman who was on vacation here to stay longer."

She stared at him, even more stunned by his admission than

she had been by his request that she stay in Hawaii longer. Her heartbeat began to drum loudly in her ears.

"You don't have to decide right now. We still have the whole afternoon, and you wanted to go snorkeling again, didn't you?"

She looked out at the tempting lagoon, trying to calm her chaotic thoughts. She'd be crazy to consider staying on this island for longer than was necessary. Hadn't she just been thinking last night that she couldn't leave quickly enough? A wave of heat struck her. She felt the familiar pressure bearing down on her chest, the clammy moisture on her skin. For some reason, it made her think of last night when Jason had coaxed and stroked her and overwhelmed her with his mastery over her body until she'd completely forgotten her childhood fear.

Who knew what else he could coax her into? It intimidated her, realizing how much power he wielded—a man she'd met less than a week ago. Still, she had to admit that if she'd met him in Manhattan or Paris or New Orleans, it would have been different. She wished he didn't live in Honolulu . . . wished he didn't embody the island paradise.

This place was associated with too many bad memories to be any paradise Lana ever imagined.

fourteen

LANA collapsed in the shallows near the shore and let her snorkel and mask float in the water. They'd spent a good hour swimming over the reef, and he'd once again been the one to suggest they take a break. After they'd had something to drink up at the boat, Lana had asked if they could snorkel again. He wondered how long she would have stayed out there if she wasn't interrupted. Something about observing the marine life seemed to calm her for whatever reason.

He took a moment to appreciate the sight of Lana wearing nothing but her tiny black panties, a clinging, cutoff wet T-shirt, and a smile. When they'd decided to snorkel again, she'd removed his huge T-shirt and started to get in the water, but he'd stopped her with a hand on her elbow.

"What's wrong?" she'd asked.

"You'll burn if you stay out in the sun for too long." He'd regretfully ripped his gaze from her beautiful breasts and grabbed the shirt she'd just removed. He'd come out of the boathouse a minute later and handed it back to her.

"You cut off your T-shirt," she'd exclaimed in surprise as she examined the now abbreviated buxom surf girl.

"It's just a T-shirt. I'd like it if you never wore a stitch of clothing while you're here, but ... well, I'll have to get over my selfishness, I guess."

She'd chuckled and put on the T-shirt. He hadn't had much of an opportunity to admire her charms in wet fabric that clung to her like a second skin while they snorkeled, but now he took his time admiring her shapely breasts perfectly outlined in wet fabric.

She noticed him watching her and paused in the action of slicking back her wet hair with her hand. Something else caught her eye, however, and she pointed toward the narrow channel that separated the lagoon and the ocean.

"Look!"

His grin was more for Lana's excitement than the dolphin's acrobatic leap into the air.

"I can't believe they were swimming so close to us. And they didn't seem to mind at all when you touched them. What kind of dolphins did you say they were?"

"Spinner. See how they spin in the air on the leap? They're regulars around here. I was a little surprised we didn't see them last night since they're night feeders."

"Do you ever see turtles?"

He shook his head as he sat down next to her. "No, they've never nested here. They always return to the beach where they were born to nest. I know of a good place where you can see them, though. You like sea turtles?"

"My father took me to the big island once. We didn't stay

long, but I remember there was a coral beach near the place where we stayed. It was shallow enough that I could swim and see lots of marine life, even without using a snorkel. There were lots of turtles there, and they just swam about, happy as can be, even with all the kids splashing around."

"Were you in Kona?"

She nodded.

"You can see the turtles on almost any beach in Kona. How old were you?" Jason asked, fascinated by her wistful smile.

"Oh . . . maybe eight. It was the first vacation I'd ever really had, although I guess it really wasn't much of a vacation. But I remember the turtles."

"I thought you said you left the island when you were four."

Her faraway look disappeared. "I said my mother died when I was four."

"And your grandmother came to get you, right?" Jason prompted, made curious by the return of her somber expression.

She sighed and dragged her snorkel back and forth in the gentle surf. "I actually didn't leave Oahu until I was eleven."

"You mean you lived with your dad for seven years before your grandmother came to get you?"

"Lots of kids live with their dad. Why do you say it like that?" she asked, her tone suddenly hard.

He rolled his eyes in frustration at the return of her defensiveness. "You told me he was an alcoholic, Lana. Would it be so awful if I was concerned about a little kid living alone with a parent who has a disease? That must have been rough for you."

She shrugged and stared out at the lagoon. Just seconds ago, her body had been supple and relaxed. Now her spine had gone stiffer than a metal rod.

"Dysfunctional families are the norm in this day and age. Look at yours," she said.

Jason's mouth fell open in incredulity. Damn, she could turn mean on a dime. "What's *that* supposed to mean?"

Her gaze skittered across his face. Her backbone sagged a little. "I just meant . . . your mom on one side of the world, your dad on the other . . . your grandmother being the main one to raise you."

"Personally, I think it was a fantastic way to grow up. Maybe it wasn't June and Ward Cleaver's idea of a family, but I wouldn't have wanted it any other way."

"I know. I'm sorry. I shouldn't have said that," she muttered, clearly frustrated. When she started to get up, he stopped her with a hand on her shoulder. Her face was tight with anxiety, so he was taken aback when she suddenly lunged forward and started kissing him. She pressed tightly against him, the sensation of her wet-T-shirt-covered breasts and erect nipples against his chest making his eyes cross for a second. He'd have called her actions desperate, but that would have implied a negative judgment on his part. Desperate or not, the woman's kiss was better than Andy Townsend's famous molten chocolate soufflé—hot, sweet, and decadent as hell.

Maybe he should have asked her more questions while her defenses were showing signs of snapping under the pressure. But he was just a guy, after all. He put his hands behind him, supporting them both on the beach, and focused solely on the experience of Lana's supple lips, nimble tongue, and hungry suck.

She ran her hand over his chest, shoulders, and arms, her movements anxious and eager, as though she thought he was going to get up and walk away and she wanted to make sure she got a good feel of him first. He lifted one hand, rinsing off the sand in the surf, before he touched her jaw.

"Shhh," he whispered next to her seeking lips. "I'm not going anywhere. Slow down."

He groaned in rising arousal when she ignored him and caught his mouth in another blistering kiss. Her caresses became increasingly frantic, exciting him to a fever pitch that nearly matched hers. She wrapped a hand around the stalk of his cock, lifting him halfway out of the water, and began to jack him with long, sure strokes. Jason broke her ravaging kiss and hissed. She wasn't intimidated by the fact that he deprived her of his mouth, however. He just watched for a minute, clenching his teeth, as she pumped him. His cock poked up halfway out of the surging water. She slapped the surface roughly on each of her strong, precise downstrokes.

He glanced up into her determined face as she continued to pound him like her hand was some kind of mechanical milking machine. She wanted to see him come and she wanted to see it *now*.

And she was going to get her way if she kept it up, he conceded.

He grimaced in something close to pain when he stopped her by grabbing her wrist. She met his eyes, looking furious at being halted.

"I told you to slow down."

"I don't want to!"

He lowered his face to hers. "I don't *care*. If you don't decide to stay, this might be my last time with you. I'm not going to waste it while you act out your issues and stage some kind of a contest to see how quick you can make me explode."

Her mouth hung open. He resisted an almost overwhelming urge to plunge between her lips and encourage her to keep right on jacking him, maybe push her down to suck on him with that hot, sweet mouth of hers. But what if what he said was true, and this was his last time with her?

"You didn't seem to mind quick and dirty too much when you practically attacked me on that ladder earlier," she accused.

"I 'attacked' you because I was horny as hell for you. You're beating my cock right now like you thought it was the only thing that was going to save you from escaping a sinking ship."

"That's ridiculous! I was doing it for the exact same reason you fucked me earlier—because I want you."

"Don't try to change the subject. Besides, if that were true, you wouldn't have any problem with stretching things out a little. Come here," he said, his voice gravely with restraint. He grasped her shoulders.

"Jason, what—?" But she didn't have the opportunity to finish when he pulled her up out of the water and encouraged her to straddle his hips with her face turned away from him.

"Put your hands on my knees."

She turned and looked at him incredulously.

"Come on, Lana. You can't change the rules this late in the game."

She looked angry at his heavy-handedness, but he knew her well enough by now to recognize the flush of arousal on her cheeks and the glaze of desire in her tilted eyes.

"It's just a game," she whispered.

He shrugged. "If you say so." He studied her while he stroked the soft skin of her inner thigh. "What's the matter? Are you afraid of what will happen if you find out it's not just a game? Is that why you're afraid to stay on the island any longer?"

"I'm not afraid," she told him through a clenched jaw.

"I think you are."

"You think a lot of things, Jason. You certainly think a *hell* of a lot of yourself, that's for sure."

He laughed. "You're the one who's going to walk away in an hour or two without a backward glance."

"And your ego is really going to be taking a hit, isn't it?" Her eyelids narrowed suspiciously. "I sure as hell would like to know what you're up to. I say that I'm going, so you have to prove to yourself that you can make me stay? Why?"

"Oh, I don't know," he mused sarcastically. "Maybe I'm trying to manipulate you until you're warm putty in my hands . . . brainwash you into becoming my slave."

"You yourself have admitted you want to make me relax . . . let go . . . do whatever you ask of me."

"But not because I'm trying to control your damn life," he nearly shouted in frustration. He took a few deep breaths, trying to calm himself. "Maybe I like you, Lana—or at least I do on those rare occasions when you're not acting like a nutcase."

He relaxed a little bit when he saw indecision flicker across her beautiful face. "Would it really be that hard for you to let go one more time? I want to taste you again," he coaxed quietly.

Her hips moved restlessly. Her lush lower lip trembled.

"Come on, honey," he prodded, stroking her thigh, inching his fingers toward her tiny panties. "Lean forward and put your hands on my knees. That's right. Bottom in the air. No, brace yourself on your feet; the sand will hurt your knees."

"Jason." She groaned, but he was too aroused by the sight of her bottom poised in the air just inches from his face to pay too much heed to her embarrassment.

His cock throbbed pleasantly in the cool water as he lowered her panties. He drew them down over her thighs and left them stretched tight just above her spread knees. His gaze never wavered from the sight of her pale, round ass and the flushed, pink petals of her pussy. He caressed her bottom warmly, turning his head slightly to catch the scent of her cunt.

"Are you comfortable?" he murmured. He blew softly against her plump labia and felt her shiver.

"Yes," she replied tightly.

"Good. You just enjoy the sight of the lagoon and the ocean, and relax while you get your pussy eaten."

She gave a snort of disgust. "Like I'll be able to *relax* while you do *that*."

"Well, you're just going to have to try, aren't you?" he challenged before he fitted his face between her widely spread thighs. He twisted his head slightly, burying his nose and mouth in humid, fragrant woman flesh. When she gasped and wiggled, he swatted her ass casually, stilling her. He nuzzled her slit with his nose and prowled with a stiffened tongue between juicy labia.

He growled in satisfaction.

He really couldn't have said if Lana followed his orders and relaxed or not. He was too busy drowning in her.

THE sun reflected off the shimmering waters of the lagoon. Lana closed her eyes in order to shut out the brilliant light. She shifted her hips, unable to stand the precise conduit of pleasure that was

Jason's tongue. It was easier to escape the blinding sunlight than it was Jason, however. He held both her hips firmly, his fingers pressing into the flesh of her buttocks. He pushed back on her ass cheeks, exposing her pussy further.

She keened in pleasure as he vibrated her clit with a strong, waggling tongue.

Her eyelids opened heavily. The lagoon flashed in her eyes like a cerulean gem as he continued to stimulate her. The position he'd insisted she take made her feel completely exposed and vulnerable. But that's how Jason always seemed to want her, Lana realized dazedly, her thoughts muddled by intense lust.

She was spread before him while he sat in the water, her hands on his knees, her feet behind them in the sand, her thighs spread wide. He held her tightly against his ruthless tongue. Every time she writhed at the unbearable torment, he either swatted her bottom in gentle reprimand or strengthened his hold on her. She had no choice but to endure while she burned at the center of a white-hot flame.

When his mouth closed over her sizzling clit and he applied a gentle suction, Lana tumbled into orgasm. She was vaguely aware that he stroked her bottom and hip while he continued to suckle her clit. She cried out as pleasure blasted through her flesh. The fact that he soothed her even as he demanded complete surrender moved Lana in unexpected ways.

"Enough," she gasped a few moments later when he continued to tongue her labia, licking off the fruits of his labor.

"Not nearly." She heard his low rumble as well as felt it vibrating her hypersensitive sex. He used his hold on her ass to widen her slit. She groaned when he dipped his tongue into her pussy and stroked her slowly. Her heart began to thump again rapidly, despite the fact that it'd been overworked by Jason Koa's love-making again and again. She firmed her hold on his knees, realizing it was going to be a long, stormy . . . delicious ride.

It felt decadent; sensually rich beyond her imagination to be poised over him like that while the sun warmed her skin and muscles, the lagoon winking at her like they shared a secret, while he used his tongue to lazily ladle her juices, soothing and exciting her at once. It didn't take him long to become more demanding, tonguing her deeply and vibrating against her until she chanted his name in a soft plea.

Lana's mouth hung agape. She stared sightlessly at the dancing blue water minutes later when he inserted two think fingers into her slit and thrust in and out. His tongue on her clit was once again demanding, delicious, and impossible to escape.

She exploded, forgetting everything in that sublime moment, existing solely *to feel*.

Her body still shuddered from the aftershocks of climax when she felt him grab her waist and pull her down to him. She'd likely be sore later from their frequent, strenuous lovemaking, but right now she only felt the dull ache of sustained arousal despite her climaxes. The cool water that filled his lap felt good against her hot pussy. She whimpered at the sensation of the wet, hard crown of his cock nudging her slit. She turned her head and watched as he positioned himself.

"Lean forward farther onto my knees."

Lana followed his terse demand quickly when she heard the hard edge in his voice. She'd learned by now what that tone meant. As usual, the evidence of his excitement made her feverish with need. He leaned back on the beach, and they found the right angle for his cock.

A moan tore at her throat as he slowly carved his way into her flesh. She melted around his steely strength. Her nerves fired a symphony of chaotic messages—pleasure, a throbbing ache, sublime friction, and sizzling heat.

"Okay?" His harsh whisper sounded like he spoke through a tunnel. *"Lana,"* he said louder when she didn't respond. He paused with his thick shaft buried three quarters of the way in her body.

Heat flooded her cheeks. She blinked sweat out of her eyes when she realized he was asking about more than her possible physical discomfort. Her facial muscles clenched in anguish. She realized he referred to the fact that he wasn't using a condom—once again.

Was she out of her mind? She usually was fastidious about safe-sex practices. The knowledge that she'd made an exception not once, but several times with Jason, left her feeling disoriented.

She'd been so right to worry about spending this time with him.

"We can't," she said brokenly.

But neither of them moved, their bodies both drawn as tight as a bowstring with an arrow notched in it. She felt his big hand lightly caressing her hip. His cock throbbed furiously inside her.

"I know that," he admitted tightly. "But I *want* to, Lana. And I usually don't let myself get so stupid."

Her vagina flexed inward with naked need. He cursed and grabbed her hips. She gasped when he fully seated himself inside of her with a hard flex of his hips. She didn't have time to revel in the exquisite sensation of him filling her to the brim before he pulled her off him. His grunt sounded guttural and a little wild.

"Come here. I need to come, and I can't wait to get back to the boat."

Lana turned around hastily, once again responding to the edge of desire in his deep voice as if a cord had tugged inside her and she had no choice but to draw closer to him, soothe him . . . grant him relief. He scooted back on the beach several feet, still in a sitting position but with his longs legs straightened now. She started to recline next to him, but he pulled her up and kissed her ravenously.

When he eventually released her, sipping her lips thirstily, Lana sensed his mixed regret and excitement. She thought she understood. She wanted to give him some measure of the pleasure he'd given her, to grant him relief, but she also wanted this moment to linger . . . to last.

His fingers at the back of her skull urged her down. She reclined next to his lap and lifted his warm, heavy cock from his thigh.

The next several minutes collapsed into an eternal moment as she took him into her mouth and sucked him deeply and thoroughly while the gentle surf rolled in around them and the sun's rays warmed her skin. She blinked her eyes open in surprise once, her mouth stuffed full of steaming cock, when a wave surged up around Jason's naked testicles and splashed into her face. When she glanced up at him, she saw that although his facial muscles were as rigid as the rest of his beautiful body, his lips curved into a small smile. She didn't want to take her eyes off his mouth for a second, overwhelmed once again by the combination of fierceness and gentleness in him. But then his hand rose to the back of her head, careful but insistent, and she was lost once again in the voluptuous fullness of the moment.

She sucked him fast and forcefully. As eager as she was, he still overfilled her. She used her pistoning fist to pleasure the flesh she couldn't reach with her mouth. He groaned, his fingers forming claws in her wet hair. She was every bit as ruthless as Jason had been with her, but he was different on the receiving end of pleasure. He never struggled, always seeming ready and hungry for what she had to give him.

She glanced up at him furtively when she slid her tightly clamped lips up the shaft, swirling, slapping, and lashing her tongue against the fat crown of his cock. He looked transfixed by pleasure, but he seemed strangely content as well, as he sat there in the gentle surf, watching her while her head bounced over his lap.

Lana realized with distant amazement that this was what he meant by living in the moment . . . giving *in* to the moment. He didn't know what was happening between them . . . had already professed his uncertainty. But he seemed so calm, so sublimely confident.

She cupped his full balls and gently massaged them while she took his cock as deep as she could. A boat revved its engine in the distance and the waves lapped gently around their bodies, but all Lana had ears for was his blistering curse.

He flexed his hips as she slid down over him one last time, his cock swelling enormously in her mouth.

"Fuck, that feels good," he grunted, his words sounding far from profane at that heated moment.

Tears slid down her cheeks as he convulsed in orgasm. For a few seconds she couldn't breathe as his cockhead squeezed into her throat, but then she told herself to calm, breathing through her nose, inhaling his musk combined with the clean, salty scent of the ocean.

Jason's semen and the sea. She wondered if the two might be entwined in her memory forever.

He shouted as his big body shuddered. Cum shot directly into her throat.

His hand on her head relented when she pushed up. She took him fast and furiously while he climaxed. His hands dropped to the beach, and he lifted his hips, giving himself to her again and again.

Even after he'd slowed, and the fierce eruptions of semen became small, sweet spills on her tongue, she couldn't make herself stop. She remembered what he'd said. *If you don't decide to stay, this might be my last time with you.*

She kept sucking him even when it was clear he was spent and only his flavor lingered on her tongue. Eventually she became aware of him calling to her.

"'Ailana," he said, his fingers caressing her scalp.

Slowly, regretfully, she slid off his length. She glanced up into his face. His damp hair bracketed his forehead, casting his eyes in shadow. He cradled her jaw with his palm. His thumb rubbed against her lower lip, and she realized he was brushing away a drop of his cum. She thought of him convulsing in her mouth, remembered how he'd overfilled her.

Before she could stop herself, she wrapped her lips around his thumb and sucked him clean. He made a low, rough sound in his throat, and she released him.

She sat up slowly. Something swept through her at that moment, a feeling of sinking shame at her greediness . . . her *neediness*.

It was a feeling she'd rather not examine too closely.

She had no idea what Jason saw on her face at that moment,

but she frequently reflected on what it must have been in the following days, given what he said next.

"You're not going to stay, are you?"

She swallowed thickly and looked out at the sparkling lagoon, avoiding his stare.

"I can't. I hope you can understand . . ." Her voice trailed off. Did she *really* want him to understand? Best not to lie. He didn't need to hear about her insecurities or the stupid childhood anxieties activated by being on this island once again.

She became hyperaware of the sound of the soft surf lapping rhythmically on the beach in the silence that followed. Against her will, her gaze was drawn to him again. His expression was unreadable. She studied his handsome face, trying to cast it in her memory.

She drew up her panties, grabbed her snorkel and launched herself into the lagoon.

fifteen

LANA followed Melanie to the departure screen at the airport. Melanie scowled as she stared up at it.

"Great. Our flight has been delayed almost two hours. I should have known this trip was going too perfectly. Do you want me to see if we can catch anything out earlier?" Melanie asked.

Lana scanned the departure board for other flights. "No, there isn't anything else going out until five. Let's just go to the lounge and wait it out," she suggested dully.

Melanie sighed. Lana couldn't have agreed more with her friend's lack of spirits. Delays on a trip were never fun, but they always seemed more depressing on the leg back home.

A few minutes later Melanie collapsed into a leather booth in the airline's lounge for preferred flyers. "Maybe I should get one last mai tai before we check out of paradise and return to the world of steel, concrete, blaring horns, and irritated people," she mused as she stared at the bar.

Lana pulled her attention away from the sight of a dark-haired woman greeting a man and an elderly lady. The man placed a blue and white plumeria lei around her neck and the woman's face lit up with pleasure.

"Hmm? Do you want a drink? I'll get us something," Lana said distractedly.

"Are you all right?" Melanie asked a moment later when Lana returned with a mai tai and a Diet Coke for herself.

"Yeah, of course. I just don't want anything alcoholic." And certainly not a mai tai, Lana added in her private thoughts.

"I don't mean that. You've seemed really out of it ever since you came back from Jason's yesterday."

Lana toyed with her straw for a few seconds before she looked up at Melanie and smiled. "I'm fine. I had a much better time on this vacation than I'd imagined I would. Thanks for letting me tag along."

Melanie rolled her eyes. "Who are you kidding, Lana? I'm the one who owes you the thanks for coming with *me*. But don't change the subject." She leaned forward with her elbows on the table. "Tell me about what happened between you and Jason."

"We had a nice time," Lana said as she took a sip of her drink.

"A nice time? A *nice time*?" Melanie scoffed. "You have a *nice time* taking a dip in the ocean or shopping with a friend. You don't have a *nice time* when you indulge in paradise with a guy who looks like Jason Koa."

Normally Lana would have laughed at Melanie's sarcasm, but

she couldn't find the energy to do so at the moment. Her gaze flickered back to the woman wearing the colorful lei. She couldn't help but remember that first night with Jason in her hotel room; the sensation of the cool, velvety blossoms tickling her aroused nipples.

The memory flashed into her mind of being buried naked in fragrant blooms, tied up and helpless while Jason tortured her with pleasure. She clenched her eyelids shut tightly.

"See . . . there *is* something wrong," Melanie accused.

"There's nothing wrong."

Melanie just studied her silently for a long moment. "He was really amazing, wasn't he?" she finally said softly.

"What makes you say that?"

"I can see it on your face. I've never seen you look like this."

"How do I look?" Lana tried to sound lighthearted, but she realized she stared at Melanie intently, as though she really wanted to hear the answer.

"I don't know exactly. Like you've either seen a ghost or been hit over the head."

"Being with him was nice, but it's over and done."

"Jason didn't want to call you, or ever see you again?" Melanie asked indignantly. When Lana didn't respond, she exhaled heavily. "Oh, I get it. You put the brakes on the whole thing. Am I right?" Melanie shook her head, her expression a mixture of exasperation and sadness. "Why should that surprise me, given your track record with men? I thought Jason might be the exception—a guy who could break through that thick hide of yours. The sparks sure were flying during our surf lesson, although it seemed at the time like you mostly hated each other.

That really wasn't the whole story, though, was it? He *got* to you. When you called me yesterday from Jason's houseboat, you sounded—"

Lana heaved a sigh of relief when Melanie's cell phone rang. She felt restless and uncomfortable enough sitting with her own thoughts, much less being the object of Melanie's scrutiny. Her volatile emotions fueled her internal chaos until it felt like a dust devil whirled crazily around in her brain.

She half listened to Melanie talking for the next minute or so, aware that she spoke to Myra Levine, Lana's publicist. Lana's gaze strayed back to the woman wearing the lei and her family. She looked unreservedly happy as she beamed at the older woman and then spontaneously hugged the man.

People who allowed themselves to be so joyful ran the risk of losing it all. Everything might turn to dust in the blink of an eye. Better to be cautious. Better to keep safe.

Lana went entirely still when she registered the thoughts. God . . . those were *her* thoughts, some of her own personal beliefs; beliefs she'd never allowed herself to focus on too objectively. It was like background music that was there all the time, a white noise you didn't even notice anymore . . . like the sound of your own heart beating.

Her eyes burned as she stared at the woman wearing the lei. For some reason, the image of the twin graves of her parents— those unattended tombstones—rose to her mind's eye.

"Myra says hi. Xanadu gave her a release date for your album: November 8," Melanie said, referring to Xanadu Recording, Lana's record label. "She says she'll call you in a week to schedule a time to discuss your tour dates." Melanie paused in the process of putting her cell phone back in her purse. "Lana, what's wrong?"

"Do you think you'd be okay flying back to New York without me?" Lana asked slowly, still staring at the beaming woman.

Melanie gaped at her. "What are you talking about?"

"I . . . think I need to stay in Oahu a bit longer."

Melanie sat back in the booth, clearly floored by the news. "Why? You don't even *like* it here."

Lana stood and began distractedly rifling through her leather tote, examining the items inside. "I already checked my suitcase. Would it be too much of an inconvenience if you picked it up at LaGuardia?"

"Lana, are you crazy? Why the hell do you want to stay here all of a sudden?"

Lana felt a little guilty when she saw the stunned, worried look on Melanie's round face. "I'm sorry. I know it must seem like it's coming out of nowhere, but it's not really. I just didn't feel comfortable talking about it. See, the thing of it is—I was born here in Honolulu. I lived here for the first eleven years of my life." She sighed when she saw Melanie's look of amazement deepen to near disbelief. "I'm sorry. I don't have the best memories of Oahu, that's why I was hesitant to come with you and . . . why I felt uneasy talking about it. But now that we're about to leave, I'm realizing how cowardly it was of me not to visit my parents' graves. Not just in the past week—for my entire adulthood."

"God, Lana, I wish you would have told me," Melanie said after a moment. "I feel awful for dragging you here."

Lana gave a brittle laugh. "It's not your fault, honey, and you know it. I'm the one who didn't feel comfortable enough to tell you everything."

Melanie just shook her head, speechless.

"Are you going to be all right?" Lana asked.

"Of course, that's not the point. Are *you* going to be okay? Do you want me to stay, as well?"

Lana shook her head resolutely. "Not unless you want to. I'll be fine."

"How much of this change of plans has to do with Jason Koa?"

Lana hesitated briefly before she answered. "I'm not sure really. I only know he was always encouraging me not to be so afraid that I ran away from the moment . . . ran away from *living* in the moment."

"Wow," Melanie breathed out as she stared at Lana, open-mouthed. "That's pretty deep advice. And you actually *listened* to him?"

Lana chuckled and nodded her head. "I *do* listen to people, once in a while."

"So you're planning on seeing Jason again?" Melanie pursued.

Lana nodded, not bothering to hide her uncertainty and excitement. Melanie's facial expression segued to disbelieving humor. The woman wearing the lei glanced around and smiled when Melanie and Lana broke into simultaneous, high-pitched laughter.

LANA called a hotel in Honolulu and booked a room while she shopped in an open-air mall for clothing. She surprised herself by choosing brightly colored dresses and unabashedly sexy island wear instead of sticking with her typical sleek, sophisticated apparel in a palette of blacks, grays, tans, and whites. After she shopped, she ate alone at a seafood restaurant near the wharf, enjoying her macadamia-nut-encrusted opah and a glass of dry white wine.

By the time she checked into the Honolulu Park Hotel it was after nine o'clock. She dumped all of her purchases on the bed and immediately went to the luxurious bathroom to draw a bath. It wasn't until she lay submersed in the hot water that she really considered her impulsive decision to stay on the island.

What if it had been a huge mistake?

Then you will have made a mistake. You'll just have to learn from it and move on, she told herself reasonably.

But her doubts not only lingered but amplified as she shaved and then rinsed in the steam shower. Despite her misgivings, she clung to her resolution—if a bit desperately—while she rubbed some scented lotion deeply into her skin. The fragrance had reminded her of the light oil Jason had used while he'd rubbed her tense muscles until she'd flowed like warm syrup beneath his talented hands.

A flash of intense heat surged through her pussy, banishing a good portion of her doubts. She thought of him standing there on the deck of his houseboat like a bronzed, naked god, pictured him waving his hand in the air between them and studying her with his intent, dark-eyed stare.

You're not just a little curious about this?

Lana was curious all right. So curious that she was acting in a completely uncharacteristic manner. And liking it, she thought as she gave herself an amused look in the mirror.

She left her hair loose and waving naturally around her shoulders and applied her makeup sparingly, only spending time and effort on her eyes, using liner and shadow to give them a smoky, exotic look. She pulled on a new sleeveless dress and fastened it around her neck. The color of it had reminded her of the azure of Jason's lagoon. She finished with a pair of delicate, silver-filigreed earrings. On the way out the door, she slid on a pair of white and silver sandals.

She caught her nervous expression in the foyer mirror as she headed out. She gave herself a reassuring smile before she reached for the doorknob and left in search of Jason Koa.

What would he think of her just showing up like this? She wondered nervously. Lana hoped it didn't seem too eager on her part . . . too desperate. God knew Jason probably had his fill of desperate women.

At this time of the night, she knew he'd most likely be at Jace's. She walked down the corridor and pressed the Down button on the elevator, her heart racing with excitement. Yeah, it was a risk, and she was a little scared, but she was going to do it anyway.

Taking a chance was exhilarating stuff.

Her gaze was caught by the flat-screen television mounted above the elevator call button. The Honolulu Park was a sleek, ultramodern hotel that Lana had discovered was popular with international businessmen. During the day television monitors on every floor broadcast the business news. Presently, a local news program was being aired. Lana was too preoccupied with her thoughts to notice the details as she waited for the elevator, but she did turn and nod in greeting to a group of businessmen who approached from behind.

"Hey . . . that's *you*, isn't it?" a Japanese American man wearing expensive looking resort wear asked as he pointed to the television screen.

Lana blinked and focused on the screen. A disorienting wave of heat swept downward through her body. It felt as if every ounce of blood had just drained out of her head. The story that followed the one that left her stunned and speechless was about a city councilwoman who had been accused of illegal hiring practices. She watched it without processing a word. The image of her own, clearly naked body, entwined with Jason's on the beach of his lagoon was still emblazoned in her mind's eye, making her blind to everything else.

Lana Rodriguez and local celebrity Jason Koa, owner of the famous restaurant Jace's have both been implicated in a sex scandal involving a high-class prostitution ring that caters to both wealthy men and women. While Koa's actual involvement in the prostitution ring is unclear, insider sources state that Rodriguez solicited sexual services from Koa while she's been vacationing in Hawaii.

The door opened and the four men clambered onto the elevator.

"Hey, aren't you coming?" one of the men asked, his voice piercing her shock. She distractedly met the gaze of a man with dark blond hair and bushy eyebrows. He gaped at her breasts covered in the thin fabric of her dress. "I might not be Jason Koa, but there are four of us here . . . surely that counts for something. And we won't even make you pay for it." The other men laughed, all of them studying her with hungry speculation.

Lana pulled on her familiar cloak of protection and straightened to her full height. The men's bravado wilted slightly under her icy stare, but they were back to making rude comments by the time the elevator doors closed.

She stood alone in the corridor, reeling from the unexpected blow.

sixteen

THE frantic beat of a Donna Summers song blaring through the speakers didn't even penetrate Jason's consciousness. He was hardly aware of the crowd or the stripper swinging around the pole on the stage, wearing nothing but a nearly nonexistent G-string. Po must not have been lying about business, because the dark, smoky room was packed to the rim.

"Where is he, Alan?" Jason shouted at Po's bartender over the noise of the music and crowd. Alan hadn't been at Hawaiian Heat as long as Manuel had been with Jace's, but Jason recognized the husky blond man, nonetheless.

"Jace . . . uh, he's back in his office," Alan said, clearly flustered by Jason's obvious anger. "But wait, I think . . ."

Jason ignored him and plowed through the crowd to the rear of the nightclub. Not even an hour ago, he'd been going through the month's receipts in his office at Jace's when someone had knocked on his door. Manuel had entered, looking tense. He'd gone over to the small television Jason kept in his office and switched it on.

"You're not going to like this," Manuel had warned grimly as he flipped stations. "They just showed it on Channel Eight, but maybe some of the other stations . . . Ah, yeah, here it is."

Jason's shock had segued to outrage as he focused on the sensationalist news bite about Lana and himself. Manuel had shaken his head in disgust when he switched off the television.

"The place is packed to the rafters tonight, Jace. Everyone in the bar is buzzing about it, but I couldn't figure out what a couple customers meant by their sleazy comments until I happened to notice that photo of you and Lana on the beach on the television . . ."

Manuel had paused when he noticed Jason's expression. "Lana's left the island. I won't even be able to break it to her in person. She's such a private person."

"Yeah, I've read that about her," Manuel muttered sympathetically. "Hell of a mess."

"Did the news station you saw in the bar mention anything about the name of the escort service Lana called?"

Manuel shook his head.

"They didn't say anything about it on this channel, either. Maybe at least I won't have to worry about Grandma freaking out over Po."

"Yeah, Lily'll just be freaking out because of you," Manuel said. He was close enough to Jason to know how the Koa clan was always trying to protect Lily from knowing Po's true profession as the owner of a modern-day brothel. "What's wrong, Jace?"

Jason slowly stood. "How could the press find out about Lana calling an escort service and not know which one it was or who's responsible for running it?"

"I don't know," Manuel answered, puzzled. "You *don't* think Po would—"

"Yeah, that's precisely what I'm thinking," Jason said before he lunged for the door.

Jason had been to Hawaiian Heat a couple times before and knew which door in the dark hallway led to Po's office. He threw open the door without knocking.

"Jace!" Po called out in surprise. At first he paused in the process of fucking a naked, brown-haired young woman. Po himself was still almost completely dressed in an expensive-looking European suit. When the woman saw that they weren't alone, she started to rise from her position bent over Po's desk.

"Don't move," Po ordered tensely. He pushed down on the woman's shoulders and resumed fucking her. Jason guessed he must have interrupted when Po was near climax, given his cousin's short, rapid thrusts, fierce grunts, and perspiration-glazed face. He smiled at Jason before he glanced down to where his cock penetrated the female's body. "Don't be shy about Jason, honey. He's seen it plenty of times. He doesn't mind, does he?"

"As a matter of fact, I do. I want to talk to you. Now," Jason seethed. Still, he knew there was nothing he could do but wait, save hose down the mating couple. He was too pissed to turn his back, so he waited with his fists clenched. He glanced once at the woman. She watched him with an almost bored expression on her face while Po slammed into her.

"Hurry *up*," Jason bit out.

Po grabbed the woman's hips and butt tightly. "Come on, honey, *move* that ass!"

The woman complied, bucking her hips mechanically as she stared at Jason. Po's face twisted into a snarl as he came.

"Not bad," he said when he withdrew his cock several seconds later. He whisked off the condom he wore and draped the semen-filled rubber over the rim of a coffee cup on his desk. "You want to try her?" He asked Jace, nodding at the naked woman. The female paused in the process of straightening, as if trying to gauge if Jason was going to take Po up on his offer.

"No, I don't want to *try* her," Jason grated out. "I want to talk to you. Alone."

Po looked up warily from pulling up his pants, obviously registering Jason's outrage for the first time.

"What's got you all fired up?"

"I said *alone*."

"Don't worry about Joanne. She knows I don't like my girls to gossip," Po said as he gave Joanne a friendly swat on the butt.

"If you don't mind your employees watching this," Jason said darkly, "then by all means, let her stay."

Po blinked as he registered Jason's threat. "What the fuck is wrong with you?"

Jason transferred his gaze to the woman. "Will you leave, please?"

Po made a disgusted sound. "Go on, Joanne. Tell Madeline I said you dance on the main stage tonight."

"Thanks, Po. You're a sweetie," she said with a flirtatious glance first at him then at Jason. She knelt to pick up a pile of clothing from the floor.

"So what's your problem?" Po asked as he idly watched Joanne step into her thong underwear.

"My problem is that my face is being splashed all over the

evening news along with Lana Rodriguez's. They're saying that Lana solicited sexual services from an escort service."

"What are you talking about?"

"You heard me. They're running a story about Lana calling an escort service, and they're implicating me in the whole thing. They're showing a naked picture of us on my beach. Some asshole trespassed on my private property in order to take it. I'm going to find out whoever is responsible for this, Po."

Joanne paused with her arms thrust into the sleeves of her dress, gaping at him.

"Shit, this is news to me," Po said. "How the hell—"

"That's what *I* want to know."

Po's eyes widened incredulously. "Wait . . . you can't think *I* leaked that story. Why would I do that? I don't want the police crawling all over this place, demanding an investigation, shutting down Hawaiian Nights and maybe even Heat."

"*Somebody* leaked it," Jason accused as he neared the desk.

"It wasn't me," Po defended. When he saw that Jason hardly seemed convinced, he put up his hands in a placating gesture. "Look, you're upset, Jace. Even if they didn't mention the name of the escort service on the news, that would still be awful risky for me to—"

"I never said they didn't mention the name of the escort service on the news."

Po went still at Jason's interruption. Was that panic he saw flicker briefly in his cousin's eyes?

"I thought you said you hadn't seen the story," Jason prodded.

Po gave an uneasy smile. "I haven't, but surely one of my staff would have told me earlier if Hawaiian Nights was getting bad press. It was just an assumption on my part that the name of the escort service wasn't being publicized."

Jason's fury mounted in the silent seconds that followed until it felt like a rabid animal clawing at the inside of his chest cavity. He didn't want to believe Po would betray a family member in such a manner, but that didn't lessen his primitive need to bury his fist in his cousin's face. The picture of his hands on the naked expanse of Lana's back, his fingers caressing her smooth, golden brown skin kept replaying in his mind. By now, half the population of Honolulu had gawked at the same image. The fact that it had been *his* arms around her and that she'd been on *his* beach made the whole debacle *his* responsibility—or at least partially.

Christ, he cringed, considering the other photos that asshole had undoubtedly taken besides the PG-13, edited version being shown on the news. Jason recalled all too perfectly the other things they'd done on that beach yesterday.

Someone knocked on the office door.

"Tell them to go away," Jason said, enunciating each word succinctly.

Po shrugged and gave him a blatantly fake apologetic look. Jason figured his cousin was actually thrilled about the interruption. "Come in," he barked. His eyes remained fixed warily on Jason, as though he expected him to pounce . . . which, indeed, Jason was considering. Jason didn't turn around when the door opened. Po's nervous expression collapsed in disbelief.

"Ms. Rodriguez. What brings you here?" Po asked.

Jason twisted his head around. Somewhere in the back of his stunned brain he took in that she wore a sleeveless button-down shirt that looked starkly white against her golden tan. She wore her hair up. The fact that she didn't wear a smudge of makeup made her look younger than she actually was. She met his stare coolly before her eyes flickered away. Jason followed her gaze and saw that she looked at Joanne, who was in the process of pulling a blue dress over her head, her large, silicone breasts bouncing around as she struggled to lower the tight garment.

"I thought you'd left," Jason said, still not trusting his eyes. Was Lana *really* standing there in Po's office at his sleazy strip bar? His brain couldn't quite make the leap. The last memory he had was of her leaning back when he'd tried to kiss her one last time as he'd dropped her off.

I think it'd be best if we didn't, she'd whispered before she got out of the car, slammed the door shut, and headed for her hotel without a backward glance.

"I watch the news," Lana said simply.

"Get out of here, Joanne," Po snapped.

Jason was only minimally aware of Joanne fumbling with her dress and hurrying across the room as she smoothed it into place. Most of his focus was on Lana. She met Joanne's eyes briefly, her face giving nothing away. But when she glanced from Joanne to Po and finally at Jason, he realized with a sinking feeling how sleazy the scenario must appear to her—like Jason and his cousin had just finished sharing Joanne.

"I'm sorry you saw the news," he said. "I wish I could have been the one to tell you about it first, but at least you're here—"

"I didn't come to see you. I came to see him," Lana stated flatly. She nodded at Po. Jason inhaled slowly. He'd thought he'd understood her considerable defenses before, but he realized for the first time he'd vastly underestimated her.

Or maybe he'd overestimated his ability to break through her walls.

"But maybe it's just as well that you're here, too," Lana finished, giving Jason a cursory glance that made his temper flare higher. She stepped farther into the room, her gaze trained on Po. "I couldn't help but notice, Mr. Koa, that while my name was made available for public consumption by your organization, there was no mention of Hawaiian Nights. You can imagine my surprise over the whole ordeal, as I was assured by a very reliable source back on the mainland that you ran a business that was highly sensitive to the confidentiality of your customers."

"Confidentiality *is* important to me and my organization—"

Lana interrupted him with a halting motion. "Spare me the sales pitch. You and I both know it's a lie."

Po looked insulted. "I didn't know anything about this news leak until a minute ago. Jason and I were just discussing it before you walked in."

"I see. Multitasking, were you?" She tilted her head toward the door where Joanne had just exited seconds before. Her voice still sounded smooth and low, but Jason caught a hint of the depth of her fury.

"Lana . . ." Jason began in a tone of quiet warning. But she ignored him, walking right past him and halting a few feet from Po's desk.

"Maybe you did tell the press about me calling Hawaiian Nights or maybe you didn't. Either way, we both know that your promise of customer confidentiality is a lie, because you saw fit to give my name to your cousin here, didn't you?"

The denial that had been on Po's tongue melted. He clearly

hadn't been expecting Lana to take that line of attack. He glanced at Jason nervously.

"Don't look to Jason for help," she said quietly. "My business is with you at the moment."

"Business?" Po asked uneasily.

"That's right. The name of your escort service hasn't been made public yet, but I can guarantee that it will be, along with all the other information on how you treat your customers."

Po flashed his patented grin and shook his head. "I don't think it's a good idea for you to go public with that, Ms. Rodriguez. You would be admitting to your own guilt, if you did."

"And what of it? You've already turned me into a spectacle. I just spoke to my publicist not twenty minutes ago. She said the story has been picked up on the mainland."

Jason cursed under his breath.

"I'm really sorry about that. I'm sorry about all this, but I was *not* responsible for leaking that information to the press," Po insisted.

"Like I said, I don't care if you were or not."

"You plan on providing my name to the press anyway?" Po asked, anger creeping into his tone.

"You would deserve it if I did. It's nothing less than what you and Jason did to me."

Jason's stomach lurched. "*Hold on*—you think I planned this with him?"

"How's business tonight at Jace's?" Lana asked sarcastically. She refused to even face him.

"What the hell has that got to— *Christ*, you think I would do this just to get some business in my restaurant?" Jason roared.

"Even bad publicity is good publicity. Isn't that what they

say?" She finally turned and gave him a blazing stare. "Anything in the name of *good old-fashioned capitalism*."

He gritted his teeth when he realized she was repeating something he'd said that night she'd come to Jace's. Of all the crap things to happen . . . "Lana, you're wrong, and you'd realize that if you weren't so upset. I'm as pissed off and shocked about this as you are."

"I'm not here for you," she repeated coldly. She turned back to Po. "I came here to speak to *you*."

"You came here to threaten me with exposure, it sounds like," Po replied. He studied Lana narrowly, his glittering black eyes lingering on her breasts.

"Get your damn eyes off her," Jason said softly.

Lana started and glanced over her shoulder at him warily.

"Everybody is full of threats tonight," Po muttered with a snarl. "You've got more nerve than I would have guessed, Ms. Rodriguez, I'll give you that. What do you want . . . money?"

"I don't want your money," she hissed. "But if you ever release the name of my friend in the same way you leaked my name, I'll go public not only with your personal information but also with the way you treated me as a customer. People who value their anonymity might not think too highly of your business any longer if they know the truth about how you *really* value customer confidentiality."

Po laughed in disbelief. "*That's* what you want?"

She just stared at him like she thought he was walking, talking slime.

Po shrugged and shook his head. "I didn't have anything to do with your name getting on the news, but if you want my promise that your friend's name will remain secret, you have it."

"For what it's worth," she said, her lip curling in disgust. She turned and started to walk out of the room. "Remember what I said, Po."

"This isn't finished," Jason told Po pointedly before he took off after Lana.

seventeen

LANA plowed through the crowd, her emotional turmoil such that she experienced her flight from Hawaiian Heat in a blur: a disconnected sensory montage of male faces, blaring music, and flashing lights, accompanied by the smell of smoke burning in her nostrils.

"Let go of me," she demanded fiercely when someone grabbed her upper arm, bringing her up short.

"What's your hurry, sweetheart? You're much too pretty to be leaving this place alone."

"I said to let go," she told the man who held her. He looked like he belonged to one of the many military bases in Oahu, given his buzz haircut. Lana yanked her arm, but his grip held strong. They were already standing close because of the crowd, but he pressed his body into hers more intimately.

"Come on, baby, let me buy you a drink."

"Fuck you." Lana hurled her entire body weight in the direction away from him, but he hauled her back against him, causing her neck to snap and her upswept hair to fall down on her right cheek. He spread his hand on the side of her neck and jaw, forcing her to look up at his sneering face.

"You're a feisty one. I like that. Means you'll keep a guy hopping in bed." Lana winced as she inhaled his whiskey-soaked breath. She pulled her free fist back to punch the smug look off the man's face, but another fist slammed into his jaw first . . . a much larger, stronger fist than her own. The man went down like a clipped bowling pin, causing other patrons to scatter in his wake.

Jason grabbed her hand and pulled her through the crowd. Lana followed without protest, her only thought to escape from the packed, noisy strip club.

Jason had to release her hand as they pushed through the revolving door exit. When they got outside, she gulped the fresh air greedily, hoping it would still her spinning head. She marched to the curb of the busy street.

"What are you doing?" Jason asked from behind her as she held up her arm.

"I'm hailing a cab."

"My car is here."

"What's that got to do with me?" she grated out between clenched teeth. He called her name in obvious irritation when she stalked past him and walked half a block, all the while searching for another cab to hail. Unfortunately, people didn't use cabs in Honolulu as frequently as they did in Manhattan, and available taxis appeared to be scarce.

All she could think of was the necessity for creating distance between herself and Jason Koa. And she needed to try and reach Melanie, to break the news of what had happened. There was no telling what her husband would do with this piece of media sleaze in the divorce courts, especially if Melanie's name got caught up in it. With Melanie being on the plane still, however, she hadn't been able to reach her friend.

She averted her gaze from Jason when he came up next to her. She'd only gotten one good look at him in Po's office, and that had been sufficient for her to know she should avoid the sight of him altogether. He was wearing a pair of jeans that looked like they'd been tailor-made for his long legs, muscular thighs and ass, and trim hips. The collarless gray shirt he wore skimmed his torso, emphasizing his athletic build and obvious strength. Not for the first time, she experienced a ridiculous wish that he wasn't quite so potent in his appeal. His blatant sexuality intimidated her as much as it pulled at her, especially now that she had even more of a reason to defend herself against it.

"Lana," he said sharply. When she refused to face him, he took her by the shoulders and turned her to face him. "I had *nothing* to do with that story being leaked to the press." They were on a well-lit, busy city street. She had no difficulty seeing how tense and furious he looked. "You can't *actually* believe I would put you—or myself—in the limelight like that just to increase business. That's ludicrous."

"Is it?"

"You know it is," he seethed.

She knew Jason thought her subsequent silence represented defiance, but in truth she was disoriented by his nearness. His eyes looked like fire and smoke combined as he stared down at her.

His familiar scent filled her nose, making her emotions froth and boil. She suddenly became hyperaware of every point of contact between their bodies: his hands on her arms, his abdomen expanding and contracting against her ribs as he breathed heavily, his hard thighs pressing against her own.

His expression altered subtly, and Lana knew he'd become aware of her in the same way.

"I want you to come with me," he said. "We can talk about it. I won't have you going around thinking I'm responsible for this. It's bad enough that it happened without you jumping to the wrong conclusions."

Lana blinked and looked away from his arresting face. She strained to find the strength to raise her defenses against him. It was harder than she thought it would be, considering how furious she'd been with him just a half hour ago. That knowledge upset her even further. She thought of his expression of incredulity when she'd entered Po's office . . . remembered the naked woman standing between Po and Jason.

Her backbone stiffened.

"It doesn't really matter what I think about it, Jason."

"What the hell is that supposed to mean?"

"It means I'll probably never know the truth, one way or another. I'll never know if you masterminded the whole thing, if you were equal partners with Po, or if you just went along with his plan for the kick of fucking a singer you happened to like. I wondered why you were so insistent while we were on that beach together, so intent on stretching it out. You wanted to offer some good photo opportunities for whoever was hidden in the trees, didn't you? So tell me: when should I look forward to being black-mailed with the rest of those photos?"

"God damn you for saying that, Lana." She was too furious and hurt to be dissuaded by his low, ominous tone, however.

"I'll never know why you did it. I'll never know, because I don't *know* you and I don't *trust* you. So why don't you just save the explanations and denials. I'm not interested."

His nostrils flared. Lana sensed his fury like a heat wave emanating off his body. He stepped closer, pushing her body into his. "So you're back to it, huh?" he said, his anger-roughened voice causing goose bumps to rise on her nape. "Back to being the mercenary bitch who only needs a hard cock, even if it is inconveniently attached to a brain. Sorry some real-life shit put a damper on your little fuck fest, Lana. *Come on*."

She gasped when he abruptly grabbed her elbow and firmly urged her down the sidewalk.

"What's your problem?" she hissed, jerking back on her arm.

"Come on," he growled. "We're about to get a different photo on the late news."

Lana turned to where he nodded down the street. A white van with Channel Eight News printed in blue on the side had pulled over to the curb fifty feet away from them. The occupants must have noticed Jason and Lana standing there on the curb under the bright lights. The passenger door flew open.

Lana responded to the tug on her elbow, jogging down the sidewalk next to Jason. Any course of action seemed preferable to standing there and waiting for reporters and photographers to accost her. They turned down a side street that was much darker than the major thoroughfaire. Before she knew it, she sat in Jason's sedan, fastening her seat belt while he whipped the car in a U-turn in the opposite direction from the reporters.

A minute later she untwisted her torso, satisfied that the white van hadn't followed Jason's rapid, serpentine progress down dark-ened Honolulu streets. He turned left onto a well-lit street that ran next to a wide canal.

"I'm staying at the Hawaiian Park," she said through a throat that had suddenly gone dry.

"You're staying on my houseboat."

"I am *not*."

"Did you register at the hotel under your real name?"

Her mouth fell open in surprise at his unexpected question. "Yes."

He studied her with narrowed eyelids. "Why are you looking at me like that?" she asked irritably.

He transferred his stare to the road. "It just seems a little strange that you would have exposed yourself in that way to a potential leak at the hotel as to your whereabouts when you'd just discovered what had happened. Where did you say you saw the news story . . . and when? I thought you said you were flying out this afternoon?"

"Why should you care?" Lana asked coldly, even as her heart seized for a moment in her chest. She'd tipped her hand in the midst of the confusion following their flight from the reporters.

It just seems a little strange that you would have exposed yourself . . .

She'd exposed herself, all right. Now her mind raced with the new reality she had to face. It was at least a remote possibility the press might discover where she was staying and converge on the hotel to hound her. Her publicist had advised her to keep a low profile at all costs until they better understood the potential threat—not only to her professional life but to her private one.

"It'll be all right for one night. If I decide to stay another night, I'll move hotels." She heaved a sigh of relief when Jason took a right hand turn and merged onto Highway 1.

She assumed he was obeying her request. She should have known better, however. He doubled-parked across the street from the Hawaiian Park and held out his hand.

"Give me your card key."

"Why?" Lana asked.

"I'm going to get your stuff," he said. Lana's back stiffened when she took in his calm, domineering manner. She opened her mouth to protest but he cut her off.

"Hotels have huge staffs, Lana. Taking bribes for guest information is more common than you might think. Maybe Po or a Hawaiian Nights employee wasn't solely responsible for the leak. Maybe one of the employees who saw me going to your hotel room blabbed, did you ever think of that?"

She gave him a condescending look.

"I didn't have a goddamned thing to do with that news leak, Lana. That's the last time I'm going to say it. I don't owe you any more explanations . . . but I *do* owe you."

He must have registered her surprise at his last statement.

He peered through the windshield. "You were with me when this all happened. I don't know specifically who the jackals were that took those pictures or why the hell they wanted to leak a story about us, but I *did* ask Po to let me fill in for one of his escorts from Hawaiian Nights. You were at my home when they took those pictures," he said gruffly after a short pause. "I owe you for the fact that I exposed you. It was unintentional on my part, but that's not an excuse."

Lana's heart thrummed loud in her ears. When she fully became cognizant of her desire to believe him, she closed her eyes.

But she couldn't shut him out. Not completely. She cautiously opened her eyes after several seconds.

"They took those photos while I was at your place. What makes you think your houseboat will be more secure than a hotel?"

He gave her a hard, sidelong look—the one that reminded her of his determined focus on the diving block.

"My family isn't going to like that news story, but they'll be the first to rally around me. Most of them will, anyway. My father is the head of security at the Pearl Harbor Navy Shipyard. After I call him and tell him you're on my boat, my marina will be more secure than the governor's mansion within the hour." When she didn't speak, he added quietly, "The guest bedroom is yours. If you want it."

"No more playing by your rules, huh?" Her sarcasm was a lame attempt to disguise the conflict boiling in her breast and frothing her thoughts. It was true what she'd said before—she *didn't* trust Jason. Or she didn't trust her reaction to him, anyway.

But her desire for him hadn't abated. If anything, her anger, shame, and uncertainty seemed to be fueling it to new heights.

She'd accused him of wanting to break her will with his dominant style of lovemaking, wanting to weaken her . . . expose her. What shamed her most was that it'd worked. She'd returned to Honolulu with stars in her eyes, ready to approach him once again with her need pinned like a flaming red flower on her breast for all to see.

She needed to find her feet again, to locate steady ground. She needed to take back the control he'd wrested from her. And there was only one way she was going to succeed in doing that.

Jason Koa was going to play by her rules before she left this damn island for good.

She reached into her purse and withdrew the card key.

"Room 2211," she said, refusing to acknowledge the look of wary surprise on Jason's face at her sudden, calm acquiescence.

eighteen

JASON didn't say anything when she came out of the guest bathroom on his houseboat wearing a pair of jean shorts and a T-shirt. She hadn't bought any nightgowns on her little shopping foray that afternoon, having reasoned that she wouldn't need pajamas.

She still wouldn't, even in this drastically different scenario from the one she'd pictured in her infantile, short-lived fantasy regarding Jason and her.

She'd heard him talking on the phone in the distance while she'd cleaned up in the bathroom, but he was finished by the time she opened the door and stepped into the hallway. She assumed he was talking to one of the five men that had greeted them when they pulled into the marina parking lot.

The spokesman's name had been Ash, a short, stocky man who had a face that looked like it was perpetually sunburned and a torso thick with muscle. Jason and he had exchanged warm handshakes. Ash had briskly outlined their plan for guarding the marina around the clock until Jason's father, Joseph, called a halt to it. He'd waved off Jason's profuse thanks, saying it was a small price to pay for the many favors Joseph and the Koa family had done him over the years. Lana had tried not to be impressed by the show of loyalty and respect afforded Jason, his father, and the Koas in general. She admitted that it would be strange for Jason to go to such lengths to protect them on the houseboat if he was the one responsible for them needing the security.

But like she'd told him earlier, who really knew the truth about that news leak and those photographs? Jason insisted upon his innocence. He'd probably go to some lengths to validate his claims.

As they'd headed toward the skiff earlier, Lana had seen a small shadow walking toward them with a spry gait. She'd thought Jason hadn't noticed, but he spoke as he untied the boat, his back to the shadow.

"How's she taking it?"

"How do you think? She's ready to shred metal with her bare teeth," Harold said dryly.

Jason's head came around sharply. "Is Grandma pissed at me?"

"No, of course not." Lana saw Harold nod in her direction. "Hello, Ms. Rodriguez. Nice to see you again."

"Hi, Harold," Lana replied.

"Harold?" Jason asked with a trace of exasperation.

"It's not your grandma who's mad at you. She's just dead set on finding out who took that picture and is calling her favorite grandson a male prostitute. She told me to have you call if I saw you before she did."

"Yeah, okay." Jason stood slowly from his crouched position. "What did you mean when you said, 'It's not your grandma who's mad at you'?"

Even in the darkness, Lana sensed Harold's uneasiness when he shrugged. "Some of your great-aunts and great-uncles . . . some cousins, too, aren't too happy with you."

"For besmirching the Koa family name?"

"Don't worry about it. It'll pass. They'll stand behind you once some of the shock passes, and you know that."

Lana had thought about that brief, charged exchange between Harold and Jason while she showered. She'd reflected long and hard on that mixture of regret and amusement in Jason's voice when he'd asked if members of his clan had thought he was besmirching the Koa name. What was it like for a man who had done nothing but heap honors upon his old, established family to suddenly be considered a source of scandal?

If he really was worried about casting his family into disrepute, why had there been that hint of dark amusement in his tone?

Lana's time alone to think and a hot shower helped her to shore up her defenses. By the time she opened the bathroom door, she felt sure she could handle this bizarre, sticky situation with Jason Koa.

Jason stood at the end of the kitchen island with his cell phone in his hand. His head swung around at the sound of the bathroom door opening. He stalked down the hallway, his gaze flickering down her body in a quick, warm assessment.

He flipped on the lights in the guest bedroom, and she followed him to the doorway. He moved aside as she stepped into the room.

"Nobody's slept in here for a while, so I changed the sheets while you were taking a shower."

"Guess you have little need for a guest bedroom given the kind of visitors you usually entertain here," she said as she walked over to the shopping bags she'd placed on a low chest when they'd arrived. The back of her exposed neck prickled when he didn't say anything. She placed the folded clothing she'd been wearing into one of the bags and turned around. He looked even taller and more imposing than he usually did in the small guest room. She'd expected the storm brewing in his dark gray eyes, but she didn't know what to make of the gleam of speculation.

"I would have been a hell of a lot more pissed off if you'd said that yesterday." The way he leaned back casually against the frame of the door alarmed her for some reason. "But I'm getting used to your particular brand of defensiveness. It's not really that different from a porcupine's, is it?"

Her mouth twisted in anger. "I don't know what you're talking about. I didn't think it was a secret that you entertained out here regularly. Surely all those sex toys, the hot tub, this Hugh Hefner–style, floating pleasure palace aren't meant to be enjoyed by the type of people who take the *guest* bedroom."

He crossed his arms under his chest and rolled his eyes. "Watch it, Lana, you're getting flustered. That Hugh Hefner thing was really lame."

"Was it?" she asked, her fury suddenly erupting into a flash fire. "You're right. Given what I saw when I walked into your cousin's office, Hefner comes off as damn classy in comparison to you."

He straightened from the wall and stepped toward her. "I'd just walked into that office sixty seconds before you did. I don't have any control over Po or the way he treats women."

Lana wouldn't have been surprised to hear the popping sound of electricity, the air had gone so charged between them. Not just from anger, either. Her breasts felt unusually large and conspicuous pressed against the T-shirt. A heavy, hot sensation settled in her lower belly and spread down over her pussy. The cotton shirt abraded her nipples. She noticed Jason's glance flicker down to her chest. The tips of her breasts pinched tight. He swallowed and heaved a sigh of frustration.

"Why don't you go to bed? Maybe after a good night's sleep you'll be a bit more reasonable. One can only hope, anyway," he added under his breath in obvious irritation before he turned to leave the room. He paused in the process of closing her door.

"Oh, and Lana . . . I don't think you have any reason to worry about Melanie."

"What do you know about it?" she snapped.

He looked like he wanted to snarl right back at her, but instead he took a deep breath, calming himself. "From what you told me, I know you're concerned about her going through a tough divorce. You probably are worried about what Melanie's husband would do with the information if he discovered she utilized an escort service while she was here in Hawaii. But I don't think whoever took those photos and plastered them on the news is concerned about Melanie one way or another. She's not their target."

"And I am?"

"Maybe. The next couple days ought to tell. I haven't quite figured out who's going to benefit from the whole mess. But I will, Lana."

Despite the fact that her heart began to thud erratically behind her breastbone, she gave him a bland look, informing him without words that a likely candidate for benefitting from this ugly affair stood right in front of her. She'd bet her entire savings account Jace's had been packed this evening.

She thought he might have read her mind when he shut the door with a brisk bang.

TWO hours later, Lana was still awake. She was more than just awake, she was wired . . . so tense that her muscles ached. The houseboat was silent except for the occasional light tinkling of the wind chimes.

She arose and felt her way toward the bureau. She groped for the items she'd placed there before getting into bed and crossed the room. Moonlight flooded into the darkened living room, casting enough pale luminescence for her to see that Jason's bedroom door was partially opened. The hinges squeaked softly when she pushed open the door farther and glided silently into the room.

She regarded him warily for several seconds when she switched on his bedside lamp to a dim setting, but he remained unmoving. She glanced down over his sleeping form, her gaze lingering on the sight of his naked body partially draped in a sheet. He slept on his back with one arm sprawled over his head and the other spread wide on the bed. His head was turned away from her, his cheek pressed to the pillow. The white sheet rode low on his hips, looking starkly white next to his sun-bronzed skin. She could see the outline of his balls through the sheet as well as the shape of his flaccid cock where it lay against his left thigh.

Her pussy tingled with warmth and anticipation. Yes, this was precisely what she wanted. What she needed. Jason—naked, vulnerable . . . completely at her mercy. After she'd made him beg, after she'd denied him, *then* maybe she'd be able to consider this whole fiasco without squirming in shame.

She wanted this supremely confident, bold man with the earth-shattering smile, this man who'd breached her defenses only to betray her so carelessly, to feel at least *some* measure of her helplessness and humiliation.

Despite the fact that she was convinced she was there for the express purpose of exacting revenge, her juices were running hot and her breathing was coming fast by the time she'd restrained one of his wrists to the headboard. She admitted grudgingly it wasn't even a remote possibility for a straight woman to see Jason Koa naked, sleep rumpled, and exuding sexuality even in an unconscious state, and not get excited.

When she reached for his other arm, his hand came up as quick as a snake at the strike. He grabbed her. Lana gave a muffled scream and stared at his face.

He looked calm enough, but his dark eyes lasered straight through her.

"Mind telling me what the hell you think you're doing?" he asked as he tugged once on his restrained wrist. She'd used a silk scarf to tie him to a wooden post on the headboard. His jaw hardened. "What were you planning on *doing*? Tying me down so you could hurt me?"

"*Hurt* you? Of course not. I've never harmed a soul in my life!"

She felt increasingly foolish under his stare. Damn it, why couldn't she have gotten this right? Didn't he deserve a little payback for what he'd done? She tried to pull back, but he tightened his grip on her wrist. She saw the second when realization dawned on his face.

"Were you going to tie me up so you could have your way with me?"

She felt her cheeks heat at being caught red-handed in the act. Anger mingled with her embarrassment. *Damn.* Why couldn't fate have allowed her this one opportunity to regain some control?

"Lana?" he demanded more loudly.

"What's the matter? You can dish it out, but you can't take it, is that it?"

"Take *what*, exactly? Do you really think I tied you up before because I wanted to *punish* you? Because that's what you want to do now, right? You want to pay me back? You want to make someone suffer for our picture being plastered all over the public's TV screens?" His voice level dropped in volume, and he leaned up off the pillow. Lana moved back warily when she realized she was just inches from his face. The amber flecks in his eyes seemed to smolder.

"You want to make me *pay* for what you've been feeling, Lana?" he growled softly.

She thought her pulse would leap right out of her throat. Once again, she tried to pull free of him. Once again, he halted her.

"Go ahead."

"What?" she asked, sure she'd misunderstood him.

"You heard me. Go ahead. Take your best shot, Lana."

nineteen

HE saw her hazel eyes widen in disbelief. She was close enough for him to catch her scent—the fresh, floral fragrance of the soap he'd collected for her earlier from the hotel room mixing with something indefinably delicious from her skin. His nostrils flared to capture the elusive scent more fully.

Onaona. Desire sliced through him, stirring and thickening his cock. Damn her, she always had an immediate, unprecedented effect on his body.

Even though he experienced a nearly overwhelming desire to turn her over his knee for her blatant stubbornness, he felt compassion for her as well. If Lana believed so firmly that she'd lost control of the situation, it was no sweat off his back if she wanted to regain a measure of it by using his body.

Yeah, it was really big of him to allow Lana Rodriguez to tie him up and have her way with him, he thought with grim amusement. He'd be lying if he said he hadn't been thinking of how to get her back in his bed ever since he realized she was still in Honolulu. Well, she was in his bed, all right. And if it wasn't under the circumstances he'd prefer, it was a damn sight better than nothing.

"Why are you doing this?" she asked suspiciously when he let go of her wrist.

"It's not a trick," he replied gruffly. "If you need me to play by your rules until you get your bearings again, I'm willing."

"Just like that?" she scoffed.

He shrugged, letting her draw her own conclusions. A blazing expression suddenly overcame her face when he didn't move. He just watched her, saying nothing while she tied his other wrist to the bedpost. She propped another pillow behind his head, her actions gentle if brisk and businesslike. She avoided his gaze when she slid off the bed and opened his bedside table drawer.

"What are you looking for?" he asked politely. "If it's not in that drawer, try the one below."

She threw him a dirty look before she slid open the bottom drawer. He wasn't overly surprised when she withdrew the ankle restraints he'd used on her previously. She wasn't in the mood for having him only *partially* at her mercy. Nope, half measures wouldn't do, Jason realized as he studied her set, determined expression as she whipped back the bed sheet, widened the straps and fastened them to his ankles. Jason scowled when she pulled him spread-eagled—not that Lana ever noticed, as focused as she was.

When he was fully restrained, she stood next to the bed and stared down at him. Her cold, assessing gaze might have made some guys wilt, but it sent a bolt of hot arousal through Jason.

His cock hardened to full readiness. Even knowing that Lana would be in charge of *what* he was ready for, and *when* he was ready for it, couldn't dampen his desire.

"If you really want to torture me, you should take off your clothes," he informed her gruffly. "It'll kill me not to be able to touch you."

She smirked at him and sat on the edge of the bed.

"How do you know this isn't all I want to do?"

"What . . . you mean just leave me tied up like this?"

She nodded matter-of-factly. "I could get my stuff and take the skiff to shore."

His eyes narrowed suspiciously. "Is that why you were so agreeable to coming with me to the houseboat all of a sudden?"

She smiled at him. He entertained a vivid fantasy about wrapping his hands around her elegant neck and squeezing.

"Ash and the other guys will stop you once you get to shore."

"What if they do? I doubt you or your father gave them instructions to keep me prisoner here."

He raised his eyebrows. "You've said you don't trust me. How do you know I didn't do precisely that?"

Her smug smile faded. "You wouldn't."

He gave her a bland look.

She seemed to reach a conclusion and stood. "You're bluffing." Her imperious gaze swept down his naked, bound body. "But either way, I do, in fact, have other plans for you."

"What are you going to do? Cover my body in honey, turn loose an army of killer ants on me, sit back, smoke a cig, and enjoy the show?"

He was pleasantly surprised when she laughed with what appeared to be genuine mirth. Despite his rising concern about her intentions, he had to admit that being in control seemed to be relaxing her a little. She'd been strung as tight as piano wire ever since she'd walked into Po's office tonight.

"Creative, I'll give you that," she mused. His gaze lingered on her lovely, curving mouth. That the thought of him being turned to a bloody pulp by killer ants brought such a wistful smile to her lips should have him seriously worried, but instead, he was consumed by the memory of ravaging her plump lower lip, sipping on her sweetness, plunging his tongue into her mouth again and again . . .

Her expression became suspicious. "What are you thinking of?"

"Oral domination."

"If any of that occurs, I'll be in charge of it."

"Fine by me," he assured, still staring at her mouth.

She straightened and cleared her throat. "Speaking of which, that gives me an idea. Remember when you said you listened to my music?"

"Yeah."

"Where do you keep the CDs?"

He told her and gave her brief instructions on operating his stereo, which had speakers throughout the boat, including his bedroom. He looked at her with curiosity when she lingered by the bed after he'd finished his explanation.

"What?" he asked, confused by her manner.

"Is there any particular arrangement that you find . . . more . . . romantic than the others?"

He gave a slow smile. "Do you mean, is there one I like to play during sex? Or wait . . . Are you asking if there's one that makes my hand look like the most tempting piece of flesh ever?"

Her irritated glance amused him. She clearly hadn't expected him to be so comfortable talking about his autoerotic moments.

" 'Escape,' " he said simply. She seemed surprised.

"Really?"

He nodded once, holding her gaze. "Your voice going husky when you sing that double entendre about him going 'down' the easy path equates to an instant erection."

Her sarcastic look told him loud and clear his response was predictable and juvenile, but Jason refused to be cowed by her prickly superiority.

"I've flattered a few dates that way, but I was too much of a gentleman to tell them they weren't responsible." He said that to goad her. The truth was, Jason didn't bring that many women onto his houseboat, despite Lana's suspicions. This was his private sanctuary, and he didn't commonly breach it by bringing casual flings here.

He glanced down her body, admiring the way her jean shorts outlined her sex. Her eyes had a glassy appearance when he looked back at her face. "Now that I know you, the theme of the song doesn't surprise me too much. Who was the other poor sucker who got to you, Lana? Is it a rarity for you to feel the need to escape when a guy gets too close, or is it a common occurrence? Is it really just me you're tying up, or am I representing the entire male population here?"

Her expression hardened. "You may think I'm jaded, but even *I* don't believe most guys would be low enough to pay someone to take pictures while I was having sex with them." One sleek brown eyebrow quirked in a challenge. "It seems you've done the impossible, Jason. You've lowered what was already an abysmally low bar."

She gave him a disgusted look when he refused to defend himself and swept out of the room.

A moment later he heard the familiar opening notes of the talented blues guitarist in her band. His eyebrows rose in prurient interest when Lana returned to the bedroom a minute later wearing an ivory satin robe. Her long, tanned legs looked well muscled and silky smooth in the dim light. The way the soft fabric clung to her slender, curvy body, and the fluid manner in which she moved was a seduction in and of itself. He could tell by the tempting, slight sway of her breasts and her nipples pressing against the fabric that she was naked beneath the robe. His cock twitched next to his thigh.

Maybe playing by Lana's rules wouldn't be such a sacrifice, after all.

He watched in rising anticipation and puzzlement when she once again opened the top bedside drawer. She must have known what she was looking for this time, because she decisively grabbed three items. Jason's eyes widened when he saw what she withdrew— a new bottle of lubricant, massage oil, and the vibrator he'd used on her just the other day.

She tossed the items between his spread legs and smiled down at him from her superior height.

"Do you like to watch a woman touch herself?"

His mouth hung open for a second at the unexpected question uttered in her patentable, husky voice.

"I *live* to watch a woman touch herself."

She laughed softly at his wholehearted response, her amusement once again seeming entirely genuine. Jason shared her smile as she fluffed his pillows, propping him up farther in the bed. Leaning over him as she was, he got an eyeful of soft, satin-covered breasts and a noseful of her floral scent. She touched his upper arm.

"Are they comfortable?" she asked, referring to his restrained arms which had drawn more taut when she raised his head and shoulders on the bed.

"Yeah," he replied shortly. Her light touch on his arm had caused desire to stab through his flesh.

She grabbed a spare pillow, went to the foot of the bed, and tossed it against the railing. He watched with rising excitement as she crawled over his restrained leg. She leaned against the footboard and tucked her robe beneath her thighs, the modest gesture striking him as humorous given the fact that he was tied up naked to the bed and a purple vibrator rested near her thigh.

It also struck him as sexy as hell.

"I'd like to amend my earlier statement."

"What do you mean?" she asked curiously as she reached for the scented oil. Hearing her voice at the same moment that she sung to him in the background in that familiar, smoky way of hers seemed a little surreal.

"I said I lived to watch a woman touch herself, but I just might die watching you do it."

She paused in her actions and studied him soberly. "You may have been born with that charm, but you've really polished it to a shine with constant practice, haven't you?"

Irritation flashed through him. Her verbal stab had hurt for several reasons—the first being that it struck a little too close to home for comfort. He *did* use his glib tongue as a tool of seduction. But the reason her insult had really hurt was *this* particular compliment had been the gods' honest truth.

Just like him to decide to be genuine with a woman who thought he was a fake at best and a criminal at worst.

She ignored his pique. In fact, she seemed to shut him out completely as she went about her business. He forgot his ire quick enough as well when she loosened her robe—still not releasing the belt entirely from her waist—and shrugged out of the sleeves. The sight of the elegant slope of her shoulders, lithesome arms, and pale, shapely breasts made him go entirely still. The realization that he was poised like a predator before it struck at prey and that he was going absolutely nowhere hit him like a stinging slap of harsh reality.

She really *was* out to torture him.

The truth was, although watching a woman touch herself was a fantasy most guys would share, he hadn't been treated to the experience as much as he would have liked. He didn't typically see a woman long enough for her to feel comfortable enough to masturbate in front of him. On the occasions where it'd happened, it'd been at his request while he was in a position to either watch or join in the process at his leisure.

What Lana was going to force him to endure was a vastly different experience.

His nostrils flared as he watched her pour some of the scented oil into her palm. She rubbed her hands together slowly, sensually spreading the oil and warming it. She opened both hands on her ribs just above her waist and moved them in sensual circular movements, smearing the oil on her smooth, golden brown skin.

Jason's head left the pillow as he strained upward so as to not miss a thing.

His cock lurched off his thigh, but Lana could have cared less.

She closed her eyes and her head fell back slightly as she slid her fingers along the underside of her breasts. He could perfectly imagine how petal soft the skin was beneath her touch. She cupped her breasts from below, her hands stroking the firm flesh all the while in small, kneading movements, slipping and sliding, molding and stroking. She held herself as though making an offering of her succulent flesh, but her closed eyelids and the flush that rose on her cheeks assured an annoyed, increasingly aroused Jason that she was wholly involved with herself.

She moved in a manner that was a hundredfold more seductive than the subtle, sensual movements that island women made with their hands while doing the hula. Her pink nipples deepened in color, drawing into tight, distended points above her massaging hands. Jason strained against the scarves, feeling a primal urge to suckle on the crests and run his tongue over the beaded flesh. He restrained a groan when she used her forefingers to trace the outline of the lower areolas of each thrusting nipple.

All the while, her low, husky voice sang to him, seduced him, and his pulse beat a primitive tattoo in his cock.

And she hadn't even removed her robe all the way.

He opened his mouth to order her to touch her erect nipples, but he caught himself just in time. He wasn't in a position to command, and as pissed as Lana was, she'd be sure to do the opposite of whatever he asked. So he just watched, helpless and dry mouthed, as she circled her forefingers around the rosy, thrusting tips, teasing him mercilessly.

If she ever gave him the opportunity, he was going to turn her over his knee for this and make that round, pale ass a pretty shade of pink.

Her eyelids opened narrowly when she heard his rough moan. He wasn't helping things by having vivid fantasies about turning the tables on her.

"What do you want?" she asked.

To have your beautiful ass under my palm, Jason thought automatically. *If I can't have that, I'd like you to slide one of those pink nipples between my lips.* But since he was doubtful he'd get either of those things, he answered, "Touch your nipples." His cock swelled uncomfortably when she did, watching him with a glassy-eyed stare all the while. "Pinch them a little . . . do what feels good," he said, his gaze pinned to her forefingers stroking the distended crests.

"It would feel good to have your fingers on me. The tips of your thumb and forefinger on your right hand are calloused. It feels so good when you touch me." Jason just gawked at her, surprised and aroused by her admission. She pinched her nipples lightly. "It would feel good to have you suck on them."

His gaze darted up to her face hopefully.

"Too bad it's not going to happen."

"Lana," he hissed in warning. He heard the wooden rods on the headboard creak in protest and forced his flexing muscles to relax.

She just smiled and lowered one hand to the belt of her robe. She released the sash with a flicking motion, and the soft satin pooled around her hips. Jason pulled against the scarves in order to better see her pussy when she spread her slender thighs.

He muttered a curse. If a man was being denied paradise, wasn't it better not to see its promise?

But his eyes remained fixed on the delicate folds of her pink flower. His nostrils flared as if to capture a hint of the juices that coated her plump labia. She bent her knees and spread her thighs wider, letting him see her glistening slit.

"Christ, Lana," he muttered thickly. His cock throbbed so acutely he hurt. Pain as well as arousal pounded in his flesh. Jason knew his body like most people might know the idiosyncrasies of a well-used tool or a piece of mechanical equipment. His muscles would be sore tomorrow from being tightly flexed without remittance. He kept himself right at the edge of restraint, preventing himself from breaking the wooden posts of the headboard.

He stopped himself, but only just.

The plastic cap opened with a click. Jason watched narrowly as she poured more massage oil into her palms.

She opened her hands on the back of her smooth thighs and began to rub in slow, hypnotic circles. After a spellbound moment, Jason realized it wasn't just his wishful thinking; her fingers really were inching closer and closer to her juicy cunt.

"Touch yourself," he whispered gruffly. "I know as well as you do how much you want to."

"I'm willing to suffer."

"As long as I am even more so. Isn't that right, honey?"

"Are you?" she asked as her fingers massaged her thigh just inches away from her slit. As she kneaded the firm flesh, she opened and closed her tiny, damp hole. "Suffering, I mean?"

Jason wondered if she could feel the burn of his unwavering stare on her pussy. "All I can think about is burying myself to the balls in you, but you've tied me to this bed, Lana. You better fucking *believe* I'm suffering."

She paused in her provocative massage and made a choked sound in her throat. His gaze flew to her face.

"Isn't that what you wanted to hear?" he queried.

"Yes."

"I think you want something even more than to see me suffer."

"What?" she whispered, looking spellbound.

"I think you want to hear two words: *don't run*." When she wrinkled her perspiration damp brow in puzzlement, he continued, "Don't give in to the urge to escape, Lana. I wouldn't do anything willingly to harm you. Take a chance. Believe me."

For several full seconds, Jason thought he'd finally gotten through to her. But then her expression hardened and she picked up the vibrator.

"You forget what I said earlier. I'll likely never know the truth about what happened with that news leak *or* about you." She depressed a button and the nubbins below the tip of the vibrator began to spin. She widened her thighs and held open her slit with one hand.

He muttered a burning curse when she went straight for the kill and sunk the vibrator into her pussy as far as it could go. A clear stream of pre-cum leaked onto his thigh at the sight of her splayed legs and the purple phallus embedded in her pussy. Frustration and arousal vibrated in every cell of his being.

She closed her eyes and manipulated the vibrator to bring her pleasure again and again. Time stretched into an agonizing eternity as she forced him to watch helplessly while she shuddered in orgasm not just once but three times.

He vowed then and there that not only was he going to convince Lana Rodriguez to trust him, he was going to get rid of every damn sex toy on the houseboat. His cock was going to fill her. *He* was going to be the one to make her firm flesh shudder in orgasm—not a piece of fucking mechanized plastic.

He was too furious with her and too damn horny to even speak when she finally switched off the fluttering wings of the clitoral stimulator and slid the vibrator out of her pussy. He felt sweat break out on his forehead when he saw how shiny the surface had been made with her juices. She'd anointed the vibrator again and again when it should have been *him* gifted with her honey. His cock felt so tight he thought he'd burst right through the surface of his skin.

She blinked several times, as though she were awakening from a dream. When her gaze landed on his leaden, swollen cock, her lips fell open. His penis lurched in excitement at even this small acknowledgment of his existence.

Pitiful, Jason thought in self-disgust.

"Welcome back. Remember me? The guy you're torturing?"

"I didn't forget you."

Jason's heart hammered louder in his ears when he heard the soft quality of her voice. Maybe a few climaxes had brought down her defenses? He watched her with wary excitement when she stood next to the bed, completely naked. A light sheen of sweat covered her golden skin. Her nipples were still distended from her multiple climaxes. She nodded at his blood-swollen, streaming penis.

"Does it hurt?"

He gave a sharp bark of laughter. "What do you think?"

Without answering him, she opened his bedside-table drawer, and Jason once again mentally vowed to get rid of everything in it. He went entirely still when she held up a black rubber butt plug and waved it in the air.

"I think I'd like you to take it in the ass, just like you made me take it the other night," she said quietly.

Jason shook his head, not at all pleased by the turn of events. "I don't take it in the ass."

But she just calmly reached for the lubricant and flipped open the cap. "You haven't before, you mean. But you will now."

For the first time, Jason flexed his muscles with the conscious intent of breaking the posts on the headboard. God knew he wanted Lana . . . more than just her body. He wanted her to trust him.

But did her stubbornness know no limits?

She knelt next to him on the bed and lowered the plug between his open thighs. He gritted his teeth, preparing to break the wooden posts and free himself once and for all.

But then she touched him on the buttocks, spreading him. The sensation of her gentle fingers made the air catch in his lungs. He went rigid, groaning roughly when she pushed the fat tip of the plug into his rectum.

"God *damn* you, Lana," he hissed. "You go too far."

"No," she whispered. He sweated profusely as he watched her lay down on her side, her head near his throbbing erection. Her exotically tilted eyes held some message that he couldn't decipher as she stared up at him. "I needed to make you a little uncomfortable, because I'm going to suck on your cock now."

Jason clamped his eyes shut and twisted his head on the pillow. Just hearing her say the words had made blood surge hot in his cock. Even though his ankles were spread and restrained, it felt as if the intrusive plug was what pried him open, keeping him vulnerable to this woman.

He once again flexed his arms, preparing to rip at the fabric, break the wooden poles on the headboard, or both. There was only so much she could ask of him . . . so much he was capable of giving.

But then her tongue swirled delicately around the head of his cock, lingering at the slit to lick up his pre-cum. When she got a taste of him, she trailed down the turgid, pulsing shaft, seeking more. He muttered a blistering curse and panted like a madman, but he remained in place, anxiously awaiting her next move, tottering on the knife's edge of agony and bliss.

She spread her lips and slid them down to the ridge beneath his cockhead. She looked up at him with desire-glazed eyes and began to draw on him like his cock was the tip of a straw, hollowing out her cheeks.

"You want me to beg?" he rasped. "All right. You have your wish, *Onaona*. I'm at your mercy. *Please*."

She responded by applying pressure on the base of the butt plug and slipping the tight clamp of her lips farther down his length. Jason gritted his teeth hard to prevent from shouting. The plug created an internal pressure on the root of his penis and prostate. It felt uncomfortable and incredibly good at once. She was right. He required the slight discomfort of the plug, or he would have come at the first touch of her sleek tongue.

Forget about her ruthless, hot suck.

Her mouth was wet bliss. He was so horny that when he eventually did explode, he'd likely incinerate a few body parts in the process. He sensed her studying him even though his eyes remained clamped closed. Sweat poured off his forehead and abdomen. It felt like his muscles would split in two from the combined friction of his primitive, naked urge to break free—to take her in the way his body and nature required—and his brain's command to restrain himself.

To leash himself for Lana's sake.

But if he didn't come soon, he was going to say hello to insanity.

He opened his eyes into narrow slits and caught her eye.

"Help me, Lana."

twenty

LANA was so hungry for him, it was all she could do not to choke herself on her monumental need. She'd read before that cock was an acquired taste. She'd long ago become a connoisseur, but Jason's cock existed in a class all by itself.

Or maybe it wasn't just his cock, she admitted as she cautiously slid his near-to-bursting flesh deeper and suckled greedily. It was the experience of seeing his handsome face tight with wild, desperate need. She'd seen it several times during their lovemaking. Sought it.

Loved it.

It wasn't until now, when she planned to walk away and leave him high and hard, that she realized it wasn't just his rigid desire for which she searched.

It was his expression of anguished pleasure when he came. It was the look of sublime satisfaction when his muscles went limp and he pulled her into his arms, kissing her with supreme passion and the promise of next time.

She ducked her head and took his cock deep, her hunger for him helping her to muffle both the power of her gag reflex and thoughts of revenge. She hummed into his flesh, hardly noticing that she did the same in the background, the notes vibrating and lingering in the throat of her recorded voice.

Her eyes blinked open sluggishly when she heard his rough groan. She felt him swell in her mouth.

The reality of the moment struck her with the final, shivering note of her drummer Jimmy's brush on the cymbals. She drew her mouth off him. His heavy cock fell to his taut abdomen with a *whap* of damp flesh against flesh.

He opened his eyes sluggishly. They widened when he saw her standing next to the side of the bed, looking down at him. She saw the moment when he realized what was happening.

Neither of them spoke as she reached for her robe and slipped it over her shoulders, but she felt the weight of his stare on her. She told herself not to meet his eyes, just to turn and walk . . . to finish the self-preserving task that she'd come into his bedroom tonight to accomplish.

But she found herself meeting his gaze, anyway.

"What are you doing?" he asked warily.

She knotted the belt of her robe with a brisk, businesslike gesture, praying he didn't notice her shaking hands. "Isn't it obvious?"

She should have been happy to see the rising anger and disbelief in his eyes, the pain of sexual torment, but she wasn't. She briefly looked down over his body. He was magnificent. She'd had the temerity to tie up a wild animal: a sleek, sinewy panther . . . a fierce lion. She noticed his powerful, flexing arm, chest, and shoulder muscles.

Her gaze darted to his. Frustration fired his eyes. Not the frustration of sexual depravation. Fury at *her*. At her stubbornness.

A loud cracking noise caused her to start. Her eyes widened when she saw his bulging muscles. She heard another popping noise. He snarled and jerked, and his wrists broke free of the splintered posts. For a panicked second or two, she just stood there, too stunned to move.

A quick glance at Jason's wild eyes, however, and she was galvanized into action. She flew out of his bedroom and down the hallway with no idea of where she was going. She only thought of escape from the feral, male beast who lunged after her.

A beast that she had created.

For some reason, she raced toward the patio doors instead of in the direction of the front door and the boat. Maybe some primitive part of her brain associated the lagoon with serenity and protection. In truth, she couldn't think of that cerulean body of water and not think of Jason as well . . . which made no sense at all, since it was Jason she ran from. She didn't really know why she ran from him, either . . . why her blood pounded madly in her veins. She wasn't afraid he would harm her. Not really.

Still, a savage voice screamed in her brain, demanding escape. And she knew it was now or never.

No time for logic. Lana ran like a frightened rabbit from a wolf. She succeeded in flinging open the patio door, but two hands settled on her waist and yanked her back inside the houseboat.

"Let go of me," she shouted, but he ignored her, lifting her into his arms effortlessly. She shoved against his chest. He responded by pushing her flush against him, breast to breast, and grabbing one of her flailing arms. Her robe parted as she struggled, causing her naked breasts to press tightly to his hard chest. The arousal that shot through her pitched her emotional state even higher. She landed a blow against the side of his head. He cursed and picked up his pace. They seemingly flew down the dim hallway.

"I'm skating on very thin ice here," he growled angrily. "If you hit me like that again, I'm going to blister your ass when I'm done fucking you."

"I didn't say you could fuck me!" she shouted petulantly against his chest. Tears flowed fast down her face. She knew she sounded like a child, but she couldn't regain her control in the midst of her potent panic. He swung her around in his arms. She cried out when he tossed her onto the bed, facedown. She scrambled to rise on her hands and knees, but Jason came down after her, covering her. He shifted his hips, sliding his engorged cock beneath her robe and up the crevice of her squirming ass. He ground against her, and Lana answered, pressing against him desperately, loving the stark evidence of his monumental need. He leaned down and spoke, his hot breath striking her ear.

"You think I'm going to ask your permission after what you just pulled?"

Lana tried to shift her weight out from beneath him, but he grabbed her wrists and pinned them to the mattress above her head. He flexed his hips again, burrowing the thick cockhead between her ass cheeks.

She couldn't move with his superior weight pressing down on her . . . his hands pinning her to the bed. She was caught.

And what a delicious trap.

"Lana?" he prompted, and she pulled her attention from the exquisite sensation of his hard cock throbbing against her asshole.

"Yes. I *do* think it," she exclaimed.

"You're right to think it." He pistoned the long pillar of his cock between her ass cheeks. "So *give* it to me."

Tears blurred all the objects in her vision.

"Ask for it, Lana," he prompted again, this time in a quieter but no less demanding tone.

"Fuck me," she whispered. *"Please."*

He grabbed his cock and arrowed it into her pussy. Lana was drenched, but he was enormous with need. He grunted in rising frustration when her body's resistance halted his bold possession. He reached down and palmed one of her ass cheeks, spreading her farther.

Lana's face clenched tight when he slid into her to the balls. For a few seconds he stayed put, his cock throbbing inside her pussy, stretching her . . . demanding she make room for him. He overfilled her, pushing at the limits of what she could take. But she *did* accommodate him.

And she wanted more. Needed it.

She wiggled her hips, wild for the friction his cock created deep inside her, not to mention the indirect friction he created on her sizzling clit. He grunted at her primitive urging and released one of her wrists to pop her bottom with his palm.

"Stop it. Do you want me to explode inside of you right this second?" he asked between pants for air.

No, she thought.

Yes.

She shifted her hips despite the restraining hold he put on her hip and ass. Now that she was here, pinned to the mattress by

Jason's big cock, the only thing she wanted, the only thing she could think of, was a hot, furious release roaring through her flesh.

He cursed and spanked her again before he held her down with both hands and gave her what she wanted.

Lana opened her mouth and keened as he fucked her like he thought the end of the world loomed at the corner of his vision. She'd teased and tormented him, and now she'd have to pay. He slammed into her ruthlessly; his cock driving into her body, making her ache when he withdrew. The headboard rattled against the wall and the mattress squeaked in protest, but still he pounded into her, firing their flesh into an inferno.

He continued to ride her . . . to master her, while he grabbed a handful of hair, turning her head so he could see her profile. Lana was so wrapped up in the delicious sensations jolting through her body that she forgot to care that he witnessed her tears.

"Do you like that? Do you like that cock?" he rasped as he smacked their flesh together.

"Yes. *God*, yes."

"You're going to have to accept me along with it, Lana." He pushed with his hips, altering the angle of his stabbing cock. He plunged into her, and Lana screamed, orgasm rearing over her. He jerked her head slightly, garnering her attention. "Say you'll do it."

"*Yes*," she cried. Her fingernails dug into the sheets. She held on for dear life as a monster orgasm shook her. She was only vaguely aware of Jason's grunt of discomfort, and then the awful void when he jerked his cock out of her. His roar as he climaxed did penetrate her pleasure, however, as did the sensation of his warm cum spurting onto her ass.

They both gasped wildly for air, as if they'd just completed the final stretch of a grueling marathon. Which they had, in a way, Lana thought wryly as she panted raggedly.

She didn't resist him when he came down beside her and rolled her body into his arms. He stretched, reaching for the bedside table. Lana collapsed onto his perspiration damp chest and lay immobile while he used tissues to wipe his semen from her skin. She was too exhausted—both mentally and physically—to resist Jason Koa for now. It was like trying to resist a charging freight train when you lay directly in its path.

Neither of them spoke as they strained to regain their equilibrium. The harsh soughing of their breath eventually smoothed, the shared rhythm and rate joining them like an invisible thread.

twenty-one

JASON existed in a cocoon of warmth and sublime comfort. He sensed Lana sinking into an exhausted sleep with him. He noticed the moment she started and stiffened in his arms. Some part of him must have been expecting it, because he spoke without thinking.

"Don't even think about moving, Lana. You're staying right there. Whether you sleep or not is up to you."

He felt her sag against him. Soon her breathing became soft and even, and he knew he'd been right to take away the choice from her. She might not be used to sleeping in a man's arms, but she was going to *learn* to get comfortable with it if he had a say in the matter.

Which, of course, was still up in the air, he thought wryly before he fell asleep.

He awoke several hours later, wondering what could have dragged him from the depths of profound slumber. The warm, soft body pressed tightly to his naked skin felt good. He raised his hand and stroked a smooth thigh, then he palmed a round ass cheek. His cock twitched. He inhaled the increasingly familiar scent—*Onaona*—and began to sink into a delicious, nonsensical dream involving Lana naked and singing "Somewhere Over the Rainbow" and gifting him with one of her rare, sublime smiles.

A cell phone rang again in the distance, pulling him from his increasingly lustful dream. It wasn't his ringtone, so it must be Lana's. The phone stopped ringing after a moment . . . only to start up again almost immediately. He sighed and extricated himself from Lana's body, scowling at being pried out of his drowsy contentment. He found her phone on top of the dresser in the guest bedroom.

"Yeah?" he answered gruffly.

A long pause ensued. *"Jason?"*

He grunted an acknowledgment, still half-asleep.

"It's Melanie."

His heavy eyelids blinked open. "Hey, Melanie."

"Is Lana okay?" she asked, the distance of a continent and an ocean unable to disguise her anxiety. "I didn't get a chance to check messages until now. I had to pick up Shawna and— Is everything okay? Lana sounded upset when she called, and she said I should call her right away."

"She's fine. There was a media leak here in Honolulu in regard to the escort service. That was what Lana wanted to warn you about before you saw it on the mainland news."

"What?"

Jason filled her in on what had occurred, making a point of assuring her that he didn't believe whoever was responsible would try and involve Melanie.

"I'm not worried about that. My soon-to-be ex-husband didn't know where I went on vacation or who I was with, either," Melanie exclaimed. "I'm worried about Lana."

"Well, she's worried about you," he replied wryly, briefly outlining Lana's confrontation with Po and the warning she gave him.

"Jeez, leave it to Lana to worry about a friend instead of herself. I can't believe this happened. It just sucks after she'd dared to go out on a limb and all by staying in Honolulu. You must know her well enough by now to realize how hard that was for her."

"What do you mean?" Jason asked, rubbing sleep out of his eyes. As Melanie talked, he slowly stopped rubbing. His hand fell to his side.

He suddenly felt wide awake.

BY the time he went back to bed, Lana had curled up into a little ball at the far corner of the bed. The sheet and blanket had fallen from her nude body. He got beneath the covers and pulled her against him, spooning her. She didn't fully waken, but she sighed and straightened her legs, bringing them into full contact with his.

Jason remained awake for an hour or more, highly aware of the soft, feminine body pressed against him, thinking of the events of yesterday, going over what Melanie had told him on the phone. The fragrance of the massage oil, sex, and Lana's unique scent filled his nose. He stroked her silky skin from thigh to breast. She kept sleeping, but Jason sensed an increased tension level in her muscles as he caressed her, as though some inner, dreaming part of her perked up in sensual awareness. He pressed closer to her warmth; his cock grew stiff next to her ass.

He continued to ponder while his body hummed with an awareness of the woman lying next to him.

She moaned in her sleep when he shaped a breast in his palm and stroked the nipple languorously. The flesh was soft when he first touched it with his fingertips. Although he couldn't see her nipple, he knew it would be a delicate pink color in it's relaxed state, fat and succulent. Just thinking about it made him salivate. As he finessed her, the nipple tightened. He ran his fingertips over the tiny bumps, and she shivered in his arms.

Melanie had revealed that Lana had chosen to return to Honolulu; that she'd planned to seek him out. He'd been floored by that fact. More stunned than he'd been when she'd chosen to seek him out on previous occasions . . . when she'd exposed herself, despite being afraid of what might happen. He'd sensed how hard it had been for her. That must have been part of what aroused him so much.

And despite it all, she'd made that ultimate step. She's stayed in Oahu. Maybe not just for him . . . but still. She'd stayed. She'd been planning on seeing him again.

No wonder she'd wanted him to hurt last night after seeing that disgusting news bite.

She would feel even more vulnerable if he told her what Melanie had said.

He grasped her hip and stroked his cock in the crevice of her ass cheeks, all the while thinking . . . scheming. Her skin felt like warm silk next to his erection.

It infuriated him all over again to consider how Lana had

done something so difficult for her—fought past her anxiety and uncertainty about what was happening between them—and returned, only to have her fragile trust smashed to bits by that crass news story.

How the hell was he going to encourage her to give him her trust again?

She's mine. I just have to convince her of that.

The thought surprised him at first, but he must have been harboring it for a while in some secret part of his mind, because the shock faded quickly enough.

Wasn't a person the most vulnerable when they slept?

The arrival of dawn cast the room in gray shadow. He slid his hand down her belly, stroking her, pleasuring her even as he accustomed her to his presence. He slipped beneath her defenses while she was the most unguarded.

Since his motivations were pure, he refused to feel guilty about that.

He pushed back a round buttock, sandwiching his cock deeply in the luscious crevice. He palmed the firm flesh, massaging it in a tiny circular motion around his burrowing erection. The heat he felt emanating from her tiny asshole made his cock throb with a dull, delicious ache.

He leaned back, reaching for the bedside table and snagging a bottle from the drawer. She continued to sleep while he lubricated his cock, but he noticed a pink flush had risen on her cheek.

He pressed close again, sliding his oiled cock between her ass cheeks and massaging the puckered, nerve-packed opening. He resumed caressing her, touching her hips and thighs, awakening her flesh even while her mind continued to slumber.

"Jason," she mumbled incoherently when his finger burrowed

between plump labia. He tickled and rubbed and played with the slick kernel of hypersensitive flesh he found.

"That's right," he whispered next to her ear before he kissed the delicate shell. "Just relax. I'm going to give it to you in the ass."

She moaned softly. He couldn't have said for certain if she was awake or asleep, but he suspected she was somewhere in between. She pressed her hips back, applying pressure to his straining cock as he thrust between her ass cheeks. Jason grimaced in pleasure.

He continued to stimulate her clit while he kissed her neck, surrounding himself with her scent. When he reached the limit of his restraint—which was much sooner than he preferred—he reluctantly withdrew from her juicy labia. Her body remained fluid and relaxed when he thrust a finger into her ass. He stroked her for a while, readying her snug channel for his cock.

She started to resonate heat like a furnace.

He couldn't wait another second to bury himself in her. He grabbed his cock with one hand; her ass cheek with the other. Her sleek body stiffened when he pushed the thick head of his cock into her ass. He felt her clamp down on the tip of his penis and tense her muscles. Her ass naturally tried to resist the invasion, but he applied a steady pressure, keeping his cock lodged in her.

Now that he was in her, there wasn't a chance in hell she was going to get rid of him so easily.

"Shhh," he whispered as he landed kisses on her neck, ear, and cheek. "You feel so good. So hot and tight."

"Jason," she groaned when he slid into her another half inch. Her muscles rippled and convulsed around him, causing his eyes to roll back in his head in pleasure.

He pressed his chest to her back, but moved his hips away from her slightly . . . giving his cock room to navigate as he slowly worked his way into her. He wanted to be slow and patient with her, the opposite of what he'd been the other night when he'd fucked her ass so ruthlessly . . . or last night when he'd given her a cock pummeling in anger over her stubbornness.

Regret from the memories gave him the strength he needed, despite his intense arousal.

He released his lubricated cock and grasped her hip, maintaining the constant pressure required to keep himself inside her. He pulsed his hips, stimulating that nerve-packed channel with just the first few inches of his cock, coaxing her resistant muscles into taking him deeper. She whimpered softly.

He dropped a kiss on her flushed cheek.

"How's that? Feel nice?" he whispered.

She nodded.

"I'm gonna give it to you nice and slow. Give me your mouth."

She turned, so sweet in what she offered despite her uncertainty. He did everything to her mouth that he wanted his cock to do to her ass. He plunged his tongue deep and possessed it utterly. He thanked her without words for coming back to him and apologized for the pain she'd experienced.

Guys weren't always the best at expressing themselves, but he hoped Lana was listening . . . because he tried.

The kiss went on—hot and electric, and all the while, he slowly worked his steel-hard erection into her tight channel. Every once in a while, he'd pause in the blissful torture and release her hip so that he could stroke her. She whimpered into his mouth as he pinched her nipples gently. His cock lurched in her ass, answering her cry of longing.

His hand returned to her hip, holding her steady while he possessed more of her.

By the time he was nearly sheathed in her, they were both covered in a fine sweat. They had to break their kiss, hungry as they both were, because they panted so fiercely.

"Touch yourself," he ordered.

She complied, moving her hand between her legs. When she moaned in pleasure, he pressed his aching balls tightly against her round ass cheeks.

"Awww, *yeah*," he gasped harshly.

Their breathing sounded ragged in the silent room. Jason held himself right at the edge of orgasm. She squeezed him in a merciless grip. Her hand moved more rapidly between her thighs. He bit at her ear then found her lips in the darkness. He brushed their mouths together.

"I don't want to hurt you, Lana. I'm just trying to reach you."

She cried out, the sound striking him as poignant, sad . . . filled with longing. She shuddered in orgasm. He shut his eyes and fucked her. Pleasure engulfed him. He held on tight to her hip, feeling her flesh tremble.

When he came, his eyes popped open as if he was seeing a different universe. His cock jerked deep inside her. Just when he thought his climax would wane, another wave tore through him then another.

He found his face pressed against her neck and cheek. He was holding her fast against him. Their skin was so damp they would likely make a popping sound when they finally unsealed their tight bond. Her heart pounded frantically in her rib cage. He licked his lips and tasted her tears.

"Are you hurt, *Onaona*?"

"No," she whispered softly.

She turned and kissed him as the pale yellow light of dawn filled the room.

twenty-two

JASON put on a pair of trunks before he dove into the lagoon several hours later. Lana felt a little guilty about that, since she knew he only donned the shorts out of consideration for her. Part of her was glad that he wasn't parading his godlike naked body around as he was wont to do. There were men in the vicinity standing guard around the area of the houseboat, after all. But part of her regretted seeing him being forced to alter his habits because of the actions of some jerk. Jason's was such a savage beauty, it seemed somehow wrong for him to be forced to cover it . . . especially here in his private paradise.

Lana never really saw the men guarding the houseboat, but she knew they were out there, nonetheless: in the marina parking lot, along the periphery of the beach . . . possibly in the foliage that surrounded the lagoon. They'd never seen the photographer, either. Surely he'd been going about his sleazy business in the thick tangle of koa and palm trees, fire cracker bushes, ficus, and hibiscus shrubs that protected Jason's paradise home.

She sat on the deck of Jason's boat and watched him knife through the water in a path toward the open sea. She'd screwed everything up last night. Royally. She'd sexually tormented him to the point of madness. She'd been determined to make her last memory of Jason Koa that of him being helpless . . . desperate with need . . . as out of control as she'd felt when she saw that news story yesterday.

It hadn't been her finest hour, Lana admitted as shame swept through her. Especially when she'd lost a great deal of her certitude that Jason was somehow responsible for those photos and that news leak. She didn't know when she'd changed her mind, precisely. Her righteous indignation must have leaked out of her while she slept in his arms. By the time he'd made love to her at dawn in such an intimate and tender manner, it had dissipated to mist.

Why wouldn't he let her talk about what had occurred between them last night? She felt as if she should say something . . . Apologize?

But hadn't he ripped through his restraints like a savage, chased her, thrown her down on the bed, and fucked her like a madman?

He did it because you asked him to fuck you . . . begged him, a disdainful voice in her head reminded her.

She wiggled restlessly against the wooden deck of the boat, feeling the tenderness of her genitals . . . the tingle. She might be sore, but just thinking about that frantic, pressured joining had aroused her all over again.

She lay down on her side in the warm sun. Maybe she drifted

off again, because the next thing she knew, Jason was returning from his swim. He straightened in the water and flipped back his longish bangs in a habitual gesture. He flashed her a smile. An ache swelled in her chest.

He was a born heartbreaker. Look how easily she'd given in to him last night, even when she'd been furious and burning to exact revenge. He'd even convinced her not to speak about the turmoil of last night, repeatedly telling her not to worry about what had occurred for the time being.

Her growing feelings for him mingled with her confusion. But her uncertainty couldn't stop her from returning his infectious grin.

"Good surfing waves. Do you want to show me your stuff?" he asked.

She shook her head. "No. I'd like to watch you, though. Aren't you worried about boats, since this isn't a public beach?"

He grabbed onto the ladder with one hand and leaned back parallel to the boat, floating lazily in the water. His long legs drifted up to the surface. Lana couldn't help but smile wider. He was such a water animal, so comfortable and playful in his movements while he was in his natural environment.

"I have eyes in the back of my head. Besides, boats out of the marina usually head farther out from shore when the waves are this high."

She became conscious of the fact that he studied her intently. "What's wrong?" she asked, glancing down over her bikini-clad body.

"Are you sure we've never met before?"

"Before?" Lana asked, perplexed by his question.

"Yeah. Like when you were a kid, living here in Honolulu."

Lana shook her head. "I don't think so. How old are you?"

"Thirty-five."

"I doubt a teenager would have noticed a scrawny little kid."

His dark eyes lowered over her warmly. "Hard to imagine you scrawny. I'll believe it when I see a picture."

"It's true. My father used to accuse me of being skinny on purpose."

Jason snorted. "What little girl wants to be skinny? I have cousins who angst over their twelve-year-old daughters wearing padded bras that make their figures so imbalanced, they look like they'd tip over on their faces in a brisk wind."

Lana laughed. "Being a preadolescent girl is no easy task."

"Did you hate it?"

"Hate what?"

"Being an adolescent."

She sighed and stared out at the sparkling lagoon. "Hated it, along with the rest of it."

"The rest of what?"

"Childhood."

She blinked at the loud splashing that accompanied Jason clambering up the ladder. He dropped down on the deck next to her, spraying droplets of water on her sun-warmed skin.

"Is that why you've been hesitant to go and visit your parents' graves?"

She continued to gaze at the lagoon and nodded. She heard his slow inhale.

"My offer still stands, you know."

"What offer?" she asked.

"I'll take you to Oahu Cemetery. I'll just sit in the car, or I'll go in with you. Whatever you want. Or you can just tell me to shut up, and I won't bring it up again."

"Thanks," she murmured, her gratitude genuine despite the tight feeling in her throat and her difficulty in meeting his eyes. He seemed to notice her discomfort and changed the subject, something for which she was even more grateful.

"I'm going in to Jace's in a bit and then to talk to a few people about the news leak . . . see what I can find out. Do you want to come with me or stay here?"

"I'll stay if it's all right. It's very peaceful here." She stared at the sunlit lagoon. "I don't like to think of your privacy being invaded by whoever took those pictures."

"You seem to have trouble believing it, but I do value my privacy. I don't mind being a public figure, and I do what I have to do to maintain my businesses. But when I'm here on this boat, it's *my* life."

She remained silent and pensive as the rippling water sparkled brilliantly in her eyes. It hit her that it was no longer a matter of not being caught in Jason Koa's trap. She'd been ensnared, tight and secure, sometime in the night. She wasn't sure how he'd done it. Maybe she'd been hooked since that moment when she'd dared to wander into his territory and seen him rise like a god from the cerulean waters.

The only thing left to do was to figure out what she was going to do about those chafing yet strangely alluring bonds.

"I believe you," she said hoarsely after a moment. "If I hadn't been so taken off guard yesterday . . . so angry, I would have been able to think straight. But now that I'm back here, now that I see you here again . . . I realize you wouldn't do something as sleazy and crass as paying someone to take our pictures. Not here. Not in the privacy of your home."

"Well, that's something I guess."

She turned to him, surprised by his tone of wry amusement. "Why do you say it like that?"

"I'd prefer you believed me because you knew me a little better, knew without a doubt I'd never pull something like that," he murmured, holding her gaze. "But these things take time, I guess."

Lana glanced away uncomfortably.

"Ah, I see. Still not willing to commit to spending more time together." He chuckled dryly as he leaned back, bracing himself on his arms. "You know you've done the impossible, right?"

"What do you mean?"

"You've managed to make *me*, Jason Koa, the guy who's usually the intimacy-challenged one, look well-balanced—relationally speaking, anyway. Next thing you know, people will be calling me sensitive."

She gave him an incredulous look, and they both laughed.

"I don't know what I'm doing here, Jason," Lana admitted, shaking her head.

"What do you mean? You're here because some asshole interfered in our lives, right?" he asked warmly.

Intently.

She looked out at the lagoon, but she still felt his gaze on her cheek like a touch. Thankfully, her cell phone starting ringing. She leapt up.

"Excuse me. That's probably Melanie. The connection is bad, and we kept getting cut off earlier."

They were cut off again, unfortunately. She was able to get

through to her publicist, whom she was talking to when Jason came inside to shower.

She switched off the enormous flat-screen television in his living room when he exited the bedroom twenty minutes later, looking casual and handsome as the devil wearing low-riding khaki shorts and a dark blue knit shirt. His hair was combed but still damp, and his wavy bangs had already fallen on his forehead. She hadn't hit the remote control quick enough, and he'd noticed she'd been watching the noon news.

"Are they still running the story?"

Lana nodded. "It's pretty much the same. They just added some archive footage of you winning a gold medal and me performing. Then they mentioned other celebrities who had been caught up in sex scandals of one kind or another."

Annoyance tightened his features. "Fricking vultures."

"Yeah. I shouldn't have looked for the feeding frenzy. My bad." She paused and tugged at the hem of the T-shirt she'd put on over her bikini. "When will you come back?"

"I'll be back by six or so. My goddaughter's birthday luau is tonight, the one I invited you to the other . . ."

He faded off. Lana paused in her fidgeting when she saw the way Jason was peering at her between thick lashes.

"What's wrong?" she asked.

"You're *going* to be here when I get back."

She swallowed with difficulty. It hadn't been a question. His tone had carried a hint of both warning and trepidation.

"Of course. I mean . . . yes, I just wanted to know when you'd be back, that's all. Besides, I thought you said last night your father's guards would prevent me from leaving," she added with a mock glance of condemnation. She'd been teasing, so it took her by surprise when he stalked across the room with a blazing look in his eyes. The next thing she knew, her breasts were flattened against a hard chest and Jason's fragrant breath was brushing her upturned lips.

"I *would* keep you as a prisoner here if it didn't interfere with my strict sense of morality."

She quirked up a brow, her gaze fixed on his mouth. "You have morals?"

"Despite what my grandmother—and apparently you—think, *yes*," he growled. His manner was playful . . . but perhaps not, Lana thought as she noticed the fire in his smoky eyes. A shiver went down her spine.

His mouth slanted over hers. He molded her flesh to his, piercing the boundary of her lips with his sleek tongue, making Lana want. Making her hurt. It surprised her, the arousal that suddenly sprang into her body, given how many times she'd come last night.

But it was Jason, and she was quickly learning the new parameters of her desire. It still intimidated her. It still made her insecure. But she'd said she'd stay, and she would.

For now.

AFTER Jason left, she showered and tossed on a sundress. While she was combing her damp hair, she heard the soft growl of a motor. The sound was nearer than that usually caused by the boats in the marina. She felt a soft thud, and the motor's hum abruptly ceased. Her stance was wary as she approached Jason's front door to check if it was locked.

Apparently she had visitors.

Before she even reached the door, however, she heard a brisk, youthful-sounding female voice speaking. The cry of a baby also reached her ears, reassuring her. Surely the person intent on blackmailing her with those photos wouldn't possess that light, energetic voice. They wouldn't have a *baby* with them. She heard Harold's calm, even reply and started to open the door. She hesitated.

It took her a moment to realize the source of her discomfort. She felt ashamed to look Harold in the eye now that her fury had dissipated and darkness no longer cloaked her. How humiliating: to know that complete strangers and casual acquaintances knew that she'd hired a man to have sex with her.

The wave of mortification passed almost as quickly as it came. Anger replaced it, stirring her pride. She inhaled deeply and reached for the door.

"You need a new life preserver," she heard Harold say as he handed what looked like a bright yellow ball with pudgy arms and legs sticking out of it to the slim Asian woman who stood on the dock. "Li'l Lil isn't so little anymore. She's busting out of that thing."

"It's probably her stubbornness bursting out of it. She sees the water and wants to be in it. She takes after Jason: a little water baby. You should see her in the pool at our condo or out at Grandma's— Oh, hello," the young woman said as she glanced around, a swath of shiny dark brown hair falling into her face. She pushed it back impatiently. When she smiled, Lana immediately knew she was a Koa.

"Hi," Lana replied, stepping closer. "I'm sorry, but Jason just left twenty minutes ago."

Harold opened his mouth to speak from where he still stood

in the boat, but the young woman beat him to the punch. "I know. I just talked to him a few minutes ago. I actually came out here to meet you." She hitched the baby—who had hair as dark and sleek as her mother's—onto her left hip and stuck out her hand in a friendly fashion. Lana noticed the woman's eyes were like rich brown velvet as she unabashedly studied Lana with a lively curiosity. She wore a tiny ring in her small, perfect nose. Other than the diaper bag flung over her shoulder and the gold nose ring, she looked like a trim, well-dressed suburbanite or a lawyer about to report for work. She wore a pair of camel brown pants, a white short-sleeved button-down cotton blouse and a pair of low-heeled pumps. Her baby was, indeed, nearly bursting out of a tiny bright yellow life preserver.

"I'm Kelly Cavanaugh, Jason's cousin. And this," she said as she bounced the baby on her hip, "is Lily."

Lana laughed when the infant turned on cue and regarded her with a somber expression that was adorably at odds with her round, chubby face, drool-wet chin, and tear-streaked cheeks. Hadn't Jason said that the upcoming luau was a celebration of his goddaughter's first birthday? Lily took after her godfather in another way besides being a water-lover; her eyelashes were thick, lush, and long. On Jason, they only seemed to magnify the singular, laserlike intensity of his gaze, but on Lily, they looked feminine and dainty.

Lana instantly felt the power of the little girl's personality. This time, she gladly gave in to the inevitable power of the Koa charm.

"I'm Lana Rodriguez. It's so nice to meet both of you." She brushed Lily's damp cheek with her fingertip, her smile widening when the caress earned her a dimpled grin. "Jason mentioned you, Li'l Lil, but he didn't tell me how pretty his goddaughter was."

"I'm surprised," Kelly said with a good-natured roll of her eyes. "He brags about her to anyone who will listen. Look, I'm really sorry to inconvenience you this way, but Lil's hungry. A mother's body isn't her own. I'm trying to wean her from breast-feeding, but sometimes it's just easier to give in to her demanding ways. Would you mind?"

"Of course not," Lana said when Kelly waved to the front door. She was a little flustered at the fact that Kelly was treating her like it was *her* houseboat instead of Jason's. Surely Jason's cousin was a much more regular visitor in his home than Lana was.

"Are you coming in, Harold?" Kelly asked as she hurried inside. "I'll be out in just a few."

"Please do. I just put on a fresh pot of coffee," Lana encouraged Harold.

Harold and Lana were sipping their coffee in the kitchen and discussing the wildlife in the lagoon—both of them pointedly avoiding the topic of the tawdry news story about Jason and Lana—when Kelly walked into the kitchen, carrying a much more satisfied looking Lily. While Harold and Lana had been careful and tactful, Kelly was refreshingly frank.

"So, how are you holding up in regard to all this crap on the news?"

Lana paused in the process of pouring Kelly a requested half cup of coffee. Her cheeks flooded with heat, but she handed Kelly her cup calmly enough. "Pretty well, I guess."

"It's not like you have anything to compare your reaction to, right? Damn press. I swear, some of those media types would throw their own kids to the wolves if it meant a good story." Lily batted a chubby hand against her mother's scowl. Kelly kissed her daughter's tiny palm, removed it from her mouth, and continued. "I was sent here on a mission from Grandma Lily."

"Really?" Lana asked, confused and a little amazed by Kelly's proclamation.

"Yeah, she's running herself ragged preparing for the luau tonight."

Harold sighed. "That woman never stops."

"She says the same about you, Harold," Kelly said wryly before she continued. "She hasn't even seen the story on the news. She refuses to watch it—out of protest, I think."

"Stubborn," said Harold.

"Yeah, well, aren't we all? And *you're* the worst of the bunch, Lil," Kelly said when Lily batted her chin in another bid for attention. She gave her daughter a smacking kiss on the cheek before she resumed. "After all these annoying phone calls from relatives complaining about Jason causing a scandal, Grandma's refusing to answer the phone. I told her we could cancel Lily's party this evening, since some people might find it necessary to be unpleasant, but Grandma said 'no black-hearted criminal' was going to ruin her great-granddaughter's first birthday luau."

Lana smiled. Lily Koa certainly sounded like a wonderful woman. No wonder Jason cherished her so much.

"She called me this morning and asked me to come out to the houseboat to personally invite you to come to the luau tonight," said Kelly.

"Considering the circumstances, maybe it wouldn't be for the best," Lana replied cautiously.

"Grandma told me to tell you she wouldn't take no for an answer. She thinks you and Jason should hold your heads high, or people are going to assume you have something to be ashamed of.

Jason told me he already asked you to attend the luau, isn't that correct?"

"Uh . . . yes, but that was before—"

"It's all settled, then," Kelly interrupted. She beamed at Lana before she set her coffee cup on the counter. "Now, I hate to run, but my babysitter has to leave in an hour, and I still have to get to the drugstore to get some calamine lotion for Kane's chicken pox."

A few seconds later, Lana closed the door after her visitors. Kelly Cavanaugh had blown into the houseboat like a gust of fresh air and left again just as abruptly. Lana found herself wondering how much of her visit had been urged by Lily Koa and how much Jason himself had been responsible for.

twenty-three

THE man paused in surprise when he noticed Jason sitting on his front stoop. Jason stood.

"Eric Knowlen?"

The man glanced around nervously, as though he was hoping someone else would step forward and claim the name. "Yeah," he finally replied.

"I was wondering if I could have a word. I'm Jace Koa."

"I know who you are. I saw you win the Hawaiian surfing championship three years ago. Those Aussies thought they knew about big waves, but they learned different at Waimea that day, huh?"

Jason laughed. "You surf?"

"Yeah, course. Been attached to a board since I was five."

Jason kept up the banter for a minute or two until he thought Eric was a little less tense about finding him waiting for him at his front door. Melanie Mason's escort from last week was Caucasian, with sun-streaked longish hair and a lean, rangy build. Jason surmised that, given the neighborhood he lived in, the rips on Eric's well-worn shorts came honestly and weren't part of his good-looking beach-bum image.

"So what are you doing here?" Eric finally asked.

Jason glanced around, but the quiet, bungalow-lined street with the poorly groomed yards was desolate.

"I understand you work for my cousin, Po Koa?"

Eric shrugged. "Surfing doesn't pay the bills. I guess it's no secret I pick up some work from Po sometimes. A guy's gotta make a buck somehow."

"And there are much less pleasant ways to make it, I guess."

"It's not what it's cracked up to be. Some of the ladies Po sends my way are real dogs."

"Guess there's a reason they have to pay for it," Jason said wryly. "That's got to be a . . . challenging aspect of your work."

Eric laughed, but his glance at Jason was wary.

"You did some work for Po last week, right?"

Eric's cautiousness segued to outright suspicion. Gone was the easygoing surfer dude. He inspected Jason through narrowed blue eyes. "What do you mean?"

"If you're like every other person on the island, you've likely seen the story the news is running about Lana Rodriguez and I."

Eric shifted on his feet. "I might have seen something about it, yeah. Thought it was a real joke—them suggesting you were a male escort."

"You know anything about who took those photographs of us or leaked them to the press?"

Jason knew immediately he'd misplayed his hand when he saw Eric's offended expression.

"What the hell? Why would you ask *me* if I know about that?"

"I just thought you might, seeing how you work for Po and all."

Eric furrowed his fingers through his shoulder length blond hair in an agitated gesture. "Dude, are you accusing your own cousin of smearing your name? Are you accusing *me*?"

Jason caught the other man's gaze and held it. "Like I said, I thought you might have heard something . . . since you're on Po's payroll. I wouldn't hold it against a guy for *knowing* something."

Eric's mouth hung open. Jason sensed his hesitancy, so he pushed.

"You didn't ask me how I knew you worked for Po."

"Po wasn't the one to tell you?"

"Nah. I got your name from Melanie Mason." He and Melanie had conversed about a lot of interesting topics in the middle of the night last night.

"Melanie?"

"Yeah. She's a nice lady." Jason was glad he'd had faith in Melanie's inherent kindness and warmth when he saw Eric's expression soften.

"Yeah. We had a good time together last week. She was one of the ones I would have spent time with, even if . . ."

"She didn't pay you?" Jason finished for him when he trailed off.

"Yes. But *hey* . . . Melanie thought I would know something about that news story about Lana Rodriguez and you? Why would she say that?"

Jason shrugged, giving the other man the impression he was hazy on the details. "She wasn't accusing you of anything. It was just a hunch she had. Something about a phone call you got one night while you two were at the Green Turtle? She said she had a great time that night, by the way."

Jason waited, allowing Eric to remember the good times he'd spent with Melanie.

"Are you sure you don't know anything about who might have taken those pictures, Eric? I'll pay you for the information if that's what—"

Eric made a slashing gesture with his hand. "I don't want your money, man. I'm not *that* bad off."

Jason inhaled slowly and reached for his wallet. He glanced up when Eric made an irritated sound. "I'm not going to offer you money. Not if you don't want it. I was just going to give you my card. Give me a call if you hear anything that might help me figure out who was responsible for this."

"I don't know anything," Eric said gruffly, eyeing the offered piece of paper. Jason kept his hand extended anyway until Eric finally took the card.

"Just in case," Jason said before he walked down the crumbling sidewalk.

LANA was nervous and not in her normal low-grade-anxiety-disorder-nervous sort of way. By six thirty that evening, she'd told herself at least a hundred times that meeting Lily Koa was *not* a big deal. Why should it be? She was just a nice elderly lady with a lot of character and charm. In truth, the picture everyone painted of Lily was delightful, so Lana couldn't understand why she was all aflutter.

She set down her hair brush, flinching at the clattering sound it made when it hit the granite countertop in Jason's spare bathroom. She emerged from the hallway at the same time Jason walked into the foyer.

"Hi," she greeted him breathlessly.

He glanced up from reading one of several envelopes he held in his hands. He studied her with frank appreciation before he tossed his mail on the kitchen island.

"Hi," he returned. "How come you're not dressed for the luau? Kelly said she convinced you to come."

Lana arched her eyebrows. "Did you send her out here to talk me into going?"

"Didn't Kelly tell you Grandma asked her to do it?"

"Yes."

He gave her a slow grin and approached, encircling her hips with his hands. He lowered his head, brushed her hair back with his nose, and trailed his lips along her neck. "Ummm, you smell fantastic. So you still think I put Kelly up to coming out here, even though she told you Grandma asked her to do it?"

"Did you talk her into it?" Lana asked. Most of her attention was on the sensation of his mouth on her skin.

"Maybe a little. All the Koa's know Kelly is irresistible."

"And when you pair her up with Li'l Lil—"

Jason lifted his head. Lana saw his white teeth in the dim interior of the houseboat. "They're unstoppable. So does that mean you're coming to the luau?"

"I was getting ready when you came in."

"So what's wrong? How come you're not dressed?" he asked, stroking her robe-covered shoulders and staring at his hand on her body in a manner that distracted Lana.

"I . . . I didn't know what to wear."

He ducked his head and nuzzled her neck with his nose. Lana shivered when he scraped his front teeth lightly against her skin. He spoke between nibbles. "Anything. It's an . . . outdoor party . . . for a one-year-old. It's hardly . . . formal." He pressed their bodies together more tightly. Lana sighed, her head falling back when she felt his hardness and heat. He sensed her surrender and began to kiss her more arduously.

She made a sound of disappointment when he lifted his head abruptly.

"What's wrong?" she rasped.

"Nothing's wrong with you. You're perfect. Unfortunately, this is going to have to wait," he said gruffly as he nudged her middle with his erection. "I need to speak with one of Lily's brothers, and he tends to come to luaus right on time and leave early."

"I'll get dressed, then."

"Okay." She tried to pull back, but Jason's hold on her remained firm. He ran his hands over her hips and ass. "Are you naked under here?"

She nodded. His penis throbbed next to her belly. She stifled a moan when his hand strayed under the hem of her robe and caressed her bare thigh and ass. He uttered a soft curse.

"If it weren't for the fact that I'm still gathering information about this news leak, I'd be buried in you within the minute."

"I'd have to shower again. Oh . . . Jason," she exclaimed when he wedged his hand between her thighs and touched her slit with a fingertip. He groaned and released her abruptly.

"Considering how damp you are, you might have to shower again whether we have sex or not."

Lana swallowed and tightened the belt on her robe, trying to ignore the heat flash that surged in her body. "Did you find out anything this afternoon?"

"Not a damn thing. Which makes it even more important for me not to miss Uncle Marcus tonight. He's the biggest gossip on the island. Knows everything. Unfortunately, he goes to bed by eight o'clock."

"I'll hurry, then," Lana assured him.

Her nervousness came back while she slipped into a tangerine-colored dress that set off her tan to good effect. She wished Jason and she could just spend the evening here on the boat alone together. How much fun could it be, knowing that almost everyone at the party was speculating on why she needed to pay for sex . . . or how she'd gone about ensnaring the favored Koa son in her trap?

twenty-four

LILY Koa lived on the leeward side of the island. Jason pulled down a narrow lane bordered by lush coconut palms and ficus bushes. When she saw the enormous house at the end of the drive, Lana laughed.

"Why do you call it a farm? It's a *mansion*."

Jason shrugged. "It's a house on a working farm."

Lana stared at the beautiful house built in the Beaux Arts style. In the distance she saw the brilliant waters of the Pacific Ocean.

"You grew up here?" she murmured in amazement as she gawked out the window.

"Yep."

He pulled behind a long line of cars and popped the trunk.

Lana thought of how he'd asked her if they might have known one another when she'd lived on the island as a child. She doubted the possibility even more now that she understood the vast differences in their families' socioeconomic statuses.

Jason retrieved an enormous package wrapped in a pink bow from the trunk of his car, and they headed inside.

The interiors of Lily Koa's home were simple but elegant with dark hardwood floors, comfortable ivory-colored sofas and chairs, and spinning fans on the high ceilings of every room. As they neared the back of the house, the sounds of talking, laughing people and shouting children grew louder. Jason led her into an enormous, airy kitchen and seating area. Opened French doors led out to a multilevel terrace. A swimming pool was situated on the lowest tier, its brilliant turquoise color echoing the much vaster body of water that took up the entire western horizon. A couple dozen kids of various ages cavorted inside and around it.

"I can't believe you grew up here. It's beautiful," Lana murmured.

Jason opened his mouth to say something, but someone called out his name.

"Jace! Lana, I'm so glad you came," Kelly exclaimed. Several people looked around with interest. Kelly approached them with a smile, her daughter on her hip. Li'l Lil was once again wearing the yellow life preserver that made her look like an adorable beach ball. Lana wondered if the little girl didn't spend half her day in the padded garment.

"*There's* the birthday girl." Jason set down the present on a table filled with other gifts and reached for his goddaughter. Li'l Lil's dark eyes grew round as saucers when Jason lifted her above his head. She giggled and waved her hands in excitement when he blew into the side of her neck.

"One year old and she's already a flirt," Jason proclaimed when he settled Lil on his hip and the little girl wrapped her chubby arms around his neck.

"You're the flirt, Jace," Kelly corrected matter-of-factly. "Lana, can I get you something to drink? Grandma makes an amazing planter's punch, but watch it; it's got a kick."

"I have experience with her mai tais. How does it compare to that?" Lana asked as she followed Kelly over to a large punch bowl on the counter.

"Just don't have any more than one, and chances are you'll remain conscious."

Lana laughed and accepted the glass Kelly offered. "Now if that's not reassuring, I don't know what is."

"Grandma will be sorry she wasn't here to greet you. She just went out to show some friends her hothouse flowers, but she'll be back in a moment. Come on, I'll introduce you to a couple people."

Lana was highly conscious of multiple stares on her.

"I have a feeling they already know who I am," she murmured.

"Well, they'd be wrong about that, now, wouldn't they?"

Lana smiled when she saw how Kelly's perfect, delicate features pulled into a fierce scowl. She understood why Kelly was Jason's favorite cousin.

Kelly sighed. "Sorry. I'm sure this is no picnic for you. Come on, I'll introduce you to Sean first—my husband. He's dying to meet you."

AFTER twenty minutes of meeting various Koa family members and several sips of Lily Koa's punch, Lana was feeling somewhat more relaxed. Harold's calm, friendly presence helped a lot, but she also met Jason's father, Joseph. Jason was like a taller, anglicized, darker-haired version of his dad. Joseph Koa had the same flashing grin. His charm had a mellower quality than Jason's potent charisma, but Lana could easily imagine a young Cornish author falling for him on her romantic vacation in Hawaii.

Much like Lana was falling for her son, she realized. Would Jason's and her affair end similarly—each of them half a world apart?

Joseph was warm and kind toward her, doing almost as much as Kelly and Harold to alleviate her anxiety. When she thanked him for arranging to have Jason's houseboat guarded, he waved off her gratitude.

"The Koas are always saying they'll guard each other's back. Unfortunately, our lives are so boring, nothing ever happens that we get to prove it. This gave us the chance to flex our unused muscles a little bit," Joseph teased.

An older teenage girl had come and claimed Li'l Lil from Jason, saying she wanted to take the baby for a swim. Lana met Marcus Koa, the gossip-loving octogenarian Jason had referred to earlier. When Kelly had pulled her away to meet someone else, Jason had remained behind talking to his great-uncle.

Lana was still highly aware of the speculative stares, but she no longer interpreted them as being hostile . . . just pervasive.

"I feel like I'm onstage," she'd muttered at one point to Kelly.

"People are just curious," Kelly had whispered. "And not just because of the news, either. Jason hardly ever brings a woman out to Grandma's farm."

She'd tried to ignore the pleasant warmth that had flooded through her at Kelly's statement.

All in all, Lana thought things were going fairly well . . . considering.

Kelly insisted that she get something to eat, and Lana thought it might not be a bad idea, considering the alcohol content in the punch. She filled up her plate with savory smelling barbecued pork, a piece of succulent ono in a lemon-basil sauce, homemade whole-grain bread, and a pear and walnut salad. She glanced up and saw Jason watching her from across the room. He gave a small nod when she looked down significantly at her plate. He said one last thing in parting to his great-uncle and started across the room toward her.

Lana saw him pause when Po entered the kitchen accompanied by the man he'd been with at Jace's the other night: Pete Makala. Both of them were wearing suits and looked highly overdressed for the casual luau.

"Jace," Po greeted. "Are we back on good terms?"

For a few seconds, Lana thought Jason wasn't going to respond. He merely studied his cousin with a stare that made Po look distinctly uneasy.

"I have no reason not to be on speaking terms with you," Jason finally replied coldly.

Po shared a smile with Makala. "That's good news, huh, Pete?"

"Sure it is," the man replied, his polished grin never wavering.

Jason looked irritated. "I don't have a solid reason *yet*."

He stalked across the room toward Lana.

"I can't believe he brought that sleazeball Makala to Grandma's house. I have a feeling Makala pushed Po into leaking that story; not that it absolves my stupid-ass cousin of anything," Jason seethed under his breath after Lana passed him a plate.

"Did you find something out from your uncle Marcus?"

"No. Nothing for certain. Still, something stinks around here, and the stench got a hell of a lot worse when Po and Makala walked in the room. Makala's been after a piece of my grand-mother's land for a few years now, and his determination seems to have grown in the past few months, according to Uncle Marcus. He's been systematically seeking out Koas that are close to Grandma; trying to find a crack where he can wiggle his way into Grandma's good graces. I've got no problem believing Makala's underhanded motives, but I can't believe Po would sell out so easily." He frowned distractedly. His cell phone started ringing in his short's pocket.

"Give me just a second, Lana, and we'll sit outside and eat," he muttered when he glanced at the caller's number. He walked over to the corner of the kitchen to take the call, so he didn't notice that Po approached Lana.

"Ms. Rodriguez, welcome to Koa Farms," he greeted warmly.

"You're grandmother has a beautiful home." She was highly aware of the increase in speculative stares from people milling about the large room and strove to say something neutral. Both she and Po knew she felt nothing but animosity toward him. It pissed her off that he dared to come over and talk to her like they were old friends.

"One of my relatives tells me you're here with Jason. You'll forgive my surprise. You seemed . . . less than pleased with him last night."

Lana met his eyes. "I've changed my mind about who I suspect is responsible for leaking my name and those photographs to the press."

"Ah, I see. And from your tone of voice, I gather Jason has convinced you that *I'm* the one who was solely responsible. Convenient for him, I'd say." His gaze lowered over her body suggestively.

"I told you where I stand on the matter last night. Nothing has changed as far as where you and I stand." She began to walk away from him, but he halted her abruptly with a hand on her upper arm.

"Since we were both in diapers, Jason has charmed every woman who comes within fifty feet of him. I wouldn't put too much stock in his reassurances."

"Jason and I are none of your damn business," Lana said quietly. She tried to yank her arm free, but Po's grip tightened.

"I guess Po feels differently."

Lana started at the snarling tone and turned around to see Jason standing close. His face looked so stark and stormy, Lana instantly thought of the brutally harsh coasts of his mother's homeland. She'd caught a hint of his fury, but Po remained clueless. He still had a fake smile on his face when Jason slammed his fist into it. Po fell back against the counter, his hand plopping in some kind of whipped cream dessert before he slumped onto his knees on the tile floor.

"No, Po here feels like *everyone* is *his* business," Jason bellowed down at his cousin, who looked like he hovered in the hazy realm between consciousness and passing out. Every occupant in the room had gone utterly still and silent, making Jason's voice vibrate resoundingly off the walls. "We're so much *his* damn business that he hired someone to take pictures of us on private property and then sold the photographs, along with some juicy little lies, to the Channel Eight News.

"Jason, *don't*," Lana exclaimed when he reached for Po's sagging form, looking like he was planning on pulling his cousin to his feet only to knock him off them once again. She grabbed his forearm. Jason didn't seem to hear her, but he had no choice but to respond when Joseph Koa joined her efforts. His father pushed him away from Po with a hand on his shoulder.

"You just about took his head off already, son. Leave him be," Joseph said when Jason shook him off.

"Do you know what that son of a bitch did?" Jason asked.

"I've got a good idea. You just informed everyone in the room," Joseph replied wryly.

Meanwhile, Po was recovering from Jason's punch. He tenderly touched his nose, smearing some whipped cream on it, and winced. He tried to pull himself up to a standing position with a hand on the counter. Makala rushed over to assist him.

"God damn son of a bitch," Po muttered under his breath, seeming to gain steam as he spoke. He blinked, trying to bring Jason into focus. "You fucking golden boy. I'm sick of you!"

Jason lunged forward threateningly, only to be hauled back by his father. "You're sick of *me*? You're the one who betrayed your own family, buddied up with your criminal pal here, and tried to discredit me in Grandma Lily's eyes so Makala could get a crack at that land he wants. Am I right?"

"So what if you are?" Po shouted. "It's not like it worked. Grandma thinks the sun rises and sets out of your ass."

Jason's eyes popped out in disbelieving rage at the open admission.

"Calm down, Po," Makala soothed diplomatically. "Maybe we'd better be going."

"I think that's a great idea," Joseph said.

"You *admit* it's true?" Jason roared, seemingly oblivious to any other comments besides Po's.

"Yeah, I admit it. And it wasn't just because of Makala, either. I'm sick and tired of *you*: perfect Saint Jace. You want to look for someone to blame for me being the black sheep of the family? Well, look in the mirror, asshole! I owe it to you that I run a strip club and sell sex to rich bitches like her." He jabbed a finger in Lana's direction. "You know why? Because *anything'd* be better than being compared to *Jace Koa*. Ever since we were kids you were the anointed one. No one can look at Grandma's books besides Jace; no one can give any sound business advice except for Jace. 'I'll ask Jace if he thinks that's a good idea,'" Po mocked in a poor imitation of what must have been Lily Koa's voice. "Just the sound of your *name* makes me want to puke!"

"*Ipo Koa.*"

They all turned. It was like a gong had just gone off in the room. Lana saw a tiny lady with liquid brown eyes and attractively styled curly white hair. She held three white orchid stems in her hand.

"What's going on here?" she asked, her tone surprisingly forbidding for one so small.

Lily Koa's dark eyes scanned first Jason and then Po. Lana thought she could have heard a pin falling on the limestone-tile floor.

"What's all this nonsense about you selling sex?" Lily demanded.

Joseph groaned softly and closed his eyes. Jason's expression collapsed. "Grandma, I'm sorry. I hit him. Po's upset. He's saying things he doesn't mean."

"I meant it!" Po seethed. His midnight black eyes looked a little deranged. He abruptly whipped his torso around, throwing Makala's hold off him. Some whipped cream flipped onto the floor and counter. "Let's get the fuck out of here."

Makala had a grim expression on his face as he followed Po.

"Is he going to be all right with Makala?" Lana heard Joseph ask his son quietly.

"You mean now that Po's blown his cover, and Makala's not depending on him anymore to get him in with Grandma?" Jason asked grimly. "Makala isn't going to dump him on the side of the road if that's what you mean. Too many people have seen them together at this point. 'Course, I can't guarantee Po's liquor license won't suddenly get pulled or that the cops won't come nosing around Hawaiian Heat asking questions about his extracurricular activities, but he'll be safe enough in the physical sense."

"What in the world are you two talking about?" Lily asked incredulously.

Jason's gaze wandered over to Lana. He still looked angry but regret weighted his features as well. Clearly, he'd let his temper get the best of him when he turned around to see his cousin manhandling Lily.

"Who was on the phone, Jason?" Lana asked, reasoning it had been the call on his cell phone that had sent him over the edge.

"Eric Knowlen. The guy Melanie spent time with last week. I talked to him earlier today, but he was guarded. He must have had a change of heart, though, because he just called and admitted that Po offered to pay him to take photographs of us out at my boat. Melanie overheard part of the conversation while they were at the Green Turtle together. Even though Eric turned down the offer, he made some comment about being a shit photographer and sort of looked guilty when he noticed Melanie had overheard. She forgot all about the incident until I explained about what had happened with the news leak. Melanie told me about it last night on the phone. It was a long shot, but it paid off."

Joseph whistled under his breath.

"I can't believe Po would do such a thing to his own cousin. You boys have known each other since you were toddlers," Lily said. Her face was pale and rigid with shock. Lana noticed that the flowers she held were slipping out of her hands.

"Here, let me help you with those," Lana said softly as she took the stems from the older woman's stiff fingers.

Lily Koa looked fully into her face for the first time since she'd walked into the room.

"Why . . . you're Mike Nahua's little girl," Lily said.

JASON blinked, sure he must have misunderstood his grandmother. The excitement must have gone to her head. Surely Lily Koa hadn't just said—

"You're 'Ailana Nahua. I never knew you when you were little, but I've seen pictures. I wouldn't need to see photos, though. You're a younger version of your aunt Patricia."

Lana's gaze shot over to Jason briefly before she glanced nervously at the crowd in the room. While the partygoers had mostly remained stock-still during the unexpected fight that broke out, currently they seemed to be surging forward like a single, many-headed creature.

Lana looked like a deer in headlights.

"Patricia is one of my closest friends. Have you contacted her, 'Ailana?" Lily asked quietly. Perhaps the shock of the fight between Po and Jason still clung to Lana, because she seemed entirely unaware of the room full of curious people.

"I . . . I don't know what you're talking about," Lana replied through lips that looked like they'd gone numb. An alarm started to blare in Jason's brain.

He'd seen her look like that before—he'd seen that *face*.

He stepped forward and put his arm around her. She hardly seemed aware that he took the orchids from her and set them on the counter. She'd lost four shades of color since Lily had said Mike Nahua's name. He thought for sure she was going to faint.

"Patricia tried to get custody of you soon after your mother passed away, but Mike kept her at a distance," Lily Koa continued, her tone weighted with sadness. "He wouldn't allow Patricia to see you and kept changing addresses, living like a gypsy and forcing you to do the same. And then his drinking got worse and worse. Eventually Patricia's husband got a job in Maui, and they moved. She didn't give up on you or her brother, but when she returned and found him—living alone and wasting away from illness and drink—he told her your grandmother had come to the island and taken you away. Patricia was furious with him for letting you go with your grandmother when he wouldn't allow you to live with her or one of the other Nahuas."

Jason felt a fine tremor vibrating from Lana's flesh into his hands.

"Other Nahuas?" she asked, her voice barely audible. Jason's tightened hold on her seemed to temporarily lift her out of her shock and bring her into the moment. She cast a furtive glance at the crowd of people watching them.

"Come on guys, give us some privacy. What are you all gawking at?" Jason barked. "*Go on.* This is Koa Farms, not the eleven o'clock news!"

But his attempts were only semi-successful. Koa family members and friends seemed to waken as if from an enchantment at his harsh words, but they still milled around and glanced back at the drama being played out by Lily and Lana.

"It broke Patricia's heart the way your father made you perform like that in public, forcing a little child to sing for tourists while he panhandled for money to buy drink. It was a *crime*," Lily said quietly, her voice shaking with feeling.

Lana made a muffled sound of dismay. She jerked in his hold, throwing his arm off her in an angry gesture. Her face was a study in misery as she turned and hurried out of the kitchen.

"Lana—*hold on*."

"Give her some privacy, Jason," his father said, bringing him up short for the second time that evening. Jason hesitated as he saw the bright orange flash of Lana's dress as she rushed out of the room toward the front of the house.

His father was right. She was such an intensely private person. The last thing she needed—the last thing she *wanted*—was another person staring at her while she suffered.

Lana had probably had enough of that by the time she was five or six years old.

twenty-five

SHOCK, shame, and confusion fueled Lana's footsteps as she hurried down the car-lined drive. All she could think of was those faces staring at her while Lily Koa exposed her secret. Lily hadn't meant to be cruel—she'd appeared to be overcome by sadness and compassion, Lana reasoned, trying to dampen her furious panic. But the words had come so unexpectedly out of Lily's mouth, striking Lana like missiles on an undefended target.

Then she'd glanced at Jason. Had that been disgust mingling with the incredulity on his face? What did he think, knowing the singer he'd previously admired had once been a freakish novelty, a frightened, helpless child with a woman's voice who performed like a pet dog doing tricks for its supper?

For its master's love.

The realization that she'd desperately wanted her father's love crashed into her with the impact of a hurricane-force wind. She staggered and hauled up short, putting her hand on the hood of a car to steady herself. She fought for air against the encroaching weight that settled on her chest.

Would it have a stranglehold on her for her whole life, this anxiety that accompanied her shame and helplessness?

No, god damn it, she thought furiously. She was a woman now, not a child. She was capable of facing her demons.

Despite her resolve, when she heard the sound of men's voices behind her, she had to resist a primitive urge to run like crazy . . . to escape. Instead, she wiped off her damp cheeks and turned around.

"What are you doing out here?" Po asked. Lana noticed that his nose was swelling and his left eye was starting to blacken. Makala dropped a stub of a cigarette onto the road and stamped it out. They must have paused up by the front of the house after they'd left the kitchen and missed Lana as she stormed out the door.

"Are you leaving?" she asked.

Po glanced at Makala uncertainly. "Yeah."

Lana straightened and smoothed back her hair. She knew she must look awful, but she wouldn't cringe in front of the likes of Po Koa. He didn't look so hot himself.

"Give me a ride into Waikiki?"

"Of course," Makala agreed smoothly.

"What about Jace?" Po asked as they walked down the drive toward the car.

"Are you worried about him having his feelings hurt if I leave without him?" Lana asked frostily.

Po snorted, which must not have been easy to do through that swollen nose. "No, I can't say that I am."

"So what are you worried about?"

She marched ahead of him on the road, ensuring Po understood she was done talking. He and Makala were just a means to get where she needed to go, and she certainly didn't plan on chatting about Jason with them.

She couldn't think about Jason right now. She needed to go back to Waikiki.

And she needed to go alone.

JASON grunted in rising frustration when Kelly and her husband, Sean, joined the others on the terrace and shook their heads grimly. They were the last members of the impromptu search party that Jason had sent out to look for Lana.

"Where the hell did she go?" he asked, raking his fingers through his hair. He'd waited for all of five minutes to go after Lana. When he'd finally ignored his father's warnings and went in search of her, however, she was nowhere to be found. The children had continued to play and enjoy the party, but several of the adults had helped him search around the extensive grounds.

"I've made a mess out of things," Lily muttered under her breath. "I was just so shocked to see her standing there in my kitchen—the girl Patricia had worried about for so many years. What a shock. And with everything that had happened with you and Po beforehand, it just all sort of spilled out of me. I had no idea 'Ailana didn't even realize she *had* relatives in the islands." She gave Jason an entreating look. He hugged her in reassurance.

"This was a hell of a mess, but none of it was your fault, Grandma." He grasped her elbows. "Look, I'm going to get in the car and search the road for her."

Harold stepped up and put his arm around Lily. "Do you want me to drive in the other direction?"

"Nah," Jason replied distractedly. "Someone call me if Lana shows up at the house again, though."

It wasn't until he was in his car and driving back to Honolulu at a brisk clip that Jason realized he wasn't searching for Lana at the side of the road. Something inside of him must have known he wouldn't find her there. He kept thinking about what Lily Koa had said. He kept seeing that frozen, terrified look on Lana's face when she realized all those people were staring at her while she was exposed and vulnerable.

He'd seen that expression before.

She'd looked like that until her father's portable recording equipment started blaring out the notes of a song. Then that little girl would open up her mouth, and her voice would flow like magic through the night, carrying her terror right along with it.

He parked his car on Kuhio and walked to the always crowded Kalakaua Avenue. The bright, glitzy storefronts contrasted markedly with the gentle twilight and mauve colored sky. Tourists from countries across the globe bustled along the sidewalk. Some were dressed in haute couture and carried shopping bags while others wore swim trunks and carried their surfboards. He heard strains of music coming from several directions. Live Hawaiian revues took place at several of the beachfront hotels every night, and the tourist board paid entertainers to perform on and around Kalakaua Avenue.

And then there were the street performers: guys doing tricks with their exotic birds; the girl who painted herself silver, stuck a torch in her hand, and stood stock-still while tourists dropped coins and dollar bills in a hat in gratitude for her Statue of Liberty imitation. There were the musicians . . . and the singers.

When Jason was still in high school, he and his friends used to come to Waikiki almost every weekend. As kids, they'd loved the energy of the tourist spot. They'd surf from morning to dusk, stroll around the beach, meet girls, goof off. When night came, they'd hang out on Kalakaua Avenue.

He might have been fourteen or fifteen we'd he'd first seen her. 'Ailana Nahua.

Course, he'd never known her name back then. He just recalled seeing her perform several times, a thick ring of tourists around her. She always drew a bigger crowd than anyone because of the unusualness of such a small, thin girl possessing such a phenomenally powerful voice. She never smiled, just sang with a heartbreaking intensity.

Jason hadn't given her a lot of thought back then, other than to admire her talent. He'd been a kid, after all, and Kalakaua Avenue and Waikiki Beach were filled with novelty performers and people trying to make a buck from tourists who were all too willing to shell out plenty to be entertained.

Once, though, his carefree teenage bubble had been pricked. It'd been the summer after his graduation from high school. He'd begun to train more rigorously as a swimmer, and he was attending college in the fall. He might not have been a man yet, but the thoughts and concerns of a man had started to enter his brain.

He'd separated from his friends, who had been too loud and too boisterous, and sat against a tree trunk, sipping a coke. Michael Nahua had arrived on the corner, carrying his amp and equipment, and the small singer trailed him with a reluctant step. He'd studied the girl more closely than he ever had on any previous occasion, obscured as he was in the shadow of the tree.

It was the first time he'd seen her when she wasn't singing with an enraptured crowd gathered around her. For the first time, he'd noticed how thin she was, how a loose thread from her dress trailed down her skinny leg, and how the hem had started to fall.

When her father had handed her the microphone, Jason had seen the terror on her face. She'd glanced into her father's face and shaken her head.

"Don't even *think* about starting with me tonight. *Sing*."

The man's voice had been harsh and hard. Michael Nahua had been tall and broad shouldered; the remnants of handsomeness were still evident in his face. The girl was as slender as a willow. There was no doubt in the young Jason's mind as to who would be forced to bend if there was a contest of wills.

Nahua had punched a button and notes had fluttered into the still summer night. When her cue came, the frozen look of anxiety on the girl's face abruptly melted as she sang.

"Somewhere Over the Rainbow."

Jason closed his eyes briefly in regret as he hurried down the crowded sidewalk. What could he have done, after all, as a seventeen-year-old kid . . . a stranger? Even her own flesh and blood hadn't been able to save her from her father's self-destruction and misery.

He'd been in such a pressured rush to find her, he found himself nearly walking right past the corner of Kalakaua and Seaside avenues. He brought himself up short when he saw her sitting motionless on a bench. Her face was wet with tears, but she didn't seem aware of it. Her eyes were fixed on the spot where she used to sing like her life depended on it.

Which in a way, it had, of course.

LANA stared at the spot of sidewalk like she believed she could make her past rise up out of the pavement. What had she looked like, standing there with that cheap microphone in her hand and singing to a crowd of strangers?

She glanced at the passersby. None of them had the hungry expression she'd imagined on the faces that had once hovered around her. A child's fears had made the crowd seem so intimidating back then, so ravenous. She'd sung her heart out in order to appease them.

In order to appease her father.

He would buy her cheap dresses in Chinatown . . . dresses that Lana was embarrassed to wear to school. They'd been gaudy and tacky, garments that her father had foolishly believed made her appear more dramatic when she sang.

Two small children holding ice cream cones darted past, frolicking in front of their parents as they progressed down the street. Lana watched them with a detached sort of wonderment.

She hadn't been any older than that little girl with the blonde braids when she started singing on Kalakaua. How in the world could the child scampering down the sidewalk be considered *weak* and helpless, just because she did what her father told her to do?

And it had been a far more complicated scenario in Lana's situation. She hadn't just performed for her father's approval. She'd done it because if she didn't, there possibly wouldn't be food on the table the next day. They might be kicked out of another apartment and have to sleep on the beach or on the floor at one of her father's drinking buddy's house.

Lana closed her eyes briefly, overwhelmed by memories. When she opened them again, she found herself staring at Jason Koa.

He stood almost exactly on the spot where she'd performed as a child. His face held her spellbound, speaking to her without words. If she had seen pity in his expression, she didn't think she could have taken it. He was seeing her exposed, after all, deprived of all the defenses he'd accused her of erecting against him time and again. And he'd been right. She'd have done *anything* yesterday to stop him from seeing her like this: naked and stripped bare.

He looked at *all* of her.

The experience wasn't what she'd dreaded it would be. What she saw on Jason's face in that brief few seconds wasn't pity or disgust or disdain.

She saw compassion and concern, regret and sadness. But she also sensed his strength, his certainty. Like a spark of electricity, it seemed to transfer to her through the warm, humid air.

Lana stood up slowly from the bench.

She hadn't been weak. She'd done what she had to do.

'Ailana Nahua had been a survivor.

twenty-six

THE wind chimes tinkled in the breeze. In the distance, Lana heard the waves breaking gently on the beach. It seemed like an eternity since she'd first sat with Jason on that spit of sand and gazed out at the sparkling lagoon, and yet it'd just been last week. Their conversation echoed in her brain.

Don't you get tired of it after a while?

What?

Perfection.

Jason opened the door for her, and she walked into the quiet houseboat. Neither of them spoke. Maybe they'd talked themselves dry after Jason had found her on Kalakaua Avenue and they'd walked on the beach. Now they walked over to the patio doors and stepped out into the sultry night. She kicked off her sandals, and they sat cross-legged on the deck, her hand in his. The moon was waning, but it still cast the lagoon in silvery light, making it look like a fey, magical place.

"I told myself I hated this island."

Jason stirred next to her. "That's not too surprising."

"I'd always felt like an outsider here. It seemed too beautiful . . . too unreal."

His calloused thumb caressed the underside of her wrist. "You're no more of an outsider here than I am. But again . . . I can understand why you were glad to say good-bye to it when you left with your grandmother."

Lana started to speak then stopped herself. "How many times?" she finally asked hoarsely. "How many times did you see me sing when I was a little girl?"

His arm brushed against hers as he shrugged. "I don't know. Maybe a dozen times. Maybe more. Does it matter?"

Lana's throat felt sore when she swallowed, like the muscles had been taxed by the storm of emotions she'd experienced tonight. Knowing Jason had seen her—naked and exposed—had been an uncomfortable yet strangely liberating experience.

"What . . . what did you think of me?"

"I thought you were an incredibly brave, talented little girl. I wasn't the only one who thought so, Lana. People were enraptured by you."

His words seemed to linger in the still, warm air. A silence stretched between them.

"It's so strange to think about having family here."

"Strange good or strange bad?"

"I don't know. Just strange . . . unexpected. Strange good. Maybe. Jason, about last night."

"Don't worry about it now, Lana."

"But I want to talk about what I did. I had no right to make you the focus of all my insecurities."

"Another time, Lana."

She gave an exasperated sigh. Her eyelids burned, and her muscles grew heavy from a growing fatigue. "You're just brushing me off."

"No, I'm not," he said as he stood and put out a hand for her.

"Well, what are you doing, then?" she asked as he hauled her up to a standing position.

"I'm just stalling. I figure as long as you haven't officially apologized for tying me up to that bed and torturing me, you won't leave. Come on. You're about to fall over. I'm putting you to bed."

LANA flopped onto her belly and turned her cheek into the pillow, but the source of her wakefulness persisted.

"Lea' me alone; I'm sleepy, Jason."

"Time to get up."

She cracked open one eyelid and saw Jason, fully dressed in board shorts and an untucked T-shirt staring down at her. She glanced outside and groaned.

"It's still dark out."

"It better be. It'd ruin all my plans if it wasn't," he said as he resumed doing something to her ribs that was between a scratch and a tickle. Lana squirmed and leaned up on her elbows, giving him an incredulous glance. He looked wide awake, relaxed, and dead sexy sitting there on the edge of the bed, tickling her and grinning like a lunatic. He'd not only awakened her from a sound sleep, he was forcing her to recall the events of yesterday . . . of last night.

Forcing her to recall everything.

No, she'd much rather seek the oblivion of sleep.

She suggested as much when she turned her head to him and dove back into the pillow.

"Uh-uh. Not going to happen. I've got a surprise for you." Lana gasped when he rolled her naked body toward him and hauled her out of the bed.

"Jason . . . I'm not in the mood for—"

"You'll be in the mood for this. Trust me."

He carried her into the spare bedroom and set her feet on the floor. Lana blinked to clear her rising disorientation while he rifled through her new clothing, withdrawing the top to the ivory-colored bikini she'd worn yesterday.

"Here," he muttered, handing her the tiny scraps of fabric. "Put this on."

"We're going swimming? In the middle of the night?"

"It's not the middle of the night. It'll be dawn in an hour or so, and if you don't hurry up, you're going to ruin my surprise."

"What surprise?"

He gave her an exasperated look.

"Oh, right. It's a surprise. I don't at least get any hints?"

"I want to show you just how real paradise can be. I'm going to pack a couple things from the fridge. Hurry up."

Lana's expression clearly told him what she thought of riddles at four thirty in the morning, but she nevertheless stepped into the bathroom to clean up, and put on the bikini and a sundress. When she stepped into the living room, Jason waited for her impatiently by the front door, a duffel bag slung over his shoulder.

"Come on," he urged, herding her out the door.

"Jason, where are we going?" Lana asked twenty minutes later as Jason soared down Pali Highway. But he answered in the same way he had the other five times she'd asked him.

"You'll see."

That was practically all he'd said to her since he'd hauled her out of bed, Lana realized. She glanced at his handsome profile, but it remained fixed and unmoving as he drove. Lana bristled in the passenger seat.

She sat upright when Jason turned and entered a small town. It was still dark outside, but Lana saw the shadow of mountains behind them. "Kailua?" she asked when she saw a sign.

"Yeah. You ever come here when you were a kid?"

Lana shook her head. She'd never been to the small town, but she knew it was on the windward side of the island. "We're going to the beach?"

"Nah. Not to Kailua Beach. We're going to the most beautiful beach on Oahu."

Ten minutes and several narrow, winding roads later, Jason parked the car in what looked like a private, upscale neighborhood. Lana peered out the window in rising confusion. Did he plan to sneak onto a private beach?

"Come on. We're going to miss it," he urged.

"Miss what?"

"The sunrise," he replied as he clambered out of the car.

"Jason, are you bound and determined to get us arrested?" Lana whispered seconds later. He led her down a private path between two enormous houses that she suspected were worth tens of millions of dollars. She shivered in the cool air. The impenetrable blackness of night that occurs just before dawn shrouded her vision. She could only make out where to walk because of dim lanterns that had been placed along the side of the path.

"No one's going to arrest us. This is a public beach. It's just a well-kept secret, that's all. Take off your shoes."

Lana slipped out of her flip-flops. Jason pulled her after him. She stepped onto sand so soft it was like walking on cool talcum powder. The sound of waves softly hitting the shore reached her ears; the scent of salt and flowers filled her nose. She had no choice but to trust in Jason's sure stride as he led her down the beach, blinded as she was.

After a moment, he stopped and she plowed into him. He chuckled softly as he put his hands on her shoulders. For some reason, his touch knocked her off balance instead of steadying her . . . emotionally speaking, anyway. He dropped one hand, but the other lowered to cradle her waist, and he drew her against him. He hadn't made love to her last night, insisting she rest after the ordeal at Lily's and Kalakaua Avenue. Lana found herself suddenly breathless with excitement as she pressed against his male warmth.

She heard the zipper on his duffel bag, but she remained pressed against his body. After a moment, he released her. She felt him lower to the beach.

"Come here," he instructed gruffly. She reached out, locating his upraised hand, and knelt on the blanket he'd spread on the sand. Neither of them spoke as he situated her in front of him, his long legs bent at her sides. He wrapped his arms around her, pulling her back against his chest. Lana felt completely, utterly encapsulated by the scent, the touch, and the heat of Jason Koa.

He pushed aside the strap of her sundress and nuzzled her shoulder with his nose and lips.

"How long before sunrise?" she asked breathlessly, highly

aware of his nibbling mouth on the sensitive skin at the back of her shoulder.

"Five minutes. Ten. More if we're lucky," he said next to skin he'd just made damp with his warm mouth. Lana shivered, and he tightened his hold around her.

"Why if we're *lucky*? I thought you were all fired up to see the sunrise?"

"Right now, I appreciate the darkness," he whispered near her ear, making goose bumps rise along the back of her neck. Her nipples tightened. As if he'd known precisely what effect he'd had on her, he began to unbutton the front of her dress. Lana held her breath when he reached inside her flimsy bikini top with both hands and lifted out her breasts. The predawn air was cool, but his hands were warm as he shaped her to his palms, massaging her softly. She felt his cock stiffen against her back.

"See, I couldn't do this, for instance, once sunrise comes. But here in the darkness, I can play with you all I want," he rumbled near her ear before he kissed it. Lana sighed as he awakened her desire, his stroking hands on her breasts causing heat and excitement to tingle in her pussy. He plucked at her sensitive nipples with his thumbs and forefingers, stiffening them further. He pushed aside her hair and buried his face in her neck, his mouth trailing across her skin. She whimpered when he kissed her ear again, creating suction. Liquid warmth flooded her pussy at the sensation.

"Prettiest tits I've ever seen. Damn shame to ever cover them," he whispered gruffly as he continued to pleasure her tight nipples. She turned toward him in the darkness, and their mouths fused.

She tasted his hunger in that long, hot kiss. The intensity of his arousal surprised and pleased her. She wouldn't have guessed it from his fixed expression and silence on the drive here. Now she realized that he'd awakened her to see the sunrise, but *this* was what he'd been waiting for . . . anticipating.

She moaned into his mouth when he lowered one hand and lifted the hem of her dress. He opened his palm along her thigh, stroking her softly. Lana burned for his touch. She shifted her hips restlessly, lost in the power of his kiss and skillful hands.

"Don't be anxious, *Onaona*." He slipped two long fingers into the top of her bikini briefs and pressed the ridge of his forefinger between her labia. He bit gently at her damp lips as though he wanted to consume her whimpers of pleasure. He began to stimulate her with eye-crossing precision. "I'm not trying to torture you. I want to feel you shake in my arms, and the sooner the better."

"Oh, it feels good."

"I can tell. You're nice and wet."

The waves hit the beach softly, but a roar rose in Lana's ears as Jason stroked her. Despite her pounding heartbeat and swamping pleasure, she still heard Jason's hoarse voice praising her as she came in his arms.

She sighed when she felt his lips on her eyelids a moment later. "Open your eyes, beautiful."

Lana lifted her heavy eyelids. He'd given her a scalding climax that left her feeling deliciously warm and relaxed in its wake. Her body had melted against his hard torso.

Wisps of gray streaked through the coal black eastern sky. By slow degrees, she made out the shadows of two hulking shapes against the brightening horizon.

"They're the islands of Mokulua, but we just call them the Mokes. One of them is a bird sanctuary."

"What is this place?"

"Lanikai," he answered softly. "It means 'where heaven meets the sea.'"

Lana watched in growing wonder as gray turned to light pink, and she could better see the black, cone-shaped Mokes thrusting out of the dark ocean. The sun turned the sky to striking shades of burnt orange, crimson, and gold. Birds sang, welcoming the new day. By the time the rim of the sun peaked over the horizon, the sky was a kaleidoscope of vivid color.

Now she saw that the beach where Jason held her was a striking pale gold. The Mokes stood like sentinels in a blue serene lagoon, their stark, volcanic appearance only highlighting the gentle beauty of everything else: the caressing breeze, powder-soft sand, and soothing surf.

The sun swelled on the horizon, dazzling her eyes with its fiery splendor.

"It's too perfect to be real," she murmured.

"It's real, Lana." He nuzzled her cheek and caressed each of her breasts before he pulled her bikini top back into place. "Take off your dress and come on."

Lana heard the gruff quality of his voice. Regret lanced through her when she realized he'd brought her so much pleasure—such an exquisite experience—and yet he was still aroused. She stood with him on the blanket and removed her dress. Jason whipped his T-shirt over his head with a fascinating flex of muscle. He shook off the blanket, slung the duffel bag over his shoulder, and took her hand.

She thought they'd swim in the picture-perfect lagoon, so she was surprised when he led her down the beach. "Where are we going?"

Jason paused a few seconds later in front of a row of kayaks. He approached a sleek red craft and set down his bag. He lifted the kayak over his head like it weighed no more than a tree branch. "I have a friend who lives nearby. He lets me keep a kayak here. Grab a couple of those," he ordered, referring to a trough of assorted double-ended paddles. "We're going out to the Mokes. There's something I want you to see."

Carrying two paddles, Lana followed him to the ocean. Once Jason had deposited the kayak in the water, he had her hold on to it while he retrieved his duffel bag.

The sun flamed brilliantly on the horizon, making the lagoon look like an aquamarine gem as they paddled out to the island. The water was so calm and clear it was like the kayak glided across ice. She could see all the way to the bottom of the ocean floor.

"Look," Jason murmured behind her. She squinted to where he pointed and saw a distant island in the ocean.

"Is it Molokai?" Lana asked in a hushed tone, recalling her childhood geography of the islands.

"Yeah. You can only see it on the clearest of days."

Jason told her to steer to the island on the right, which he called Moku Nui. At one point, as they neared the island, Lana saw a dark shape moving near the surface of the crystalline water. She spun around to look at Jason in excitement.

His slow smile was just as potent to her heightened senses as the Lanikai sunrise had been.

More so.

Jason directed them to the back of the tiny island.

"It's beautiful," Lana exclaimed as they lifted the kayak onto a white beach dotted with large black volcanic rock. The only other likely inhabitants on the island were the Wedge-tailed Shearwater birds—the true locals on the protected seabird sanctuary.

"It's called Shark's Cove." He saw her expression and laughed. "Don't worry. It's a misnomer. I've never seen so much as a pygmy shark out here. But there's something else swimming around in this cove."

"I know," Lana said, grinning in response to his small smile. She nodded at his duffel bag. "Did you bring the snorkels?"

"What makes you think I'd bring the snorkels?" he teased.

Lana laughed and grabbed for the bag.

They stood in the warm shallows of the cove to adjust their masks and snorkels. Lana looked up at him in growing excitement to see if he was ready and saw that his mouthpiece still hung around his neck. He reached behind her and unfastened her swimsuit top.

"You won't be needing this. There's no one here but us and the birds."

"And the turtles," Lana added as he untied the strings around her neck and bared her breasts to the balmy breeze.

Jason's teeth flashed white in his face. He balled up her bikini top and threw it up onto the beach. "They won't mind."

She went utterly still when he reached up and caressed her right breast with a feather-light touch. He stared at his hand cradling her flesh for a spellbound moment. He looked like he was about to say something—do something—but then he nodded toward the cove and they plunged into the warm waters.

It was magical. They snorkeled all over the serene, sunlit cove. Lana saw a myriad of marine life through the crystalline twenty-five-foot depths, but it was the turtles she followed. Despite her excitement at seeing her old childhood favorites, she was constantly aware of Jason swimming beside her, hyperaware of every brush of their water-lubricated skin and his light caresses. He touched her everywhere while they swam, but he made it clear that he'd bared her breasts for a reason, occasionally gliding his fingers along the sensitive skin at the sides of the mounds or skimming over her sensitized nipples. After almost an hour of swimming in the idyllic, sun-dappled cove with him, Lana's entire body hummed pleasantly with sexual arousal.

Most of the turtles swam way below the surface, but once, one large green one ventured up into relatively shallow waters. Jason surprised her by quickly sliding his snorkel off his mask and pushing it into her hand. He shot into the depths with a powerful kick, pushing the water aside with his strong arms. Lana watched him approach the wary turtle—which must have been close to five feet in length. She thought for sure the animal would swim away from him, but it must have recognized a fellow inhabitant of the sea.

She watched, spellbound, as he put one hand on the enormous shell, and the ancient creature obliged him with a short ride.

Lana surfaced when she saw Jason swim up for air. He broke the surface, flipped his bangs out of his eyes, and found her with his gaze. He laughed.

"That was amazing," Lana said as she swam toward him.

"I think I recognize him," Jason said, referring to the green turtle. "He's been here before. Give me the snorkels, and you take a dive. He's still down there."

Lana opened her mouth to reply when something caught her eye. Her grin widened. "No, he's not."

She removed her snorkel and pushed it along with the other one toward Jason's outstretched hand. The turtle paddled its huge clawed feet not three feet below, looking for all the world as if it patiently waited for her. She dipped just below the surface and stretched out her hand. The area between the thick ridges of the shell felt surprisingly smooth despite its weathered, ancient appearance. The turtle's feet moved, taking her on an exhilarating, surprisingly swift ride.

Jason and Lana walked onto the warm white sand minutes later. He spread out the beach blanket and they sat on it side by side.

"You're still grinning," he said.

"I can't help it. That was wonderful. It was as if he knew precisely what he was doing, like he was fully conscious of us . . . like he was *playing*."

"Does that surprise you?"

"Yeah, it does. How could something seem ancient and innocent and young at the same time?" She laughed, still under the spell of the enchanted morning. She caught Jason's eye. "Thank you for bringing me here."

He turned toward her, his hand opening over her damp rib cage. "Welcome to paradise, 'Ailana."

The early morning sunlight magnified the amber flecks in his dark eyes. Lana stared up at him, her mouth hanging open. His hand moved on her wet skin. All of the repressed desire she'd been feeling all morning flooded to the surface. He kissed her, his lips cool from the ocean water. Inside, his mouth was hot. Lana shut her eyes and lost herself in him.

He lifted his head a moment later. Lana opened her eyes, dazed by the sight of Jason cast in golden sunlight and shadow. He cupped a breast.

"I've been hard as a rock for the past two hours straight," he mused as he stroked her.

"Well, why don't we do something about that?" He held her wrist, restraining her, when she reached for the fastenings of his board shorts.

"I'm like a bomb that's about to explode. I don't want to do anything that I'll regret, like I did the other night."

The silence stretched.

"I'm the one who should be regretful. Not you," she finally murmured.

He studied her intently for several seconds, still shaping her breast to his palm and finessing her nipple, making it difficult for Lana to concentrate. His other hand lowered. He cupped her sex. "Are you sore at all?"

She blinked, surprised by his question. It took her a moment to comprehend what he meant.

"No. It was two nights ago, Jason."

"I fucked you hard enough to make you sore until next week."

Her pussy throbbed against his hand. Leave it to Jason to say something like that and turn her on instead of repulse her. She pressed closer. "I'm fine."

"Right," he said doubtfully. He came down over her, forcing her to lie back on the blanket. He shifted his weight until they were belly to belly, groin to groin, and Lana knew firsthand that he hadn't been exaggerating about his state of readiness. She stroked his muscular back, reveling in his weight, his power . . . the sheer maleness of him.

She exhaled sharply and then gripped his hair desperately when he lowered his mouth to a nipple. Her vagina clamped

tightly when she glanced down and saw his cheeks hollow out a
he suckled. Pure pleasure lanced through her pussy like a light
ning strike, leaving a sharp ache of longing in its wake.

As aware as she was of her own acute desire, it was Jason'
need that motivated her first and foremost. She could feel th
long, straining pillar of his cock along his right thigh ... coul
sense how much he'd been hurting. The fact that she'd *wante*
him to suffer with that ache just two nights ago made her all th
more wild to alleviate it now.

She burrowed her hand beneath the low waistline of his boar
shorts, pausing to sink her fingers into a smooth, muscular as
cheek, before she trailed around to his front. Despite his earlie
attempt to restrain her, he lifted his hips, granting her access t
him. A low groan of excitement and impatience vibrated into he
breast. Lana tugged at the drawstring and tore open the Velcro
fastening of his trunks. She shoved them down over his hips an
reached for his cock.

He lifted his head and hissed against her damp, distende
nipple when she stroked his length. Her excitement mounte
when she felt how hard he was in her palm, when her fingertip
traced the swollen veins that ran along the stalk.

He hadn't been kidding. He really was about to explode.

"I don't want to fuck your pussy while you're sore. Can I fuck
your breasts? They've been driving me crazy," he muttered tightly.

"'Course you can, baby," she whispered, more moved by th
evidence of his need than she'd known she had the power to be
She regretfully released his erection, flinching in stark arousa
when it fell heavily against her swollen, naked labia. She trans
ferred her hands to her breasts, pushing the firm flesh up an
together.

His gaze shot to her face, and Lana knew he recalled, like she did, the moment when she'd played with herself to torture him, held up her breasts and pinched the nipples, taunted him with what he couldn't possess.

"Come here. I'm all yours," she whispered.

His hot eyes lowered to what she offered. She squeezed her breasts lightly and ran her fingertips over the stiff crests. He stood and shucked off his damp shorts. Her pussy tingled and burned at the awesome sight of his bronzed, muscular body lowering down over her. She bit her bottom lip and squeezed her thighs tightly together to contain the excitement that throbbed in her pussy. He lifted his heavy erection into his hand and rubbed his thumb over the fleshy cockhead, smearing it with a coating of clear pre-cum.

"I'm going to last about three strokes," he admitted gruffly as he positioned himself.

"I didn't last much more than that when you touched me on the beach this morning."

She said nothing more, just parted her breasts so that he could slide his cock in the valley between them. He felt hot, heavy, and unbearably exciting resting there on her chest. He made a low, growling sound in his throat when she pushed her breasts around him, burying him in her flesh.

"Fuck," he muttered as he thrust. His eyelids clamped closed for a few seconds before he opened them again, his gaze zeroing in on her breasts. "You're so soft. That's right, play with your nipples . . ."

He plunged his cock between her breasts in mounting excitement.

Lana loved his fixed, glazed expression as he watched his cock thrust between her breasts again and again. His penis looked dark and ruddy next to her pale breasts. He lasted longer than he predicted, but his arousal was too great and of too extended of a duration to last for long. He put his weight on his hands behind her head and thrust hard enough to make her breasts bounce up again and again as his pelvis smacked against the underside of them.

He thrust one last time and grunted gutturally. He kept his hips flexed, his testicles pressed tightly to her breasts, the cockhead reaching all the way to her neck. Lana closed her eyes, overwhelmed with a desire so immense it felt tangible. His warm cum spurted on her skin. She lowered her chin in an instinctive gesture, allowing the warm fluid to gush on her jaw. A fat globule landed on her lower lip.

She sought blindly with her mouth, coating her lips, tongue, and throat in his taste.

She kept her eyes closed when he sank down next to her, listening to the sound of his rough breath blending with the gentle surf hitting the beach. Her fingers delved into his tousled hair while she caressed his perspiration-damp skin with her other hand, soothing him.

A full, potent feeling surged in her breast. For a moment, she thought it was panic. She relaxed by slow degrees when her heart continued to beat slow, even, and strong.

twenty-seven

THEY made love to each other again and again on that secluded beach, despite Jason's initial concerns for her well-being. Lana discovered that even after they'd gone back to shore and drove back to Honolulu, she carried the memory of that sunlit morning like a secret treasure she could touch and admire any time she chose. Something told her that even after she returned to Manhattan, the gift that Jason had given her would be there, deep inside her.

He drove back through the mountains. When they crested a peak and looked out over the metropolitan area, Lana broke their silence.

"Do you think Po will try and blackmail either one of us with those photos?" she asked.

"Not a chance," Jason said.

"What makes you so sure?" she asked as she studied his profile. Just the mention of Po's name made his handsome face tighten with annoyance.

"Everybody in the Koa family tried to protect Lily from the knowledge of Po's occupation. Po knew that perfectly well when he created that news leak. He knew that even if I thought he'd had a part in it, I wouldn't take my suspicions to Lily."

"But then you got angry at him at the luau and Po got pissed in return, and your grandmother found out what everyone was trying to keep from her."

Jason nodded. "Yeah. I regret it, but there's nothing I can do to change that now. Lily will recover. She's tough as an old mule, and a good sight more stubborn than Po. She'll more than likely railroad him into making an honest living in the next several months."

"So you think Lily will be the one to keep Po from black mailing us?"

Jason gave her a quick glance of dark amusement. "Yeah, but not directly. Po just knows that if he ever goes so far as to try and blackmail us, I've got nothing to stop me anymore from informing the cops of what he's up to. Hell, I'd be all too happy to do it. Grandma will end up catching wind of it if I turn him in. I may not have much pull over him, but it's amazing how much pull his portion of Grandma's inheritance has on him. He's not likely to risk that just so he can blackmail us."

They crested another mountain. Lana looked down over the entire metropolitan area and the Pacific Ocean. It looked so small from up here . . . so much less complicated.

"I think I'd like to go to the cemetery," she murmured.

His head swung around.

"Now? You're sure?"

Lana nodded with more certainty than she felt. Still . . . she knew she was ready after spending the morning in Lanikai.

THEY stopped in Chinatown and bought two bouquets of fresh flowers. Oahu Cemetery was a historic graveyard located just outside of Honolulu. Lana possessed few memories of the cemetery from when she'd come there as a child to bury her father, and she recalled even less from her mother's funeral. As an adult, she realized her parents were laid to rest in an idyllic setting in the lush Nuuanu Valley. The graveyard was laid out on acres and acres of immaculately landscaped grounds.

To my beloved wife, Christiania Elizabeth Nahua.
My spirit flies with you.

Lana sat and thought as the craft made its way across the harbor to Jason's home. *My spirit flies with you.* Michael Nahua had lost a vital part of himself the day his wife had passed away. He'd been devastated. He saw himself as an empty shell, and yet he remained on this earth, forced to exist in a sort of purgatory.

Forced to remain behind with a daughter who was a daily, hourly reminder of what he'd lost.

"It wasn't an excuse for him to treat you the way he did," Jason said after he'd pulled up to his boat and stood to secure the skiff.

"No," Lana agreed. She met his eyes. "But I understand him a little bit better now, I think."

He stepped onto the deck of the houseboat and put a hand out for her. He stopped her when she started to walk toward the door. She turned to him, a question in her eyes.

"Are you going back to Manhattan soon, Lana?"

"I'll have to . . . in a few days, anyway. I need to start planning my tour."

He stared at her with eyes like smoking embers. She stepped closer and opened her hand over his angular jaw.

"But last I checked, there are plenty of flights to New York everyday. Surely you could make your way onto one of them. And I'll be back, Jason. That's one of the things you've taught me. I have as much right to paradise as anyone," she said softly.

He gave her a slow, satisfied smile before he grabbed her hand and led her inside.

headline
ETERNAL

FIND YOUR HEART'S DESIRE...